YA
SME

Smedley, Zack

Deposing Nathan

DEPOSING NATHAN

DEPOSING NATHAN

ZACK SMEDLEY

PAGE STREET
PUBLISHING CO.

PAGE STREET
PUBLISHING CO.

Copyright © 2019 Zack Smedley

First published in 2019 by
Page Street Publishing Co.
27 Congress Street, Suite 105
Salem, MA 01970
www.pagestreetpublishing.com

Distributed by Macmillan, sales in Canada by The Canadian Manda Group.

23 22 21 20 19   1 2 3 4 5

ISBN-13: 978-1-62414-735-7
ISBN-10: 1-62414-735-6

Library of Congress Control Number: 2018956358

Cover design by Meg Baskis, book design by Sara Pollard for Page Street Publishing Co.
Cover image Shutterstock © Rudchenko Liliia
Author photo by James Ferry

Printed and bound in the United States

For my incredible parents, Mark and Debbie
Smedley, with immeasurable love.

My writing is the product of all I am, and
every word belongs to you.

DAY 1

1

What you have to understand about Cam—and this is important—is that up until he jammed a shard of ceramic in my gut, he was the best friend I've ever had. I know why I'm here, Mrs. Lawson, and I know what you want me to say. But you're not going to like it, because the fight wasn't just Cam's fault. If anything, it was mine.

■ ■ ■

Run. It's Her.

She's almost here—any minute now. I'm in my front yard, swallowed by the shadow of my house as my eyes dart between the front windows. No lights on. Ten minutes before She finds us—probably less.

Runrunrun.

Cam is farther down the sidewalk. Unlike me, he's perfectly

still, blocking the path between me and my front porch. His feet are rooted to the spot: steel girders in cement.

When I realize he isn't going to say anything, I decide to.

"Out of my way, fag."

Shit—that's my own voice. I tighten my lips, but the word lingers in the air between us.

A wry smile jumps to his face. He spreads his arms wide. "You had a three-hour bus ride—"

"Don't start."

"—a *three-hour* bus ride to come up with something."

"You think this is the time to screw around?" I cut him off. "Come on—move. I need to get inside."

"I'll move once you talk to me about what happened," he says. Serious, now. And the way he says it—*what happened*. All delicate, like the words are dangerous.

"Listen, I'm not kidding," I tell him. "She's going to be home any second."

"Better talk fast, then."

"Oh, blow me."

"Right here?"

"*Stop* joking!" I shout, stomping my foot in his direction. He doesn't flinch. I want to do something, anything, to wipe that confident smirk from his face. "Jesus, why are you still here? You get to go home to mommy and daddy and have them coddle away all your shit—"

"Yup!" he jumps in. "That's exactly how it works! *Hey, Mom and Dad, you're going to get a call—"*

"Stop talking."

"Nate—"

"Stop." My eyes latch back onto my house. Still nothing.

Cam steps forward, almost extending his hand but not quite. "Dude, come on. Let me help."

It doesn't even surprise me when he switches gears. I'm expecting it.

"No." My voice cuts through the air. "Just go home."

He doesn't. Instead, he takes another step forward and touches my shoulder.

"Get the fuck off—" I try to hit his arm away, but he jumps back and I end up mostly swatting empty space. Right as I shove past him, he grabs a fistful of my shirt collar.

"Nate, we promise—"

There.

My fist plows into his jaw before he can finish the word. He stumbles back, his hands flying to his face. Blood. I don't give him time to recover. I hit him again in the stomach, even though my fist is throbbing. As he doubles over, my front leg snaps up, catching him in the side. He yells and topples to the ground.

Everything after is a blur. I don't stop to think or plan my moves, I just pummel again and again with my fists, my elbows, my feet. He's yelling in pain now, a messy stream of blood is smeared across his face, his glasses are broken; he's begging me to stop, and I still don't.

This boy on the ground is Cameron M. Haynes, the same person who stabbed me. But this is the first piece you're missing—the stabbing only happened after I beat him half to death.

Whether you like it or not, Mrs. Lawson, the truth is that Cam's not the only one who did something wrong. And if you still think it's more his fault than mine, then you really need to hear this. I'm just getting started here.

2

"**S**top talking, Nate."

I do.

All eyes in the room—and there are a lot of them—turn to Aunt Lori, seated beside me. Each of her fingers is clamped on my arm, coiled tightly around it like tiny serpents.

"Stop talking," she repeats. I'm sandwiched between her and Dad, who watches the exchange without interjecting.

"Excuse me," says Mrs. Lawson, her voice ringing with authority. She points her pen at Aunt Lori, then me. "Would you like to let Mr. Copeland finish his statement?"

I blink when she says my name. It's another reminder of how serious this is. In here I'm not Nate, I'm "Mr. Copeland." And I'm not answering questions for a job interview or college app—I'm in the smallest conference room of the state's attorney's office building giving a *statement.* Technically it's for a deposition, which is the same thing as a testimony except it's a recorded interview instead of a courtroom interrogation. Apparently it's rare to do depositions for criminal trials, but my family was like 90 percent moved out of our in-state residence when this all happened, so I was dubbed enough of a flight risk to preserve it all on the video camera currently leveled at my face.

Go, me.

Mrs. Lawson—the prosecutor running the show—is a steely black woman in a suit, heels, and a wheelchair. Her face is gentle, but she wears a permanent scowl that's been burning a hole in the table since early this morning.

She taps her pen against her notepad, then repeats the question to my aunt.

"Would you like to let Mr. Copeland finish?"

My aunt and father share a look. As always, Dad is the one who drops his gaze.

"We need to have a word with Nate in the hall," Aunt Lori says.

"I don't think that's necessary," says Mrs. Lawson.

"That's our call. This is his father, and I help raise Nate," Aunt Lori snaps. "He's not feeling well."

Mrs. Lawson sighs through her nose like, *get over yourself.* Then she turns to me. "Mr. Copeland—may I call you Nathan?"

"Nate's fine."

"Nate." She fixes me with a rare smile. "How're you feeling today?"

I open my mouth to say something, but Aunt Lori's grip on

my arm tightens until my fingertips prickle, so I shrug instead of speaking.

"Are you feeling up to this?" Mrs. Lawson asks.

I nod, eyes on the table.

"And you're aware that if you need anything—a glass of water, an attorney, or even to stop for the day if your injury starts bothering you—you can ask, and we'll accommodate you?"

Another nod.

"Perfect." She turns to my aunt. "I think Nate can handle himself."

I bob my head a third time. And of all things—of *all things* that might've set Cam off—the excessive nodding is what does it.

"Okay, seriously," he says to me from the other end of the table, hand outstretched. "For fuck's sake, say *something*."

The adults give a small collective gasp. Like I figured, Cam is leaning on his first and favorite defense mechanism: acting like a little shit. His tie is thrown over his shoulder, and his pencil has been tracing a lazy cartoon of Shrek on his notepad for the last twenty minutes. His parents—seated along the wall behind him— are burying their faces in their hands. The next chair over is Cam's attorney, a silver-haired man who looks ready to choke someone.

"Mr. Haynes," Mrs. Lawson says to Cam, putting on her most professional smile. "Good morning."

"Top of the morning—"

"Keep this shit up and I'll have you removed from this deposition. You got that?"

"Oh, come on, Nora!" Cam's lawyer protests.

"Come *on*, Nora!" Cam echoes, pouting.

They start bickering about whether he's legally allowed to sit in on this, which apparently he is. Meanwhile, I feel a sharp pressure over the wound on my stomach and realize I'm pushing my hand against it. It's just about fully healed, but I still have to hold my front if the pain gets bad enough. It didn't exactly help that the surgeon had to cut the area open wider to pull the pieces of ceramic out. Between that and a sepsis scare, I was in the hospital for almost two weeks.

Aunt Lori notices my arm has escaped. She lifts it back onto the table, giving my hand a pat.

". . . you've got two hours; I've got four," Mrs. Lawson finishes, glaring at Cam's lawyer. "So tell your client that weaponizing the back talk isn't going to get us anywhere."

"I'm taking that as a compliment," Cam pipes up.

"It's not."

"I'm taking it as one anyway. Is your last name really Lawson? You're a *lawyer* named *Lawson*?"

"We're getting back on track now," Mrs. Lawson snaps. She scoots her wheelchair back a few inches, turning to fix her X-ray eyes on me. "Nate, a few minutes ago you said, quote, 'Cam's not the only one who did something wrong.' What did you mean by that?"

I hesitate. "There's a lot to it, I guess."

"I'm going to need you to do two things for me. I'm going to need you to stop guessing. And I'm going to ask you to elaborate on 'a lot.'"

"Okay."

"Perfect." She points to me, like, you're my guy. "So let's start back at the beginning of your friendship."

"Okay . . . why?" I ask.

"Because Cameron has been charged with breaking West Virginia Code Chapter 61, Article II, Item 9, Subsection a. The exact wording of that law makes a distinction between a *malicious* attack and an attack carried out without intent. The first is two to ten years in prison; the second is one to five."

Cam's dad is crying softly. I don't look at him.

"Now this is what's called a discovery deposition," Mrs. Lawson explains. "My mission here is to understand the context of what sounds like a . . . complicated dynamic between you two."

"Yeah."

"I'll ask you some questions, which you'll answer as best as you can." She reads from her notes in a rapid-fire monotone, like she's delivering a sales pitch. "We've already gotten your name, address, and background info on the record. I asked if you're currently on any medication that could affect your testimony; you said you've been taking 7.5/300 milligrams of Verdrocet for pain management but stopped this morning. As the court officer reminded you when you were sworn in, you are under oath. Knowingly making any false or incomplete statements is a felony, and you can be charged with perjury. Understood?"

"Yes."

She clicks her pen. "Then let's get started. You met Mr. Haynes . . . when, exactly?"

"Um." I clear my throat. "I met Cam the first day of eleventh grade. I'm not sure when that was."

"August twenty-sixth," Cam adds from across the table, sounding bored. "We're all sitting here today because of a biology project."

3

'm jolted awake first thing in the morning by my alarm clock, followed by Aunt Lori shaking me.

"Nate," she whispers. "Naaate? Time for school."

"Hmmf," I mutter into my pillow. My code for, "Euthanize me."

"I made French toast for your first day. Junior year! Come on, scoot your boot."

I spend the next half hour remembering how to tug on my school uniform, then washing down my French toast with half a quart of iced tea. The only plus side of the morning is I get to drive to school in my newly purchased, severely used 2003 Passat, i.e., the consolation prize for busting my ass all summer wrapping burritos.

It isn't until I'm sitting in AP Biology that I even wake up. Some older lady—"Call me Mrs. Koestler!"—introduces herself as our teacher and passes out the syllabus. She goes over what's going to be expected of us "young pioneers of knowledge."

Pretty soon, everything blurs together, and I tune it all out. My brain jumps back in around here:

"So I want you to pick a partner to get this knocked out by the end of next week. That gives you the weekend to take your time and make it look stellar. Go ahead and pair up while I take roll."

Everyone turns to their closest buddy. Of course, this is the one class where I don't know anyone. I sigh and let my head fall back, staring at the ceiling.

I'm in the middle of trying to figure out who would die if one of the fans fell down when I feel something poke the top of my head.

That something turns out to be the pointer finger of the guy from two desks over, who's now standing over me.

"You should probably try to look busy," he advises, sliding into the seat next to mine. "Considering Mrs. K's syllabus looks like a legal document that was shat out of a '90s typewriter, I kind of doubt she's going to be one of our more chill teachers for the year."

I have no idea what to make of this. I glance the guy up and down—he's got enormous black-framed hipster glasses under a mess of dirty blond hair spiked up. His uniform is way too loose on him. I can tell he's short, even shorter than me.

"Are you a new student here too?" he continues. He holds out his hand, all proper. "Cameron."

"Nate," I say, shaking his hand. "And no, I'm not new here."

"Really? You seem like it. Do you not have any friends in this class?"

"Not in this one."

"Gotcha." He slides his glasses up his nose, then starts drumming on his kneecaps. After a few seconds of this, he takes a breath and says, "Well, would you like to be friends, Nate? You seem nice, and it's like fucking shoot me if I need to ask Mrs. K to assign me a project partner."

I'm caught off guard not only by his directness, but by the way he says the first part. *Would you like to be friends, Nate?* Like it's an actual question instead of a formality.

I figure it would be rude to say anything other than, "Uh yeah, sure."

"Good stuff." Cameron rummages through his backpack, digging out a notebook. Its front cover is, I can't help but notice, almost entirely occupied by a cartoon ladybug.

"What I get for letting my parents do the school-supply shopping," he explains. "It's either this ladybug or a fish that looks like Samuel L. Jackson."

I blink a few times, making sure I heard right. Sure enough, he pulls out a second notebook, this time with a cover picture of the sternest goldfish I've ever seen.

"What?" I ask.

"Say 'what' again!" Cameron belts out in a comically deep voice, making me jump. He shoves the notebook in my face for emphasis. *"I dare you; I double dare you, mothafucka! Say 'what' one more goddamn time!"*

His impression gets me to smile, which gets him to smile

back. We both relax a bit. I catch him letting go of something—this little touch of nervousness that he'd been keeping concealed.

"I mean," I tell him, deciding to play along. "It's not *not* Samuel L. Jackson."

"*Right?* That's what I'm saying."

"Why is he so angry anyway?"

Cameron tilts his head a little, studying the picture. "Bad parenting. His fish daddy was cold and distant. Now Fish Junior comes home every night to a wife who pretends to love him, but really she's only staying for the kids."

"Excuse me!" Mrs. Koestler cuts into our conversation. I realize the room has gone silent in the past handful of seconds. "I hope this is a discussion about biology? Yes, no, maybe?"

I'm trying to think of an exit strategy when Cameron takes over.

"Oh, definitely. Nate and I were debating the best way to scan for the BRAF V600E mutation in thyroid cancer. I was saying how the best way is to use IHC detection with the VE1 antibody, but Nate pointed out that real-time PCR had better trials. It was a pretty heated debate."

Which of course throws her completely off. As she sits there trying to come up with new lines, the class seizes the opportunity to devolve into noisy chatter. The whole time, Cameron is wearing this subtle look that almost scares me—a sweet, smiley version of *Ha ha! Eat shit.*

Once the bell rings, I turn around and thank him for saving

my ass. He shrugs without smiling.

"No worries, man. I'm honestly a little stressed about my first day here, and you're the only one who's talked to me so far, so I appreciate that. Not too many juniors want to be friends with a fifteen year old."

I scan him up and down. "You're fifteen and in AP Bio?"

"Skipped a grade."

We both shoulder our backpacks. I follow him out of the classroom and down the hall.

"How did you know all of that science-y stuff back there?" I ask him.

"Self-study. Next year I'm applying to a BS/MD program, and they might make me take the MCAT. A thousand merry fucks to the MCAT." When he catches me squinting at him, he rephrases. "Trying to get into medical school."

"Well that's . . . impressive," I say, even though I don't know half the abbreviations he just used. This is why I'm uncomfortable talking to people who are clearly brilliant—I feel like I have to take notes just to hold my end of the conversation. Meanwhile I fall into the camp of "decently smart in every class, but exceptional in pretty much nothing."

"What do you want to study?" Cameron asks as we turn a corner.

"Nothing we study here."

"What is it?"

"It's—well, okay." I feel a strange discomfort, like I'm

bringing light to something that's supposed to stay hidden. "I've always thought about maybe, like, painting? I'm not sure how I'd make a career of that though."

"Get an art degree."

"I also have no attention span and hate school. What do I do in that case?"

"Get an art degree."

"Tell that to my dad and aunt," I say, slowing my walk since we've reached my next class. "They need to approve my college choices before I apply."

"Seriously?"

I shrug. "They know what's best."

"You're okay with them dictating your major?"

"They know what's best."

"You don't think that's a bit dictator-ish?"

"They're dictating because they know what's best."

"I see," he says, chewing on his lower lip as he studies my face. "Last question."

"Sure."

"Are there now—or have there ever been—tiny men inside of you operating you with controls?"

Thing is, Friday night dinners are essential in my family's household. That's probably because my dad works as an air traffic controller, so he keeps bizarre hours.

You wouldn't guess his profession by looking at him, by the way. With his shaved head, earrings, and numerous arm tattoos, you'd think he's the lead singer of an all-dad '80s cover band.

Sometimes he'll be home every evening for a week, but it's much more common to go two or three days at a time without me even seeing him. But every Friday night, damn it, we're going to eat together as a family. So unless I basically give written notice, the three of us are expected to be in the kitchen at precisely six o'clock to pray, eat, and swap weekly updates. Clockwork.

"When's your friend supposed to be here?" Dad asks as we sit around the table, shoveling down steak and overcooked potatoes.

"Not really my friend," I say between bites. "Just a partner for a project."

"Fun way to spend Friday night." He chuckles. "Was Aria busy?"

"No, but I need to get this thing done."

"You and Aria have been seeing a lot of each other anyway," adds Aunt Lori, attempting a thin smile. "I'm amazed you aren't sick of her."

"We're dating. Is that illegal now?"

"Hey. Attitude, sir," she cautions, giving me a warning look. I can tell it's been one of her bad days. She's still in her work suit, but her hair is down and thick bags are latched under her eyes.

As if on cue, we're interrupted by the ringing of her cell phone. She pulls it out, glares at the screen, and answers.

"Tell me you fixed it," she says, climbing out of the chair and excusing herself from the table.

Dad turns to me and mouths, *Rough week.* I wince.

As Aunt Lori disappears into the dining room, I hear her snap, "If that's what you wanted, you should've drafted it right the first time. The next time I want to hear from you is when those nondisclosures are on my goddamn desk. And for the record, I don't take meetings with you. I set them."

Meet Aunt Lori: senior litigator at Garner-Stowell who lives out of a briefcase, has one of those "My Kid is an Honor Roll Student" bumper stickers, and would like to speak to your manager, please.

And I guess the bumper sticker sums it up: I'm not her kid, but I may as well be. Dad says between that and her helping us out around the house, we should be understanding of the "rough weeks."

The doorbell rings just as Aunt Lori hangs up.

"That's Cameron," I say. "We'll be in my room."

"Are we too embarrassing to be introduced?" Dad says, bolstering the question with exaggerated sobs. I roll my eyes and head for the door.

"What's up?" Cameron says as I let him in. He's in a loose tank top and his blond hair is damp. "Sorry I'm wet. It's drizzling a bit."

I poke my head outside, looking for his car. "Wait. Did you walk here?"

"Yeah, man. It's good exercise, and I don't have my license. It's only like three miles."

I look down and notice a jacket draped over his arm.

"What's that for?" I ask. "It's summer."

He ignores this. "Should I take off my shoes?"

I nod. He's just finished slipping them off when Dad and Aunt Lori both step into the hall. Cameron straightens up.

"Hi!" he says, extending his hand. "You must be Nate's mom and dad."

"That's my aunt," I say automatically, pointing.

"Oh! My mistake."

"It's no problem. How are you, Cameron? So good to meet you," Aunt Lori fires off, turning on her smile as she crushes his hand. There are guests in her house, which means Fun Aunt is on duty.

"You can call me Cam," he says, though he nods to indicate this is more directed toward me.

Once all the introductions are over, I lead Cam down the hall to my bedroom.

"First-floor room? Lucky," he says, bouncing up and down a little as he closes the door behind us.

"It's all right," I say, clearing a space on the floor for us to sit. "So how'd your first week go? Did you get lost yet?" Our school is infamous for its complete mess of a layout.

"Nah," he says, waving off the thought.

"Really? Pretty much everyone does at first."

"I made a point to memorize the map."

I frown at him. "There's *no* way you can memorize that whole thing."

"Well, I mean. I did."

"How?"

"I just remember everything."

"Ha ha," I say, but I can tell by Cam's face that he isn't joking. I raise an eyebrow at him, and he says, "It's called eidetic memory. You wanted to know how I knew all that biology stuff, right? It's because I can recite the research paper."

"Like word for word?"

"Pretty much. Yeah."

I'm basically speechless at this. He catches my expression and says, "For the record, no, it's not fun to have."

"BS," I say, careful not to cuss in my household. "That's awesome."

"You wouldn't be saying that if you had to deal with it."

"Why not?"

"So, does your aunt live here like, full-time?" he asks, once again ignoring my question.

Once I realize he isn't going to answer me, I say, "Yup. She moved in when I was younger. My mom died in a boating accident when I was seven. Her sister came here to help us out."

This happened long enough ago that I stopped feeling self-conscious about bringing it up. For a while, I was afraid people would label me as "the kid with the dead mom." But now, I'm comfortable enough to say it flat, like I'm providing information rather than asking for pity.

Cam takes this in, and I appreciate him sparing me the sympathy treatment. Instead he says, "Oh! So your aunt and your dad aren't like . . . together?"

"God, no. Ew."

"Right. And this is your girlfriend?" He's pointing toward a framed photograph on the dresser of me next to a girl with a huge smile and an auburn braid falling over her shoulder.

"That's her," I say. "Aria Harrington. You know her?"

"Nah. Just moved here, remember?"

Right.

"She has your freckles," Cam observes. He's resting his chin on his right hand like he's studying a painting. "Or, you have hers. Which is it? You both have freckles. Except your hair is black instead of brown."

I snort, pushing my bangs out of my eyes. "Do you just like

saying things that are obvious?"

"Oh, one hundred percent. You know how much I love the sound of my own voice."

"I don't, actually."

Cam gives me a knowing nod and says, "You'll learn."

He says it like he's joking, but I'm starting to wonder if he is.

5

By 11:30, my brain is melted.

"I can't read another word," I tell Cam. We have my TV on in the background, an empty bowl of popcorn between us on the bedroom floor, and a tri-fold poster splayed out in front of us. A diagram of an ecosystem is drawn, albeit half done, underneath a title that reads ADAPT, MIGRATE, OR DIE.

"Not your favorite subject, huh?" Cam asks, sitting back on his heels.

"Absolutely not." I massage my eyelids. "I can't believe you want to make a career out of this."

"This is one hundred percent different from what I want to do with my career."

"How so?"

"Well, for starters, I'd be in Hopkins' research lab instead of AP Biology, and I'd be doing adoptive T cell research instead of making a poster."

Once again, he's used a phrase I've never heard before. "T cell . . . ?"

"Cancer research," he clarifies. "T cells are part of your immune system, but they're bad at getting rid of cancer sometimes. In these new studies, researchers use a stretch of DNA called a CpG oligonucleotide—"

"Too many words—"

"—to modify the expression of an activating receptor called OX40."

"English, I'm fucking begging you."

"They could give you injections that supercharge the shit out of your T cells and you're cancer free."

I blink, then gape. "Seriously?"

"Seriously. Science is pretty nifty." He stretches his arms, stifling a yawn as he climbs to his feet. "And on that note, we should probably call it a night. I'm surprised your dad and aunt haven't kicked me out already."

I explain to him that they act like old people and go to bed at like 9:00. Dad's in the master bedroom—the nights he's not working anyway—and Aunt Lori has a bedroom-office across the hall from him.

"But we have an open-door policy," I add, brushing off my legs as I stand up. "So they're allowed to walk in here anytime without knocking."

"You're joking."

"Nope."

"God, dude. I mean—okay, I guess I don't have room to talk," he says as he packs up his stuff. "My parents can be controlling too."

"Yeah?"

"But for me it's more like, '*You're not leaving this house without a jacket, even if it's eighty-five degrees out.*'"

"Ah," I say. "So that's why you were carrying a hoodie?"

He bobs his head, then pretends to slit his own throat. "My favorite part is that cold weather doesn't even get you sick. But my parents are all like, 'Well then, why is it called a *cold*, hmm?' Great defense, you fucking idiots."

An awkward pause hangs in the air, like when someone takes a joke too far and everyone else stares at their laps uncomfortably. I get what Cam is saying, but I also can't imagine being so blatantly rude about my dad and aunt. It's like he's showing it off.

But, I mean, I do get what he's saying.

"Aunt Lori's the same way about my homework," I say, opting to bridge the gap. "She tells me, '*Not to breathe down your neck, but I need to look over your calc answers every night.*'"

Cam zips his backpack and we share an understanding eye roll, back on track now.

"So . . . not to breathe down your neck, but—" He leans forward and makes a show of blowing hot air on the back of my shirt collar, causing me to jolt by reflex.

"Oh—sorry!" he says, eyes widening. He laughs behind his hands. "I didn't mean to do it that much."

I grin back, shrugging it off.

Then Cam gets the same look that he had when Mrs. Koestler tried to put him in his place—subtle, dangerously intense defiance.

"You should join me," he suggests.

"Huh?"

"Like right now, when I walk home. Join me for the first mile or something, then you can turn around and come back here after."

"No way I'd be allowed to." I try to decide how to explain to Cam that it takes one to three business days to get permission to do anything outside my house. Before I can, he says, "Oh, I didn't mean like, tell them."

I scoff, but he calmly glides over to my window and lifts the blinds.

"What're you doing?" I ask.

He drums his fingers on the glass. "Seeing how easy it would be to slip out this opening. I think we're in luck."

"Absolutely not. Dad and Aunt Lori would murder me."

"Relax. We're only going to lay in the rain and shoot some heroin."

"Cam—"

"I'm kidding; there's no rain."

"Will you listen to me? I know my aunt seems chill, but she's got eyes in the back of her head."

Cam ignores me, dislodging the tabs keeping the window shut.

"And aren't your parents worried that you're not home yet?" I add.

"Normally yes," he says. "Except they're camping in Pennsylvania right now. They like to call the house phone to check in, but I programed it to redirect to my cell."

"When will they do that?"

"Remember the call I got at ten o'clock?"

I sigh into my hands. It astounds me that Cam can go about this like it's no big deal: lying to parents, sneaking out of the house. It feels like he grew up in a different world than me. Hell, I didn't even know you could reprogram a house phone.

"Look at it this way," he adds. "If our parents are going to treat us like little kids, we might as well do something to deserve it."

I'm about to point out how shitty that logic is when he heaves my window open. The sounds of a summer night—crickets, leaves rustling in the trees—spill into the room. Cam pops the screen out and sets it behind my desk, staring at me over his shoulder.

"C'mon . . . one loop around the neighborhood. We'll drop you right back here," he pushes.

I'm not doing this. No way. *No.*

He takes a fistful of my shirt and yanks so I'm facing him—the summer night to his back, his eyes on fire.

"Adapt, migrate, or die," he tells me.

6

As soon as we're out the window, Cam announces the game: we both try to guess how many bullshit catchphrases our parents have in common.

"I've got one," Cam says, jogging backward along the sidewalk. "I'll be Aunt Lori. Ready?"

"I don't—"

"WHO ARE YOU TEXTING, young man?"

I laugh, then bite the inside of my cheek. "I take it your parents nag you about that too?"

"Hoh yeah," Cam says. He snaps his fingers as he spins into a forward walk.

Okay, yeah, I'm going along with him. I can't figure out why— maybe it's because I've never tried something like this, or maybe some part of me knows that Cam would never have shut up until I'd agreed. By now my adrenaline is pumping, and I keep throwing paranoid looks back at my yard as it shrinks in the distance.

I do have to admit, the scenery is nice. The summer air is that perfect temperature, and the ambience of crickets echoes all around us now.

"I can't quite figure out your deal," I tell Cam.

He cracks an amused smile. "My deal?"

"With your parents. Why do you hate them?"

"I don't hate them."

"Okay, but you don't seem to respect them very much."

"I have as much respect for them as they do for me. Wasn't my idea to aim low in that department; it was theirs."

He says all this in a brisk deadpan, like he doesn't even have to think about the words before they're out of his mouth. The more I talk with him, the more I realize just how many ideas he's got marinating in his head—like a computer with too much information and a bad attitude. It's intimidating.

I opt to change the subject. "So where'd you move here from? I never asked."

"Virginia," Cam answers, segueing into the new conversation without missing a beat.

"That's cool. Which part?"

"Richmond," he says. *"Sic itur ad astra."*

"Oh—wait, what?"

"That's the city motto on the official seal and stuff," he explains. We turn the corner, starting the loop back to my house as promised. "It's Latin for, 'thus one journeys to the stars.'"

"I didn't even know cities had mottoes," I say. "So you grew up there?"

"Actually, I grew up in North Carolina. I've seen a little of everywhere."

"Oh." I, meanwhile, have lived in the same bedroom since the day I was brought home from the hospital. "Why'd you guys leave North Carolina? You get bored or something?"

Cam, for once, misses a beat. He even falters a little on the sidewalk. "Well, actually, uh—my parents wanted to move after Chloe, my sister, died."

That wrenches me to a stop. I look him up and down, mortified. "Oh my God—I'm sorry."

"No, you're fine dude, you're fine," he says, eyes straying off to the side. He picks his walk back up, seeming even more embarrassed than me. "I didn't mean to like, drop heavy shit on you."

"It's okay," I say way too fast, because it really is. "I mean. Because of my mom, like . . . I get it. Was this recently, or . . . ?" Shit, there I go again. I shouldn't be asking this kind of stuff.

"Nah," he says, with a casualness that sounds exaggerated— like he's letting me know he doesn't mind talking about this. "She was five, and I was in elementary school when it happened. Same as you."

I don't ask any more questions, and he doesn't elaborate. We walk in silence until we're back to my house. When we reach my backyard, neither of us goes to climb back in the window. We just stare at it, unmoving.

"Well." I finally break the silence. "Good talk."

"Good walk," Cam replies. "For the record, that was the most you've said since I met you."

"I don't do that much talking."

"You should."

"I don't have much to say."

"Well in that case, do you mind if I ask you something weird?"

"No."

"Did you start at Catholic school before your mom died, or after?"

Even though I'm ready for something random, this still catches me off guard. What's his point?

"Before," I tell him, tentative. "Why?"

"Just curious." He steps back so he's leaning against the trampoline in the middle of the yard. "I started after."

I see what he's getting at. And the truth is, I grew up with a Catholic education, but it didn't really start to *mean* something until after that day. Most kids my age only go to church because their parents force them to—especially at our private school. But it isn't like that for me. I pray every night, and when I go to mass, I consider it sort of like a conference with . . . myself? God? I'm still not sure on that one. But when I decide how to act, I picture it like I'm being observed. And if any of this sounds strange, try telling that to a seven year old who spent his time growing up without a mom and wondering where she went after she drowned.

I tell all this to Cam. He listens without interrupting. When I finish, I'm leaning against the trampoline with him.

"So yeah, complicated subject," I finish.

"I didn't mean to—"

"I know. And it's cool if you're not religious or anything."

He cocks an eyebrow. "I am though."

I give him eyebrows right back. "Really? But you're like, super into science."

"You say that like those are antonyms."

"A lot of it just seems contradictory."

"A lot of it isn't though," Cam says. "Like, for example, the watchmaker analogy argues that God exists, and that was supported by Newton and Descartes. Plus—"

"But evolution," I interrupt.

"Yeah, I mean, obviously evolution is a proven thing," he says. Now he's clearing the brush off the trampoline. "But scientists still don't know what happened during the Planck Era—the first ten-to-the-negative-forty-three seconds of the universe. So for—"

"Sorry," I interrupt again, pointing to the trampoline. "Are you getting up there?"

"If we're getting into developmental theories of the universe, I'm going to be sitting down for that one."

"This is a sitting kind of conversation?"

"You better believe this is a sitting kind of conversation."

So we hop up on my old trampoline and both lie back so we're sinking into the mesh, staring up at the sky, and holy *shit* are the stars gorgeous. I mean, they look the same as always, but it's a clearer night than I've seen in a while.

"So what was I saying . . . oh right, well, an example would be deistic evolution," Cam continues, arms folded behind his head. "That's the theory that God created the world, then let evolution take things from there. And there are a few other theories along that line."

I wish there were a way—without being weird—to tell him how much I like hearing about this stuff. What Cam just described is more or less what my view on this has always been, but I never knew there was a word for it. Nor have I ever really talked to someone who would know that.

"So you *are* Catholic, then?" I ask. It's the kind of question that would've been out of place to ask him ten minutes ago but doesn't feel like it now.

"I'd say I'm a solid two on the Dawkins scale," he says. "But probably more accurate to say I'm ignostic."

"Agnostic?"

"*Ig*-nostic. It says the whole debate of whether or not God exists is kind of pointless because the word *God* doesn't have a universal definition. Some people think it means the same thing as 'consequences,' or 'statistics,' or whatever force created everything. It's all the shit that's out there, and *that's* what scientists study. They map galaxies and develop models, and it's all just so, so . . . huge." And Cam sweeps his whole arm across our view, tracing over every star.

"I don't usually talk about this kind of stuff," I say.

He snorts without looking at me. "I can tell."

"I don't mind it though."

I let my arms rest at my side, studying the sea of tiny lights above us. *There's one. And another. Another. Another.* I think about what Cam just said about the size and scope of the universe, and it hits me for the first time how seriously incomprehensible all this is. Countless stars. Countless galaxies. God. All of it. Us.

A wave of overwhelming calm crawls from my feet to my head—warming my blood, cradling my body as I feel every muscle relax. I breathe as deeply as I can, closing my eyes and trying to find words for the feeling. Floating while staying anchored. Flying without moving. Whatever it is, it builds and builds, and finally the sensation is so intense that I release this huge, stupid grin.

Cam notices and laughs tentatively. "Doing okay?"

"I feel like I'm on drugs," I tell him. "I feel like this is what it's like to be stoned."

"Eh, it's kind of similar. I'm a lot more giggly."

I open my eyes. "So you've been before?"

"Stoned? Once. Wasn't really my thing. You?"

"No," I say, because holy shit would Aunt Lori have my head if she even suspected I tried drugs or alcohol. "I like this though. I like feeling . . . floaty."

"Sounds like you'd probably like being high, then," Cam says. He sounds pleased with himself that I'm having such a good time. "It gets you in the mood to just say, 'fuck it.'"

"Isn't that what we're doing right now?"

Cam rubs his chin, thoughtful. "Nah. This is like, level two of saying 'fuck it.'"

"Oh boy. How many levels are there?"

"Ninety . . . six," he decides. "But in fairness to you, this is pretty normal behavior for me. My family is full of campers. Stargazing and having deep conversations is a monthly activity."

"So what does level ninety-six look like for you?"

"Leaving." He says the word without an ounce of hesitation. He lets out a puff of air, clearly invigorated. "Like sometimes I want to just pack all my shit, drive someplace out in the middle of nowhere, and set up my own campsite by myself. No parents. No people."

"When I was younger, I fantasized about something like that," I say. "I saw people selling toolsheds at the hardware store, so—this is so weird, but I wanted to buy one and live out of it. Like a small house."

"Now *that* would be something," he says, smiling at the idea. "I could never actually do it though. I'd miss the people too much."

I nod, thinking of Aria, Dad, and Aunt Lori.

"Your perfect memory wouldn't help with that?" I ask.

Cam spits out a dry laugh, so it's more of a bitter-sounding cough. "The memory is the whole problem."

"I don't get it."

"I'll try to explain," he says, sounding like he's had this

conversation a million times before. "So . . . easy example, have you ever had a breakup?"

I pause. "I met Aria at the start of tenth grade, and we broke up during winter break. She thought she might like this douchebag named George."

"Fucking George, I swear."

"Right?" I huff. "Fuck George."

"She didn't, I hope."

"Nah, it was just a small fight. We got back together this past summer. So more of a break than a breakup."

"Okay, well. *I* had a breakup a few years ago," Cam says, holding his palms toward the sky like he's examining his nails. "Granted I was twelve, but stick with me. I'd grown up with this girl, and she and I had the cute neighbor thing going. We did that version of middle-school dating for a few months until her family—military—moved to Texas. And we had this last day together where we watched movies the whole afternoon—"

"Please tell me you had your first kiss that day."

"I did," Cam says. "Normally I recommend waiting for a soft, romantic part of the movie to kiss the girl. However, if you're an idiot like me and picked *Gladiator*, just go for it whenever his family isn't being crucified."

"Smart."

"It was cringeworthy, and I totally missed her mouth, but . . . it was cute-awkward, right? Then she left for good, and I started missing her as soon as she did."

"Makes sense. It's still fresh."

"That right there—that's exactly the problem." Cam taps his temple. "For me, stuff is *always* fresh. I guess it eventually fades into the background, but . . . well, it takes a long time. A really long time."

"Wow." I chew on that. "So does it hurt to relive bad memories?"

"Yeah. It hurts more to relive the good ones though."

Damn.

"There are some days—really important ones—where it's the anniversary of a vivid day from way back when. And I can't do much but sit and like, *think* about this thing that happened, that isn't happening anymore. Stupid."

"It's not," I say.

"Fair enough. Annoying, then."

"Well, when's the next one of those days? We can find something to do. To take your mind off it."

Cam gets really quiet at that. He turns and stares at me until I'm staring back.

"Hey. You have no idea how much that means to me," he says.

"Why?"

"Because no one's ever offered that before."

I bop him on the head with my palm. "No one's ever sat down next to me in class and declared that we were friends."

"Eh. You were an easy target."

Of all things, that makes me laugh in a way I can't stop. Like it's been building for the whole night. I laugh until it hurts and when Cam notices, he chuckles too. "What is it?"

"This is just . . ." I trail off, shaking my head.

"How're you feeling now?" he asks me. His words soften. "Still like you're on drugs?"

I let myself sink back into the feeling of floating. Simplicity. Riding the wave of euphoria, less intense now but just as powerful because *maybe it can stay like this. Maybe I can feel like this again now that I know what it's like. Maybe I can start hanging out with Cam, and maybe we'll do this again. God, I hope we do.*

Sic itur ad astra.

"I feel like myself," I finally tell him.

Beside me, my new friend smiles at the sky.

"Mother*fucker*."

If you wake up and this is the first word out of your mouth, chances are you're already off to a bad start. In my case, I repeat it a few more times as I sit straight up on the trampoline and rip leaves out of my hair. Then I smack Cam in the shoulder as hard as I can, pointing to the sun peeking above the tree line.

"Hey! We fucking overslept!"

Cam's eyes snap open. He joins me in scrambling off the trampoline.

"Dude, I'm so sorry," he says as we bolt toward the house. "What are your Aunt Lori and dad going to say?"

We don't have to wait long to find out. As soon as we tiptoe through the back door, we have about five seconds of relief before we spot Dad and Aunt Lori seated in the living room. Dad is dressed for the day, but Aunt Lori is still in her purple bathrobe. She's sipping from a cup of coffee, her face entirely neutral.

Cam and I freeze, deer-in-the-headlights style.

"Good morning, gentlemen," Aunt Lori says.

I assess my options and decide to come out swinging.

"We just went out to the backyard," I stammer. "Last night. We needed a thing for our project. We got distracted and fell asleep. We are so, so sorry."

Aunt Lori's eyebrows crawl upward. "What was it?"

"Huh?"

"What thing did you need from the backyard?"

Cam opens his mouth to try. "It—"

"HOLD up there, Cam." She raises her voice on the first word to cut him off, but keeps the pleasant tone. "I was talking to my nephew."

I turn feebly to Dad, who has his gaze fixed on us. I deflate.

"We wanted to get fresh air outside last night, and we fell asleep." I get it all out in one breath. "That's all."

Aunt Lori is nodding thoughtfully, like I've told her an intriguing bit of trivia. She lets out a long sigh through her nose, setting down the coffee and lacing her fingers together.

"Cam." She turns to him. "Mr. Copeland and I were just saying how glad we are that Nate has someone to hang out with besides his girlfriend. We like you, and we want you to feel welcome here. But," her voice darkens, "it's important to us that Nate only has friends who are good influences. So if you two break the rules together again, we're going to have a different discussion. You hear me?"

Cam nods. "Totally understand. I'm so sorry."

"It's all right." She doesn't sound *quite* satisfied, but thankfully Cam doesn't press further.

"We just need to finish the project this morning," I say.

"I think that's enough for one weekend," Aunt Lori says, which is what she always tells me when she means, *if you had fun yesterday you can't have fun today.* "Cam is going home now. Do you need one of us to drive you?"

"No, no," Cam says, sounding jittery. It's my first time seeing him on edge. "I can walk. I'm really sorry, again."

I walk him to the front door, out of my dad's and aunt's sight. Before he steps out, he tries to repeat his apology to me, but I wave it off. "Don't worry about it."

"Okay," he says, hushed. "Phone number?"

I murmur it to him, and he nods, promising to text me. I close the door behind him.

As soon as it locks, I realize that I've now sent home the one thing preventing me from getting chewed out. Dad and Aunt Lori would never bitch at me in front of guests.

I head back to the living room, bracing myself for the firing squad. My hands rattle behind my back.

"Sit down, bud." This from Dad.

I collapse onto the couch across from the two of them.

"First time sneaking out, or just the first time you got caught?" Aunt Lori asks. Her eyes have narrowed into slits. The snake eyeing its prey.

"I've never done it before," I say, not sure whether to nod or shake my head. The words tumble out of my mouth. "It was an accident."

"So you, what, tripped and fell through your window screen?"

They rail on me for a few minutes but, honestly, it's a tame treatment compared to what I was expecting. It helps that Dad is here—Aunt Lori dials it up when it's just her and me. They take away my cell phone for a week and give me what they call the "open-door penalty," which is where they disconnect the latch from my door so it can't close. I'm also not allowed to attend Aria's dance recital tomorrow.

Dad finally says that's it and slinks off to take care of my door. Once he's out of earshot, Aunt Lori grips my shoulder, stopping me mid-stride out of the room.

"Listen. You don't like our rules, that's fine," she says. "But for every day you deal with us, you get a roof over your head and food in your mouth. You want to make it on your own, at sixteen? Be my guest. I guarantee in ten years you'll be a high-school dropout with no car, a disappointed mom watching over you, and a job where you scrub shit off the floor of GoMart bathrooms for nine bucks an hour. I wouldn't screw this up if I were you."

8

The plan was never for Aunt Lori to move in with us, by the way. At first, she just came down for the funeral services when my mom died. She noticed that Dad was overwhelmed with managing things on his own, so she offered to stay with us short-term to babysit me. That took all of two weeks to turn into cooking, and cleaning, and doing some legal work on the side to help us out with the bills.

"You're a godsend," I remember Dad saying one night.

Cut to three months later: Aunt Lori, fresh out of a messy divorce, needed somewhere to stay. From there, the deal was sealed. Months turned into years, and at some point, the guest room turned into "Lori's room." It was never meant to be permanent, but that's what it became.

I can still clearly remember the day I first met her. That's pretty remarkable, seeing as it was the summer before my second-grade school year.

I'd never seen her before; in fact, I'd never even known my mom had a sister. Then one day, this hip thirtysomething woman with straight dark hair comes hustling through the door, earrings jingling, waving like she's being introduced on a game show.

"Hi, everyone! Bill, it's so good to see you. Oh, how are you holding up? Come here." I remember seeing her hug my dad for a long time. Then she turned and knelt down to my eye level. I caught the smell of vanilla and wondered if she lived in a bakery. She wasn't my mom, but she felt like *a* mom, at least.

"And you must be Nathan. Do you know who I am?"

I shook my head.

"Sweetie, I'm your mom's sister. You can call me Aunt Lori. Can I call you Nate?"

I nodded. I was too young for any of this to excite me much.

"Awesome. Nate, I'm so sorry about what happened to your mom. I loved her more than anything. But she's with the angels now, and we're going to get through this together, all right?" Then she reached into her bag and pulled out a lollipop. "Now, I don't know if you like candy, but if you do . . ."

Then a goofy grin split across my face, and Aunt Lori was my favorite person in the world.

■ ■ ■

"OhmyGodIdidn'thearfromyouallweekendIwassoworried!"

I'm caught in the blast zone as soon as I step out of my car

Monday morning. The very cute source of the explosion is my girlfriend, Aria Harrington, who has her auburn hair tied back and her hands bolted to her hips.

"I'll pay for your bagel this morning?" I offer, my hands raised in surrender. I try to kiss her, but she ducks away.

"I don't care about a bagel! Were you in a *coma*? I was worried about you!" she says.

Let me be clear: biting off my head like this isn't something Aria normally does. Sure, she frets about everything from test grades to the color of her nail polish, but she rarely takes it out on me. Well. Unless it's my fault. Which in this case it absolutely is, because I was a no-show for her recital yesterday.

"I'm sorry," I tell her. "I'm super, super sorry. I got grounded on Saturday."

She wrinkles her nose. "Not funny."

"No like, actually."

"You? *You.*"

I tell her the whole story and add how well that went with my parents. (I've gotten in the habit of referring to Dad/ Aunt Lori as "parents.") I leave out my aunt's last comment about my "disappointed mom," since it still makes me a little sick to my stomach.

By the end of the story, Aria is clutching my hand and patting it. We're still leaned up against my car in the school parking lot.

"I'm sorry, dude, that sucks," she says. She stands up on her tiptoes and kisses me on the cheek. "No bagel required."

"I missed your recital. We can both owe each other."

"Deal." She squeezes my arm, and we walk toward the gas station to buy our breakfast.

This early-morning food routine is something we did every day last year. It's actually how we met: back in tenth grade, before I could drive myself, my parents would drop me at school way early. To kill time, I'd walk to the mini-mart across the street and get some cheap breakfast food.

Turns out a girl from my homeroom came up with the same solution to the same problem. After a few instances of bumping into each other, we got talking. Then we made a point to consume our feast together every morning, slowly opening up to each other. She was the first person I told about my love of painting. Before long, Aria was gas station breakfast girl.

Girlfriend sounds a lot nicer, but anyway.

Since I have a car now, we eat our food in the front seat. Morning radio talk-show hosts yammer out of the old speakers as Aria and I continue our conversation.

"Not going to lie, I'm a little happy to hear about your escapade with this Cameron person," she tells me, stealing a sip of my coffee.

"You're happy I got grounded?"

"No, but I'm glad you got out of your little bubble." She pokes my cheek. "Maybe Cameron can get you to stop being . . . you know. Allergic to fun."

"Yes, being grounded is exactly the motivation I need to do something like that again."

Aria shrugs. "Your aunt needs to loosen up a bit."

"Try telling her that."

"Yeah, no thanks. I don't want her hating me."

Aria finishes her food, reaches into her backpack, and pulls out a small orange medicine bottle. She tries to obscure my view even though she's shown it to me a hundred times: Lexapro, twenty milligrams. Also known as anti-anxiety medication.

We've had a lot of important breakfast conversations, she and I.

9

As if being grounded isn't punishment enough, the world decides to get one last jab in by hitting me with the stomach flu a few nights later.

There are a few silver linings to this. First, me being sick is one of the few situations that transform Aunt Lori into a superhero. I don't know who decided to give a lawyer medical training, but she knows exactly how to take care of me. She wastes no time getting me the proper medicines, making me a balanced dinner, and watching HGTV with me until I fall asleep.

"Anything you need during the night, you wake me up, okay?" she tells me that evening, stroking my hair as I feel myself sink into an Imodium-filled coma.

So that's nice of her, I guess.

The other advantage of my illness is that I'm home from school Thursday. Which means that instead of slogging through an AP Bio lecture, I get an empty house to myself.

I don't waste the opportunity. My first order of business is to retrieve my cell phone from its home away from home, i.e., a shoebox in my aunt's bedroom. I make note of its exact position, since I know she'll check later to see if it changed. I'm also careful not to walk through the entrance hallway—we have one of those Wi-Fi security cameras that records any movement. It's only on during school hours, so normally I don't have to worry about it. Aunt Lori likes to "joke" that she and Dad are going to use it to spy on me, but I have no doubt they'd love to do it for real sometime.

I flop down on my bed and open a private browsing tab. Three days with that unlatched-door policy has taken a severe toll on my masturbatory career. Plus it might help cure my flu-induced achiness.

I owe it to my personal health, you see.

And I know, I know: I'm a hypocrite for being a practicing Catholic and choosing to do this stuff. I'll admit that, as wonderful as the naked women on the screen are, they fuel a steady moral quandary that's been on the rise—uh, no pun intended—since I was twelve. Would it be better if I only pictured Aria? Probably not, since it'd be without her knowledge—not that it doesn't still happen. Any way you frame it, the whole thing is an ugly subject.

I'm about to get rolling when my phone buzzes with a text from an unknown number. Probably Cam, I figure.

So is this a case of actual illness, or are you just allergic to HAVING FUN LEARNING ABOUT BIOLOGY, you young pioneer of knowledge?

Yup, that's Cam. Unless Mrs. Koestler spent her weekend learning how to use a cell phone.

I punch in a reply.

Really sorry I'm not there for the project—actual illness. Everything on my inside wants to be on my outside. The only thing I've been able to eat today is like a gallon of applesauce.

He answers a few minutes later.

Unforgivable, applesauce boy.

Me: Soo am I missing anything important?

Him: Well, you're missing Ms. K's speech about eukaryotes. If this woman gets any more fired up, she's going to achieve liftoff.

I snort. PLEASE get a video of that. I really hope she doesn't get any creamier as the year goes on.

"Damn it."

*CRANKIER not creamier. Fucking hell.

Cam replies to that one almost instantly: HAHAHAHA autocowrecked.

Yeah yeah, shut up.

Oh God. You're not living that one down. Ducking autocorrect.

I smile at my screen, grateful that he's at least making me forget how groggy I feel. Even if he's being an ass about it.

He isn't even done yet. Do you like your teachers on the creamier side, Nate?

Me: Sigh :P

It's unusual for me to use emojis in texting. Maybe it's my sickened state.

A few minutes later, Cam says: Welp, I should get back to focusing on the lecture. I'll send you my notes later. Keep eating that applesass . . . it has a thing called pectin that'll help your stomach.

Me: Will do, thanks.

Him: No prob . . . catch you later!

I go to set down my phone when he adds: Don't get too creamy ;)

10

"Still don't know why you need to wear that," Aunt Lori says, ruffling my hair as we walk through the parking lot and into church. She's talking about my bow tie, which is part of my weekly attire for the Sunday service.

"Let him overdress if he wants," Dad says with a chuckle. "You got a hot date after this, bud?"

I roll my eyes. I don't blame them for not understanding my thing with church—most people don't, not even Aria.

My family runs into hers on our way into the building. I wave to her and Asher (her twin brother), who has her green eyes and auburn hair. They both beam at me. I pull out my phone—recently returned—to a texting conversation I've been having with Cam. Most of the Edgecombe Academy kids are here, and since Cam is new, I invited him to sit with us.

Aria and I are about halfway back on the left.

A few minutes later, I spot him coming in with his parents and flag him down. Dad and Aunt Lori both look a little tense, but the trampoline incident was over a week ago, so I hope they're over it by now.

"What's up," Cam says, taking a seat next to us. Then he looks past me. "Hi, there—Aria, right?"

She puts on her smile, shaking his hand. "Nate said you go to our school?"

"Yup! Cameron. Friends can call me Cam though."

"Friends . . . wait, does that include me?"

"Depends." Cam rubs his chin, glancing between me and her. "According to Nate, you have friend-like tendencies, so we can give 'Cam' a try. I'm not married to it, though, so no pressure."

"Be as mean as you want to him," I tell her.

Cam picks up the bulletin for today's service and starts reading it over, nodding to himself. I almost ask him if he's even been to church in the past few years, but I decide that's kind of a rude question.

I attended with my mom just about every week from kindergarten up until she passed away. Dad didn't really go before that, but he and Aunt Lori started joining me afterward. Most of my classmates are there because they get dragged by their parents, but I actually look forward to it. No joke.

And I *know*, the Catholic Church has its image problems. I know nothing about it is perfect, and it's not the norm for someone my age to have mass hymns like John Michael Talbot's "On Eagle's Wings" in their music library.

Church has always been the one place where I can really *think*. I think about how well my life worked out when honestly, I never did anything to earn it. I think about my classmates who've broken their bones or had to get surgery, when I've never had so much as a cavity. I think about my old babysitter, Ms. Susan, who worked sixty hours a week to manage our town's soup kitchen, only to lose her kids in a car accident and her husband to an OD a year later. I think about my Dad's college roommate, whose daughter was killed in a school shooting. I think about a list that goes on and on and on, and I can't know what it's like to be on it because I never have been, and I wonder *why*. Sure, my mom passed away, but then my aunt stepped in to help us. I have a loving family unit. A beautiful girlfriend. And now a new friend in Cam. How can I not show up to church for one hour a week to reflect on my way-too-shielded life? To thank God for it and ask what I can do to be better?

When I turned seven, as preparation for First Communion, my mom gave me a prayer journal called *Dear God*. Every night for the next year, I wrote my bedtime prayers in it. *Dear God: Thank you for the extended recess today. Dear God: Thank you for my mommy and daddy.* Stuff like that. And it's a bit embarrassing, but I've gotten myself a new prayer journal every year since, and I still write my prayers down each night.

And every week I'm here, alongside all my classmates and

neighbors and teachers—all of us, together on our own list that goes on and on and on—wondering why we're here and the others aren't. Turning to the same thing for answers to all the same questions.

11

DEPOSITION EXHIBIT 1

Dear Violet,

Don't kill me . . . sorry it's been so long. I got caught up with the first few weeks of school. I know your trip was like a month ago, but how was the beach? Did your dad actually go in the water this time? XD

Also, I made a new friend. His name is Cam, and he's pretty weird, but in a good way. I met him in biology class about a month ago, and we've texted pretty much every day since. Definitely the closest guy friend I've ever had. My dad and Lori are happy I'm spending less time with Aria, which I don't get.

How's your school year been? I know tenth grade is kind of the worst, but as a survivor, I can tell you it's worth getting through.

You totally owe me a lunch. I paid for smoothies last time. When do I get to see you next? Lori has a conference coming up, so I should have some more free time than usual.

Talk to you soon!

Love,

Nate ☺

12

I decide that I like being Cam's friend. Which is good, because I get the feeling that he wouldn't take no for an answer if I told him to leave me alone.

He becomes fast friends with Aria and Asher, so he fits right in at our cafeteria table. I half expect him to ditch us for other friends in a few weeks, but he doesn't really socialize with anyone else. Which makes sense, I guess—it's obvious that Cam is totally in his element with the three of us. Soon we get to see all his little quirks. For example, with almost every conversation, he'll throw in some tidbit about himself . . . no matter how obscure.

"How was your day, Nate? Aria? Asher? Mine started great because I had waffles for breakfast. Speaking of: What's your favorite breakfast food? Favorite color? Do you take showers in the morning or at night?"

I try to give him a break because he claims it's not him, it's his perfect memory. Once I answer minor questions like those, he'll remember the answers forever, and that's his way of getting to know people.

He's like the collector of secrets, or something.

In just a few short weeks, my whole social life has transformed. Every school day is the same routine. Gas station breakfast with Aria: check. AP Bio with Cam: check. Lunch with them and Asher: check. Random study sessions, after-school hangouts, mass on Sundays. Check, check, check.

Saturday nights are the ones that are just mine and Cam's though. Aria's dance practice is then, so Cam will ask me to join him for nighttime adventures, which are usually activities as simple as getting ice cream or going to the mall. Every week I'll be sitting in my room, sketching out rough ideas for paintings, when the doorbell will ring. There'll be Cam on the porch, jacket in hand, with this look in his eyes.

"You down to do something new?" is what he always asks.

"You mean your level-ninety-six adventure?"

"Yeah, that thingy."

Whatever, Cam.

Every time, I'll put up a little fight before finally rolling my eyes and saying, "Fuck it." Like it's our secret password.

And every time, when the night is over and I drop him back home, he'll turn to me and we'll have the same exchange:

"Nate? Thank you."

"What for?"

"Just being my friend."

■ ■ ■

Dear God: thank you for Cam. Help my family to like him more—
he's not as bad as they think.

13

The first Friday of October, the usual cafeteria crew—Cam, Aria, Asher, and I—are sitting at our table in the back corner of the lunchroom. Aria is finishing a math assignment, I'm pretending I know how to help her, and Cam is showing Asher how to make sculptures out of apple cores and drinking straws.

"You guys are coming with us tonight, right?" Aria asks, to both me and Cam. She's talking about the football game.

"I'm down," Cam says. "Might need a ride though."

"I gotchu," Asher says. Nodding toward Aria, he says, "Mom is loaning us her car. We can pick everyone up. You need a ride, Nate?"

"Huh?" I stiffen. "Oh. I'm not going."

"To the *homecoming* game?" Aria says, gawking at me. "Come on. Spend time with usss."

"I'm going to the dance with you guys tomorrow," I point out. Normally I despise school dances, but this will be the first one

I go to with Aria, so it's a bit of an exception.

Cam jumps in. "What you're forgetting, Aria, is that Nathaniel is chronically immune to having fun."

"Exactly," she says, beside him. He leans so he's right behind her and waves a scolding finger at me.

"Eat shit," I mutter to him flatly.

"Already am," Cam says, sliding his half-empty lunch tray at me. "Be a lamb and put that in the trash where it belongs."

"You're not going with it?"

We're now close enough friends for this to be a typical exchange.

"Behave, boys," Aria scolds.

"Thanks, Mom," I tell her.

"Dude. That's your girlfriend," Asher says, cringing. Cam sucks in air through his teeth.

■ ■ ■

The three of them are on my ass until I agree to go to the football game, which means they'll be at my house around 6:00 to pick me up. Unfortunately, a roadblock in the form of a very unhappy aunt presents itself around 5:50.

At first when I hear her slam the car door, slam the front door, then slam her briefcase on the kitchen counter, I assume it was one of her bad days at the firm. It's not until she finds me in my room that I realize I'm involved.

"There you are," she says, barging in without knocking. She

closes the door behind her and sets an envelope beside me on my bed. She waits for my reaction, sipping water from a wine glass. When I don't immediately pull out my earbuds, she yanks my phone out of my hand.

"Whoa," I say, sitting up. "Um, hi."

"Open that," she says, nodding to the envelope and pocketing my phone. I gulp once when I see it's from my school, and twice when I read what's inside. It's my interim grades, which are sent home the middle of each quarter.

"Crap," I mutter.

"Is that what all those Cs stand for? C-c-c-c-crap?" Aunt Lori stutters at me.

"They're interims. They don't mean anything," I say. Time for damage control.

"Oh? I guess the school just wants to waste paper, huh?"

"I guess."

She tilts her head, eyeballing me over the rim of her glass. "Well? Is that it? The school just wants to waste paper?"

"I don't know."

"You don't know? You just said you 'guess.' Which is it?"

I make the mistake of dropping my eyes to my lap. I'm jolted by a *smack* to the side of my head. Not hard, not abusive or anything, but it still stings my eye.

"Look at me when I'm talking to you." Aunt Lori rips the letter out of my hands. "We've never seen this from you before. And I *think* I figured out the problem. Any guesses what I came up with?"

"No."

"You don't know?"

"*No.*"

"See? You're getting better at this. Admitting flaws and asking questions, bud. That's all it takes."

"Okay," I say, gritting my teeth so hard it hurts.

"So, ask me."

"What do you think the problem is, Aunt Lori?"

The serpent flicks its tail: a warning.

"Don't you dare give me attitude, mister. The last thing I want to do is play the bad guy here, but this is important. There's only one influence on you that's changed recently."

I pause, then see what she's getting at.

"This has *nothing* to do with Cam," I say, a little too quickly. "Most of the time we spend together is studying anyway. He's really smart."

"Well, since you're a C student now, maybe you aren't the best person to decide what 'smart' means," she says with a snicker, like I'm supposed to find that really funny. "These need to be As by the end of the quarter."

I dig my nails into my palms—I'm almost out of calm. "They're really high Cs. Almost Bs."

"Am I asking what they are? No. I'm telling you what they need to be."

That sends one last rush of anger prickling up my spine, and my mouth acts without permission from my brain.

"You don't need to say it like that, okay? *Okay?* I get it."

As soon as the words are out of my mouth, Aunt Lori angles her cup and throws the ice water straight in my face. I jolt, my head snapping back against the wall with a sharp *thwack*. The biggest ice cube nails me right in the eye, which starts to throb.

Below, the doorbell rings.

"That's Aria and Asher," I splutter, trying to dry myself with my sleeves. Aunt Lori's mouth snaps shut, and she frowns. Can't have mean Lori around when guests are here.

I pocket my wallet and head for the door, still dripping. "I'll be home by eleven."

"You'll be home by ten. If you're even one minute late, you can forget about going to the dance tomorrow," Aunt Lori calls after me. When I don't respond, she adds, "I swear to God. I'll shred your goddamn ticket."

I plow out my front door without looking back.

14

I don't say much during the drive other than to tell Aria how much she's just saved my ass. I take care not to mention that Aunt Lori is blaming Cam for my grades, since I figure he would probably burst into tears right there in the backseat. That would be especially messy, considering he currently has green and yellow stripes—the colors of our school—painted on each cheek.

It's dark outside by the time we get to the football game, but the field glows under the stadium lights. The bleachers are packed with screaming teenagers, most of their faces and arms decorated.

Cam—jacket in hand, per his parents' mandate—leads the way. The crowd jumps up, cheering again, and Cam joins right in, turning to me and flailing his arms. Oh yeah, in addition to his face paint, he also has several beaded necklaces, which he waves in my face.

"Yo, cut it out," I mutter. I can tell he's trying to cheer me up, but Aunt Lori officially trashed my mood for the evening. All I want is to take a nap alone somewhere dark and quiet.

Asher splits off to smoke pot with a few buddies, so the rest of us sit, with Aria between Cam and me. We buy hot chocolate, Cam offering his whipped cream to Aria. She grins at him. I catch an exchange between them that I haven't seen before— a shared look, something private that doesn't include me. I can tell it doesn't mean anything concerning, but it piles on to my already bitter attitude.

I'm slightly cheered up when Aria takes a blanket out of her backpack, allowing her and me to cuddle for the second half of the game. I even manage to convince her that you're supposed to kiss your boyfriend every time there's a touchdown, though this doesn't help much when your school's football team is a joke.

Aria rests two fingers on my kneecap, making me jolt.

"You okay?" she asks, promptly yanking her hand back.

"Yeah, no, you're fine, just . . . caught me off guard," I say, snuggling closer to her. I'm seriously out of it tonight.

"If you're sure," Aria pats my knee, a teasing smile creeping to her face. "Don't want another. You know. Boathouse Incident."

"Oh my *God*, that's never going away."

"Never. Never ever."

Okay, fine—story time. The first month of every summer, our school sponsors a weeklong trip to Covenant Lake Camp, a Christian summer camp for grades 9 through 12. Cut to this past June: Aria and I, having recently rekindled our relationship, were both on this trip and decided it was the perfect chance for a bit of . . . private time together. The boys' and girls' sites were kept separate, for obvious reasons, so we agreed to each take a spontaneous stroll down to the lake at midnight.

(For the record, the unambiguous hypocrisy of hooking up at a Bible camp is not and never was lost on me.)

Long story short, Aria and I ended up in the boathouse, which was perfect since it had walls on three sides and an open view of the lake. We started making out, both getting handsy for the first time ever, and it was *fantastic*. Better than I ever pictured. Only it was a bit too fantastic too quickly, because I had my—let's say, grand finale—before she even got my shorts unbuttoned.

Once she was done pissing herself laughing, Aria assured me it was okay, maybe even for the best, and we called it a night. The guilt ended up setting in for us both over the next few days, and it screwed us up enough that we haven't done anything since. But man, does she still love to tease me about it.

I guide her hand back onto my knee, pointedly not jumping this time. She flashes me an exaggerated thumbs-up.

Cam, meanwhile, has mellowed out and is ignoring us. The game has a few minutes left on the clock when I realize he hasn't spoken in over an hour.

"Hey," I say to him, leaning across Aria. "How're things?"

"Things are dandy," Cam says, but he sounds worn out. It's a strange tone for him.

"You sure?" Aria asks. She senses something is wrong too.

"You seem all bummed."

"Nope—bumming-free zone," Cam tries, but he isn't looking at either of us. He stands up, fidgeting. "Be right back."

His first two steps are slow, careful. Then he breaks into a half run and hustles down the bleacher steps, past the concession stand, and out of sight.

"What's up with him?" I ask.

Aria gives me a look. I go, "What?"

"Don't you think you should . . . you know, help him?" she says. "You're his best friend."

I figure that's a strong phrase to use for someone I've known a month, but I should probably still check on him. Aria shoos me off, and I amble down the same route Cam took.

I find him the first place I check: the deck of the trailers. Our school is too poor to afford all the classrooms it needs, so some of the classes are held in these trailers with a huge wooden patio connecting them all. It's directly adjacent to the field, which is why I look there first. Sure enough, Cam is sitting in the back corner of the deck, up against the railing. The overhang shields him from the moonlight, and his legs are tucked up to his chest in the fetal position.

I approach slowly, tapping on the rail to let him know I'm there. If he sees me, he doesn't react.

"Cam?" I say tentatively. He still doesn't move.

Then in a wobbly voice, he says from the shadows, "How's it going?"

"I was going to ask you that. What's up?"

"Well, I guess you're getting to witness me dealing with memory stuff," Cam says. "You remember when I told you certain days are significant anniversaries, and it puts me in really weird moods?"

It takes me a second to know what he's talking about. Then I snap my fingers. "Right. That. So you're having a . . . I don't know what to call it. Memory attack."

"Wrong word but right idea."

"Okay. Well, what can I do?"

He turns to look up, giving me a grimace that's both pained and grateful.

"Can I maybe tell you about it? Sharing the memory would help. If you don't mind."

I nod, sliding down until I'm sitting right next to him. I pull my arms against my chest the same way his are—it's chillier down here.

"Today is October sixth," Cam starts. "Which is the day they diagnosed Chloe—my sister."

I suck in a breath, not sure what to say. I go with, "Shit, dude. Has that been on your mind all day?"

"Kind of."

"But you seemed so . . . peppy. You were waving your arms and stuff."

"I try to distract myself," he says. "Which works sometimes. But I don't know, the game was winding down, Asher had left, you and Aria were basically a human knot—"

"Hey!"

"Just an observation, not a judgment. But anyway. Chloe."

"Yeah. So how'd you find out? That day."

"I overheard my parents freaking out about it," he says. "So, like, the worst way possible. They'd just gotten home from the hospital, and they thought I was asleep because I stuffed a towel under the door crack so it looked like the lights were off."

"That was smart."

"I was a sneaky little shit. But anyway. I could hear my mom crying. And I mean, she wasn't just sobbing . . . this was something different. Hysterical. And she didn't say outright what had happened, but I picked up enough buzzwords that I Googled it the next day. So it's like, I didn't actually find out that night. But I knew something had happened with Chloe. And I remember the whole next month, my parents kept it from me. They pretended everything was fine. And I don't know, I just . . ." Cam falters, and I can hear his voice slipping.

"It's oka—" I start to say, but he continues, cutting me off.

"I just wish my parents gave me enough credit to tell me, you know? Because during that month, them not telling me was enough to make me think it wasn't true. Because I didn't want it to be true. Obviously. And when I found out that it was, I was . . . completely livid with them." His fists clench. "It was like they'd just taken away a month I could've spent keeping close to her. And the way it played out, just . . ." His shoulders twitch.

"Remembering this. It's a lot."

"It's okay," I say, which I'm aware is both lame and generic advice.

He squeezes his head between his hands. "It just sucks for right now. It'll pass, but it sucks."

"I know." I sort of pat his shoulder, which normally I'd never do. He still has his arms and legs pulled up against himself. Above us, a light rain patters on the steel roof.

"Please don't tell anyone," Cam says, his gaze pleading with mine. "About this. I . . . I don't usually share this kind of stuff. I've never told anyone this, come to think of it."

"Of course," I say. "I'm glad you did."

"Could I be alone now? If you don't mind. Sorry. I don't mean to be—"

"It's okay." I let go of his shoulder and climb to my feet. I take a few steps when he calls after me, "Nate?"

I turn back to him. He looks so small, curled up on the floor.

"Thank you for being my friend," he says.

"You don't need to keep thanking me for that, Cam."

"I know. But I feel like I should."

"Why?"

"Because no one's ever helped me like you," he tells me.

■ ■ ■

After that night, every few weeks, Cam has a memory attack,

and we go through the same routine. We sit together, wherever we happen to be, and I stay until he gets through it. Normally, he wants to share the memory with me. I just sit there and let him.

Sometimes he cries. I let him do that, too.

15

Thanks to my talk with Cam, I get home from the football game at 10:08 p.m.

I tiptoe into my room to find my ticket for the dance sitting on my desk, torn in half a dozen pieces.

From my doorway, Aunt Lori sips her wine.

"Shame," she croons.

16

Dad does everything he can to change Aunt Lori's mind, but I know it's a lost cause before he even tries. While she gets groceries that morning, Dad slips me my phone and says I can call Aria—who, naturally, throws a fit. I've never felt so helpless, trapped in my bedroom like a caged animal while she sobs about how I'm going to miss dinner. And pictures. And the whole evening that's been planned for a month. Eventually she has to hang up because she's having the start of an anxiety attack, and that's the part that kills me because I know I'm the direct trigger for it even though she tries to tell me I'm not.

For the first time since the Trampoline Sleepover Incident, I consider sneaking out. Unfortunately, as strict as Aunt Lori can be, she's equally clever. She opens my door every ten or fifteen minutes, pretending she's asking me a question. There's even a tender smile. But there's also this look in her eyes that says what she's doing, and that she knows I know what she's doing.

A mutual understanding we share: the hand of Aunt Lori giveth, the hand of Aunt Lori taketh away.

I spend Saturday night eating reheated lasagna, then crawling into the shower—the one place I can be alone—and soaking for over an hour, smacking the wall tile until I can't feel my palms.

■ ■ ■

Aria doesn't speak to me at church on Sunday. Cam tries, but I ignore him.

17

DEPOSITION EXHIBIT 2

Dear Nate,

It's about time! I was starting to think Lori strangled you for failing a test or something.

That's cool to hear about Cam. Does this mean you've started pulling the stick out of your ass? Maybe he can help you ;) JK. I'm happy for your bromance.

It's been SO LONG since I've seen you! I'm glad you want to hang, but I'm under total lockdown for the next month. My dad found the Oxy under my bed, which isn't a big deal since it was just leftover from my surgery a few summers ago, but he found out I was selling it and threw a fit. It didn't help that I came home from a house party extremely not-sober a few days later.

I know, I know, you're going to lecture me. I PROMISE I'm behaving here.

I'll let you know next time I'm free. Winter break for sure.

Love,

Violet ☺

18

"Who's Violet Cantrell?" Cam asks me one day.

I close out the email from her, covering my phone with my hand. "No one. Someone I'm not allowed to see anymore."

"Scandalous. Why's that? Aunt's rules?"

"It's a long story, but pretty much. She also goes to boarding school eighty miles away. I don't feel like explaining it."

I can tell Cam is a little thrown by me not sharing with him, but I don't apologize for keeping certain things to myself.

"Someone's a little brusque today," he observes, but he drops it.

We're studying on his bedroom floor with music on in the background. It took two weeks, but Aria stopped being pissed at me for missing the dance, and I stopped being pissed at Cam for getting me grounded in the first place. I think we collectively decided that it was too exhausting to work out who was to blame for what, so we let it all blow over.

Cam gets to his feet and sways back and forth, clapping to the song blasting from his speakers—"Mr. Maker" by the Kooks.

"Having fun?" I ask, peering over my Spanish homework.

"Tons of it. You try!"

"No thanks."

"Why not?"

"Because I'm, you know, straight."

"But oh no, it's alright! Mr. MAKER, he'll be fine!" Cam is singing over me, just so badly. He grins. "Come on! Try it once. If you hate it, you'll know to never do it again."

To demonstrate, he puts both of his hands over his head and twirls on the spot, then collapses onto his bed laughing like a maniac.

I really don't get him sometimes.

"Ask me again on your birthday," I tell him. "That can be your present."

"You trying something new is my birthday present?"

"I live to serve."

"Do you find it weird that every year, you pass the day of your death without knowing it?" Cam says, like this is a normal segue. "Today's October twenty-third; maybe you'll die on October twenty-third eighty years from now."

"I live to be ninety-six? Neat. I hope I die in my sleep."

"Hm." Cam folds his arms behind his head, thoughtful. "I assumed you'd die from being too uptight."

"Does that kill people?"

"It can. Tycho Brahe was a Danish astronomer who was so determined to be polite that he refused to get up to pee during some banquet. He died when his bladder burst."

"Ew, dude." I shudder. "What would people even say at my funeral?"

"I'm not sure about anyone else, but I personally would stand over your coffin and whisper, '*Looks like urine trouble.*'"

"I'm going to punch you in the dick if you ever make such a bad pun again."

"You can try, but West Virginia health code requires me to warn you that its sheer size would suck your hand right in. Like quicksand."

Cam proceeds to make slurping noises while I laugh and swat at him with a nearby pillow.

Once we both settle down, he looks out the window and says, "If I had to pick, I'd die like Martin of Aragon."

"Who?"

"So in 1410, this guy named King Martin of Aragon died one evening when he ate an entire goose."

"That's what killed him?"

"No, no," Cam says, waving off the thought. "After that his favorite jester, Borra, enters the bedroom. King Martin asks where he's been. Borra replies, '*Out of the next vineyard, where I saw a young deer hanging by his tail from a tree, as if he were punished for stealing figs.*'" Cam does the impression in a purposely awful English accent.

"Let me guess: Then Borra stabbed him."

"Nope. That terrible joke made the king start to laugh, which caused indigestion because of the goose he ate."

We blink at each other.

"So what then?" I ask.

"What do you mean, what then? He fucking died."

"So, just . . . *what*?"

"So, I want to die laughing and full of food." Cam is back to looking out the window.

"That's pretty weird, man."

"So am I."

■ ■ ■

That night, when I'm alone in my own room, I try dancing to the song.

I'll never tell Cam, but I like it.

19

"Is it fair to say that Mr. Haynes was a source of tension in your household?"

It takes me a minute to realize that Mrs. Lawson is talking to me. I shift in my seat and glance around the deposition room. All eyes are on me. Cam's parents are quiet, while Cameron himself is still acting bored, twirling his pencil on the table. Aunt Lori's fingers are snaked around my bicep. I flex against her hold. It doesn't loosen.

"Tension?" I ask.

"Sure," Mrs. Lawson says. She props an elbow against the table. "So far you've outlined two occurrences in which the actions of Mr. Haynes caused disagreements between you and your parents."

"Everyone fights with their parents," I point out.

"Yes," Aunt Lori pipes up. The spotlight shifts to her, and she repeats, "Yes. He caused tension among all of us."

"Happy to help!" Cam calls across the table, flashing a toothy grin. Aunt Lori clenches her jaw, looking ready to rip out his throat. The grip on my arm clamps down so hard that I stifle a grunt. Meanwhile, Cam's attorney just shakes his head, eyes closed.

"May I give you some pro bono advice, Mr. Haynes?" asks Mrs. Lawson.

"I literally cannot wait for this," Cam says, cupping his chin in both hands.

"I know acting like a petulant child is fun for you, but to a jury, I guarantee it'll come off as obstructive. Because at the end of the day, you aren't as cute as you think you are."

Is she seriously trying to fix his attitude? She'd have better luck getting him to plead guilty.

Cam smirks at her. "Was that an insult, or a joke?"

"Does it matter?"

"Not really. You're bad at both."

"*Cameron,*" his lawyer begs, just so, so tired. "Remember what we talked about. Respectful tone."

Mr. and Mrs. Haynes are crying again.

I think back to the transcript I read of the day when Cam was the one being questioned by Mrs. Lawson. He wasn't deposed or anything, but he was offered the chance to provide his account of the assault.

"No," he had told Mrs. Lawson, unreadable. She hadn't even asked him anything yet.

"No, you don't wish to provide a statement? I'm doing you—

and your attorney—the courtesy of considering a plea deal, Mr. Haynes. That doesn't work if you say nothing."

"No."

"What the hell is this?" Mrs. Lawson had snapped to Cam's lawyer. "If you expect—"

"No," Cam had repeated softly, and that was pretty much the end of that discussion. He hadn't said a word when he was arrested, and he wasn't about to start.

Present-day Mrs. Lawson picks her pen back up and turns to me.

"What was the next significant interaction you had with Mr. Haynes?" she asks.

"Halloween," I say, after a second. "Meghan Richter had a party."

20

Meghan Richter is a five-foot-one Girl Scout with mousy brown hair, huge hazel eyes, and a report card that's been full of straight As since the day she was born. She's the model citizen; the one who reminds the teacher we had homework or stays late to chat about the lecture of the day.

There's no nice way to say it: Her party is one hundred percent what you'd expect from that description.

Which, don't get me wrong, isn't to say it's lame. It's just that when most people hear "high-school party," they picture a living room full of music, people dancing, and—depending on the host—alcohol.

As it is, when Aria, Asher, Cam, and I knock on the front door of Meghan's house, we're offered candy and shown down to the basement by her mom. There we find Meghan and three other girls from our school, all clustered on the couch watching some old horror movie on mute. I pick up the theme from *Ghostbusters* playing out of a Bluetooth speaker on the table.

"Hey, guys!" Meghan says, scurrying over and giving us each a little one-armed hug. She's in an orange dress with black polka dots all over it, carrying a red Solo cup full of sparkling cider. She gestures to Aria and I. "You guys look so cute!"

I assume she's referring to our matching orange pumpkin shirts that Aria made me wear to match hers. Asher went for true minimum effort and is in a black shirt that just has the word *costume* on it. Cam, on the other hand, is in white-and-orange tie-dye with black skinny jeans and candy corn–pattern socks. It's strange to see everyone wearing clothes that aren't school uniforms.

Cam steps forward, then crosses his arms and huffs, "Your parents will be home the entire time tonight, right?"

"Uh, my mom should be," Meghan says, looking a little startled. "Why?"

"Good," Cam says, surveying the room. "Because I've been to *way* too many parties with alcohol and drugs. I get it—that can be fun. But you know what's more fun? Having parental oversight to keep anyone from indulging in the Devil's Drink and/or Lucifer's Lettuce. Do we agree?"

Everyone looks around like, *wtf.* Then Cam bursts out laughing.

"Holy shit, I'm just fucking with you," he says, his arms as wide as his grin. "Can you *imagine*? What's up, Meghan."

Of course that gets everyone cracking up, and Cam is in the spotlight for the rest of the night. As usual, he strikes that balance between sarcasm and respect, taking just the right jabs at people to let them know they can be chill.

"By the way, I love your socks, Cam," Meghan says. It's a few hours later, and we're all sprawled out on the couches, chatting.

Cam salutes. "Thanks! They're very Hallow-weeny."

"Hollow weenie?" I arch an eyebrow at him.

"No, that's you," he says, then mimes dropping a mic, all exaggerated. Everyone laughs, including Aria, who's sitting in my lap snuggled against my shoulder. She checks her phone, then lets out this sudden gasp.

"What is it?" I say, looping my arm around her waist. She twists away.

"It's . . . they released listings for our spring recital."

Everyone sits forward. Asher says, "How'd you dooo?"

Aria bites her lip, then shakes her head rapidly. The partygoers frown, exchanging nervous glances. Aria stares at her phone for a while.

Finally, she says to her lap, "Not good enough." Then a few deep breaths, followed by, "Sorry . . . I'll be right back. Just . . . sorry."

As she clambers up the stairs, I hear her smack her own arm, hard, and choke out, "FUCK!"

Cam follows her, I follow Cam, and Asher follows me. Pretty soon all four of us are in front of Meghan's house. Aria is leaned up against her car, Cam patting her on the shoulder. I step forward to try to help, but as soon as I do, she crumples to the ground.

"Whoa," I say. "Are you—?"

"Don't try to stand up," Cam interrupts, shoving me back so he can kneel down beside her. He helps her reposition so she's leaned up on the car tire. "Hey. You need to catch your breath."

"I'm fine," Aria says, but it's coming in between controlled gasps of air.

"You're having a panic attack," he says, studying her eyes.

"No I'm not."

"Yes you are. If you want to get technical, it's called a cued panic attack in response to an extrinsic trigger. Common in people with any of the five subtypes of anxiety."

Aria frowns, puzzled and a little guarded. "I-I never told you about that."

"Self-study. Plus my mom used to get panic attacks when I was younger. I know what they look like. Hey, try to breathe slowly. Do you have medicine you take when this happens?"

"I—yeah. Lexapro every day. And other fast-acting stuff for this. But I left it at home."

"That's okay," Cam says, although he looks a lot more worried by that. "Do you remember what that one's called?"

"Alprazolam."

"Xanax. Do you remember how much?"

"No. No. What do I do?" she asks, wide-eyed.

"I'm going to ask you something. This is really important."

"Okay."

"Take as long as you need to think it over."

"All right."

"What's your name?"

She sniffles weakly. "Aria Harrington."

"Are you cold?"

She rubs her bare arms, shivering. "Yeah."

"Just sit tight. Asher, start up the car and get it warm. Not burning hot though. Nate, ask Meghan for a cup of water without ice. Also get Aria's purse and my wallet. We left those downstairs."

"No no no," Aria gasps. "We're not leaving because of me—"

"We were talking about socks. That party was over anyway. I was trying to find a way to leave."

"Really?"

"Yeah. I owe you."

I try to look at Cam, because I can tell he's lying. He just waves at me and Asher to do as he said. Asher climbs into the car, but I don't move. I'm still processing the fact that my best friend is the one comforting my girlfriend instead of me. It feels like an out-of-body experience, but I can't stop it. I don't know what to do.

Cam waves again, so I sprint inside and do as he said, shouting a quick apology to Meghan. When I return, I find Aria standing once more, taking slower breaths. Cam is hugging her from the side, his body twisted so she can lean on his shoulder.

"Drink this," he says, handing her the cup of water I give him. As she sips, he says, "Listen. There'll be other recitals. I bet the spring one will suck anyway. That's why you weren't a good fit for it."

Aria laughs, rubbing her eyes. "Maybe."

"What was the theme of it?"

"Um . . . 'A Night at the Movies,' I think."

"*Pfft*," Cam scoffs. "Well, there you go. You're officially saved from being a dancing bucket of popcorn. Imagine what that would look like."

He puffs out his chest, which gets Aria laughing. I meet Cam's gaze, which is grim. I wonder what expression I'm wearing.

"You're *talented*. You'll be in other shows. And we all love you," Cam says to her. "Is there anything else you need from us? Because if not, we can go home now."

She doesn't answer. But as I go around to open the door, she leans and I hear her whisper to him, "You're amazing."

The four of us climb into the SUV. And we go home.

21

"**A**sshole!"

The yell is loud enough to jolt me awake from the other side of my bedroom door. I sit bolt upright in bed and glance at my clock—1:28 a.m. It feels like I just got in the door from Meghan's party, even though that was hours ago.

I start to wonder if I dreamed the noise when I hear another shout, clearer this time, from the kitchen. It's Aunt Lori.

She's sniffling.

Normally I'd rather approach a wounded panther than an upset aunt, but I decide I can't go back to sleep like I didn't hear her. So I pull on a shirt and tiptoe into the kitchen.

Every square inch of our table is covered in legal documents that make me gag just looking at them. Aunt Lori is in one of the chairs in her purple bathrobe, hunched over a laptop. The screen frames her face in hot light.

"Aunt Lori?" I murmur tentatively. I try not to startle her, but she still jumps.

"Why are you up? Are you okay?" she asks, glancing around the room like she's checking for intruders. It looks like she hasn't closed her eyes in ten years.

"I was sort of going to ask you that," I answer.

"Oh." Her shoulders relax, which only makes her look smaller. "Don't worry. Sorry if my yelling woke you up. I just . . . just dinged my toe on the table leg, is all. It's fine now."

And I want to be like, *Yes, quite convincing. As you know, I'm six years old and very slow.*

"Will you sit with me for a minute?" she asks. She sounds so unfocused, I almost want to ask if she knows what she's saying. Instead, I take the seat beside hers. My nose catches an aroma that I recognize from church—red wine.

"This looks horrible," I observe, sweeping my arm across the sea of paperwork.

"You have no idea." She groans and rubs her eyes, drawling, "Garner-Stowell hasn't . . . been doing the best lately. A few months ago, they put me in charge of restructuring the firm. They couldn't even—well anyway. I just got an email letting me know that one of our senior partners is leaving and taking his clients. That's several million in revenue."

Which, of course, I feel bad about and all. But all I can focus on is that this might be our first conversation in weeks where she's not talking to me like I'm the problem.

"I'd never want to be a lawyer," I say.

"Hey, you know what?" She wags a finger at me. "You never know. Not at your age."

I hesitate, almost thinking I can tell her about the painting stuff. It's not that I want to make a career of it, because it's not exactly a steady job, but still. I just want to see what she thinks. Except I already know what she thinks, so I hold my tongue.

"Did you know at my age?" I decide to ask. "About being a lawyer, I mean."

"Hmm," she says, sounding genuinely intrigued by the question. She folds her hands in front of her mouth. "You know, it's complicated. The short answer is yes. But it was . . ." She pauses. "Your grandma, she was—well, she wasn't a lawyer, but she was the head of an insurance agency. She had a lot of nights sitting around all pissed off. Bunch of papers around her. I always saw her and thought, *Whatever happens to me, I'm not going to end up like that.* And my friends' parents, you know, they all liked their jobs. But Grandma said that was part of the system too— everyone pretends to like their jobs. And I thought . . ." Aunt Lori gives me a rare, rebellious smile. "I thought, *shut the eff up, Mom, I'll show you.* So that's what I wanted to be—a lawyer who's not a, you know . . ."

"Corporate tool?" I offer, when she seems to lose the word.

"Ex-*actly.*" She knocks on the table for emphasis. "But then there was this one night—I was twenty-four, so this was a few years back—they had me put together a proposal for one of their bigger clients, this pharmaceutical company . . . but we had to get it to them before this other firm did. Brought it home, killed myself working on it . . . and about halfway through, they told me we didn't get it to them in time. And I mean—I was *pissed*. Crying, swearing, you know . . ."

"Yeah, I'm sure," I say.

She points straight forward. "I saw my face in my window, and oh . . . my God. The resemblance to her was scary. It—"

"Her?"

"My mom. I looked *just* like her . . . not even kidding. And I think that was when I just kind of accepted that I wasn't going to be that working adult that broke the mold. Nothing I could do."

"You could keep trying," I offer. Softly, because I don't want to make her more upset with the suggestion.

Aunt Lori shakes her head. "The only thing I could've done was learned all this sooner. Known what to expect." She meets my eyes for the first time since she started telling the story. "That's why I'm tough on you, sweetie. I know I am. It's for a reason. It really is."

"I'm sorry," I tell her.

"Yeah, well." She lets out a long breath, studying the table. "I know I've been . . . going overboard. These past few months."

"It's fine," I say, pretty much by reflex. Truthfully, I just can't believe I'm hearing any semblance of an apology from her.

"Hitting you wasn't fine," she says, abrupt. Even in her

drunken state, she adopts a firm tone of conviction. "When I talked to you about your grades. I knocked you on the cheek. That wasn't fine."

But it's like, if she felt so bad about it then, why is she bringing it up now?

"I know I'm not the *fun* parent, Nate. But no matter how much I nag, I promised myself I'd never hit you. I cried for hours after you left that night."

As you tore up my homecoming ticket, you mean.

"Your grandma and grandpa would hit me with an electrical cord when I was little." She says it in a more fragile voice, and the words take a minute to process.

"What?" I say.

"That's why we don't go up to Grandpa's house for Thanksgiving."

"But they *hit* you? That's illegal, right?"

"They don't need us for Thanksgiving anyway." She isn't really listening to me. "It was just different in those days . . ."

Suddenly I feel sick. "And . . . my mom? Did they—"

"God, no, honey." She pats my arm, then grabs it to steady herself. "No. Only me, the big sis. And you know, as soon as I was eighteen, I took her. With me. We both got out of there."

I want to have a stronger reaction to all this, but it isn't registering with me yet.

"But that's enough of that," she says, wobbling to her feet. She's still using me as a crutch. "Let's get you back to bed, all right?"

I let her walk me to my room.

"I didn't have it like you do," she whispers before she leaves. Talking to ghosts no one else can see. "I never found them . . . I . . . wanted to find them."

I don't know what she means by that.

"I'm sorry, Aunt Lori."

"Don't be. But it just . . . it makes me so sad to see you having fun sometimes. You can understand that, can't you?"

■ ■ ■

Dear God: Please help my aunt.

22

It's a bit careless of me, but I let it go two whole weeks before I end up talking to Cam about the Halloween incident. Mostly this is because I'm scared to tell him what I really think: that I'm not cool with how close he and Aria got that night, even if it was to comfort her from a panic attack.

I don't exactly know why. I think it has something to do with my concept of Aria and our relationship. To me, "girlfriend" means "girl who's my best friend that I enjoy getting naked with." Not that she and I have exactly done that, but I sure as shit have thought about it ever since the Boathouse Incident.

The point is when I saw my best friend having a panic attack, I feel like it was my job to be there to comfort her. Instead, my other best friend did that for me. Something just felt . . . off. Like I was in the way. And I know I have nothing to worry about between Aria and Cam. But being aware that a worry is irrational doesn't get rid of it, you know?

Anyway. I don't plan to bring it up with Cam, but the second Friday of November, he randomly starts a conversation. I'm lying in bed around midnight when my phone buzzes with a text from him.

Dear neighbor: What foul force has driven ye, in this Godforsaken hour of the night, to mow your lawn.

I snort.

Lawn care is important, Cam.

Then I bite my lip and decide to just go for it. I add, Also . . . so. Can I tell you something awkward?

He replies almost immediately.

Awkward away!

Which is when it hits me that there isn't a way to do this without being blunt. I have to remind myself that Cam and I have known each other for a couple months now. Being strangely direct is something of our specialty.

I type, backspace, retype, and finally send: Honestly, it bothered me that you were so close with Aria at the Halloween party. Touching and holding each other and stuff. Don't mean to be a dick, but yeah.

I wince at the screen all the way until he replies a few minutes later.

Oh . . . I didn't realize. That really was just me comforting her as a friend. Like, I hope you don't think I was trying to be romantic?

He then adds:

So just being direct here, I think I did the right thing. I wanted to help a friend, and I'd never try to come between you guys. But I get it, man. Appreciate you telling me, and I'll respect it in the future.

He closes it out with a thumbs-up emoji. I reread the whole thing, a little impressed. The guy may be a total drama show when he's in a crowd of people or rambling about the meaning of life, but when it comes to solving problems, he's refreshingly down-to-earth.

He sends a follow-up: Is there any reason you waited so long to tell me?

Me: Guess I just didn't want an argument. I didn't know if we were close enough to bring it up.

Him: Well, best friends argue. May as well get good at it. And not close enough, seriously? We've told each other basically everything about each other. Except for literally like, shoe size or dick size, lol.

I don't have time to react to that one, because as soon as it pops up on the screen, my door slams open.

"Hey!" Aunt Lori barks. For a bizarre second, I think she somehow knows what Cam and I are saying. But she just scans me up and down and says, "Bedtime is midnight on weekends. You're ten minutes over."

"I'm going to sleep now," I tell her, tucking the covers under my chin.

"I see that phone in your hand. Who are you texting?"

"Aria," I lie. It sounds forced, and for a second, she rubs her chin like she's reaching a verdict. My hands start to shake under the covers when she says good night and closes the door.

When I look back to my phone, I see that Cam sent a follow-up.

I can tell you that 7.5 is one of those numbers ;)

I stifle a laugh, since Aunt Lori could still be listening at the door.

Me: Bullshit.

Him: Nope. Don't care if you believe me, of course.

Me: Well, duh. You couldn't prove it unless we were, like, changing clothes.

I realize my heart is thumping in my ears. I put my phone next to my head and jump when it buzzes.

Well, correct me if I'm wrong, but I can think of one or two things besides changing clothes that would do the trick. Right?

I smile at the screen.

Me: Goodnight :)

Him: Right?! ASDFGHKALKD. You're just going to leave me hanging?

It's like I can hear him saying it in his facetiously whiny tone.

Well, you know me, I write, and I can't stop smiling. It feels like he and I are speaking in our own secret code. Saying things we couldn't say to anyone else. Making jokes that we're only comfortable sharing with each other.

That I do, he replies. Goodnight, Nate :)

23

"I have a weird question for you," I tell him one night.

"I'll have a weird answer."

We're driving back from the movie theater on the last evening of Thanksgiving break. "Sons and Daughters" by the Decemberists, one of Cam's indie artists, is playing through my car speakers.

"So, you spend most of your time thinking about memories," I start. "Things that already happened."

"Not most of my time. But a lot of it, yeah."

"Events like that night we fell asleep on the trampoline."

"I remember."

"Do you miss it yet?"

"Sometimes. Is that your question?"

"No," I say. "My question is: While something is going on, are you able to tell how, like . . . *important* it's going to be later?"

"Most of the time, yeah."

"How do you gauge that?"

"I can usually just tell when it's that kind of night," he says, leaning against the car window. "*Ser-en-dipity*."

"Is that another one of your fancy words?"

"Not my word, obviously. But yeah."

"What is it?"

"It means, 'finding something beautiful while looking for something else.'"

"That's nice. I think."

"I live for that stuff," he says. "*Those* events—those are the ones I really remember. Like maybe you're just sitting around having a boring night, or getting lunch by yourself—"

"Or doing a bio poster."

"—or doing a bio poster, yeah, exactly. And then you meet someone new or it turns into a great night out of nowhere. Those are the best. That's what I remember. What do you think?"

"I think you'd make an excellent stoner."

"I'm serious."

"Me too."

He sighs and lets his head fall back against the seat, like he's trying to get something out of me.

"So those great nights," I continue. "The surprises. Where do you find them?"

"A lot of my recent ones have been our hangouts, honestly. It's always different with you."

"Good different?"

"Most definitely. Even if you're not the blast-music-with-windows-down type."

In response, I give him a challenging look. Then I put down both of the front windows—only halfway, because it's below freezing outside—and turn up the volume knob until my ears hurt, then one notch after that. I grin at his stunned laugh.

"ALWAYS DIFFERENT!" I shout as he gives me a thumbs-up. God, I can't even hear myself!

And from there we drive in comfortable elation.

"Serendipity," Cam repeats, mouthing it to himself over the noise. This time he says the word slowly, like he's trying to savor every trace of its meaning.

24

DEPOSITION EXHIBIT 3

Dear Violet,

Happy (late) Thanksgiving, and Merry (early) Christmas! I know, it's still like a week away. Are you guys going anywhere for the holidays? I'm not sure if you're still grounded.

On that note . . .

I won't pretend I love your life choices, but as long as you're being careful I can't really stop you. I wouldn't recommend disclosing details of illegal drug transactions over email though. Aunt Lori is one step away from tracking my account.

Speaking of which, she's been more intense than usual. Apparently her law firm is losing money, so maybe that's it? I know for a fact she's not fond of Aria, and she definitely isn't a fan of Cameron. To be fair, she did say she would "think about" letting Cam and his family do a joint dinner thingy with us for the holidays. I've never met his parents, but I hear they're really uptight, so . . . maybe they'll fit right in. I just want to make sure Lori doesn't force me to cut off Cam like she did with us.

Speaking of which . . . winter break, right? Coffee or something? I haven't seen you in six months.

Love,

Nate ☺

25

Because all of our extended family is either dead or not talking to us, Dad and Aunt Lori agree to have Christmas dinner with Cam and his parents.

They invite me over early to help set up, so the plan is for me to drive separately. I'm just about to head out the door when I get a picture message from Cam of his family Christmas tree. The caption reads: Merry Christmas, Nate—see you in a few! Also, when am I getting my Christmas nudes? ;)

I grin, replying with a picture of our fireplace and a message that reads: Right after I get mine :)

I've just grabbed my car keys when my phone goes off again. 2 New Picture Messages.

My stomach flips over.

There's no way—obviously he didn't. Not even Cam is bold enough to send me pictures of his dick an hour before Christmas dinner. But I'm sure as hell not risking it by opening the messages in the living room.

I bolt into the downstairs bathroom, lock myself in, then open the images. I let out a breath I didn't know I was holding and laugh at the stupidity of it: The first is of a bunch of presents with the caption Merry XXX-mas! The second is a picture of his stocking with the caption Hung with care ;)

■   ■   ■

I ring the doorbell twenty minutes later. I'm greeted by a tall blond woman with a thin smile and Cam's deep brown eyes.

She leans toward me and shakes my hand. "You must be Nathan! It's so good to finally meet you. Merry Christmas!"

I'm in the middle of replying when she's joined by a short, balding man with a scraggly beard. He grips my hand in both of his and says, "Good to meet you, young man! Merry Christmas."

"Hello, sir," I say. "Merry Christmas."

"Ah, cut all that 'sir' crap—makes me feel way too old. Come on in."

So Cam's parents aren't quite the terrorists he made them out to be. They point me down the hall, where I find Cam in his room. He has a cardboard fireplace with stockings set up under his window, and I recognize The Piano Guys Christmas album over the speakers.

"Well, that looks familiar," I say, pointing to the stocking from the picture message.

"Merry Christmas!" Cam says. It's been a week since we've seen each other because of break, so we do a bro hug. He points to my attire. "Look at you, all fancy."

I'm still in my button-down and bow tie from morning mass. Luckily he's been forced to dress up too—or maybe he chose it—because he's in a red dress shirt with a green sweater-vest pulled over it, and a tie to match. His hair, normally spiked up, is neatly combed over to one side.

"I thought I saw you this morning, but I couldn't tell with all the crowds," I say. "Too many token Christmas-ers." This is my term for the people who only go to mass once a year. In reality, I don't mind them, because it means people sing the holiday hymns extra loudly and it adds to the sense of community that I love so much.

Cam leads me to the dining room, where we help his parents get set up. Celtic Woman holiday tunes are playing on an old stereo from the den, and he sings right along. And it's just such a cozy mood, listening to classic carols in our holiday formal wear and sipping hot chocolate that Mrs. Haynes makes us. It makes me feel warm from my head to my feet and reminds me of all my favorite parts of winter.

"Go ahead and set the table, if you could," Mr. Haynes tells Cam. "Remember, use the big plates."

"Yup, I've got it."

"And forks on the left."

"Yup, I've got it."

"And you'll want to make sure those are evenly spaced, so—"

"Have I mentioned this yet? *I've got it.*"

"Oookay," Mr. Haynes says, hands up. Then, obviously not able to resist, he adds, "Last thing: spoons on the right."

Cam's hand hits the table—hard.

"What's that?" he asks his father.

"All I said was, spoons on—"

"What are spoons?"

Mr. Haynes rubs his beard, sighing. "Cam—"

"*I HAVE GOT IT.*"

Mr. Haynes glares daggers at him, but he shakes his head and disappears into the kitchen without pressing the issue.

"What can I do?" I ask Cam, trying to avoid an uncomfortable silence. "I can help your mom cook, or—"

"Don't bother," Cam spits. "They won't let you touch the stove."

"Oh. What's wrong with it?"

"It does this weird thing," Cam says in a grave whisper, stepping closer so our faces are inches apart. "When you turn the knob that says 'heat,' it gets really hot, and that's a concept that could be challenging to grasp for young adults like you and me."

Despite myself, I smirk. "You're not allowed to use the stove?"

"Nope. And there's no such thing as a simple conversation like, 'go ahead and set the table.'" He shoves a bundle of spoons into my hand as he brushes past me. "Put those wherever the fuck you want."

■　■　■

I give Cam a few minutes to cool off, then rejoin him in his bedroom. Aria—who was also invited to this shindig—is on a ski trip with her parents, so Cam and I video chat with her. In the background, the movie *Home Alone* is playing on Cam's TV, which we continue to watch after signing off.

I don't notice it at first, but he's quiet for most of the movie. We're both sitting on his bed, and I turn to poke him in the shoulder.

"Still pissed about your parents?" I ask.

"Not really. I'm pretty used to it."

"You're just all quiet," I say. "Is it . . . memory stuff again?"

Without responding, Cam gets up and closes his door. Then he plops back down and says, "Sort of."

"Do tell."

He bites his lip, eyes fixed on the TV. It's the very last scene of the movie where the old man is hugging his granddaughter.

"I'm not sure how to phrase this," he says. "But to start, it's Chloe again."

"All right. What about her?"

"Just . . ." He takes off his glasses to rub his eyes. "She *loved* Christmas. Like—really loved it. Especially the holiday movies like this one."

"So the movie's what made you think of it?"

"Kind of? Somewhat. But it's also just the holidays in general. Like, this is the time when you look back on the past year and think about everything that's changed, and you set aside differences to just . . . love the people around you. It just makes me think of her, is all. I don't know, man."

"It's okay to cry if you need to." We both know I don't have to tell him, but I say it anyway.

"I'm good. But thanks." He collects himself, then slides off the bed. "I need to give you your gift anyway."

"You got me a gift?" I ask, with an immediate sinking feeling in my chest. I didn't think to get him anything other than a card, and not even a good one.

"It was literally ten bucks," he says. He opens a cabinet underneath his bookshelf and pulls out an object the size of a soccer ball draped in a black towel.

"Come here," he says.

When he pulls off the towel, I see that it's a one-gallon fish bowl, complete with a live goldfish and a paper background taped to the side.

I laugh, glancing between Cam and the fish.

"What's this for?" I say, confused.

"Your Christmas present," he tells me. "You remember our first conversation with the fish on the notebook? Samuel L. Jackson?"

I take a second look at the background taped to the bowl and realize it's a printout of the famous scene from *Pulp Fiction*.

"You told me your parents wouldn't let you get a fish, and I figure they can't forbid it if it's a gift from someone else. This was the angriest one at the pet store." Cam makes a fish face at me.

Then he hands me the bowl and says in a little voice, "Nate, meet Sammy."

Oh my God, he's serious. He actually had the balls to purchase a pet for me without asking first. Normally this would raise a million concerns, most of them related to how my dad and aunt will feel about this. But I'm too swept up in how thoughtful of a gift the stupid fish is.

"I didn't get you anything," I say, feeling an order of magnitude worse than before. I set the bowl down on the nearest shelf.

"Ah," Cam says. I think I see a twinge of hurt on his face, but it's gone almost at once. "Luckily, ebullient hugs are an acceptable form of currency."

So we hug, and I get that feeling where I want to say something, but I can't come up with anything meaningful. I almost think I've got it, but then the moment passes and all I manage is, "Thanks for this."

Cam steps back, a smile playing at his lips.

"You too," he says.

26

Dad and Aunt Lori show up at dinnertime, and the adults swap all their greetings and gripes about the job market and the weather. Aunt Lori is, of course, charming as ever. She even leads the prayer before we start dinner. No one asks about it, but I notice that there's an extra place set at the table beside Mrs. Haynes.

Once we've all served ourselves, Mr. Haynes asks Dad, "So what is it you do, Bill?"

"Air traffic controller," Dad says, then gives him the spiel outlining what that's like. "How about you?"

"Contractor," Mr. Haynes says. "I've been between projects for 'bout a month though. Tougher market around this time of year."

"Or anytime," Aunt Lori adds with a charming grin, and everyone chuckles.

"But it's all good stuff," Mr. Haynes continues. "I had time to put some work into the Charger we're restoring in the garage. And Cameron and I got a good portion of the deck built, since I was home to work the power tools."

Cam leans toward me and explains, "Circular saws fall under the category of too dangerous and complex for me to ever operate alone, like a nuclear reactor or electric stove."

"Cameron," Mrs. Haynes says, in that universal mom-warning voice.

"So dude," I say to Cam, trying to change the subject, since I can feel Aunt Lori's evil eye on us. "I think I'm going to do some painting tonight."

It works. His eyes get wide. "Like, on an actual canvas? That's so cool, man! Your first ever!"

"Painting?" Dad says. He and Aunt Lori exchange this look, like, *how adorable.* "Didn't know you were into that."

"Kind of," I say with a shrug.

"It's definitely . . . artsy," Aunt Lori remarks, her bullshit smile still stuck to her face. "Next thing we know, you'll be taking up modeling. We should've gotten you heels and a miniskirt for Christmas!"

"Ha ha!" Cam belts out, in complete contradiction with the scowl he's wearing.

This is followed by a horrifying half second of dead silence.

"Cameron," his mom repeats in that same warning tone.

"Yes?" he challenges. Both of his parents shoot him a sharp look.

"We apologize," Mrs. Haynes says to Aunt Lori, putting up a hand like a traffic cop. "Going through a bit of a phase."

"Oh no no no, of course. We've had to deal with that ourselves," Aunt Lori says, because why not turn this into a two-for-one special?

"So you've gotten the *eye roll*," Mrs. Haynes says in a deep voice, coupled with an imitation.

"The *eye roll*," Aunt Lori takes over. "And they just can't live without the *Internet*..."

"The Internet! The Internet!" cries Mr. Haynes. "And the texting . . ." he adds, while a googly-eyed Mrs. Haynes jackhammers an invisible phone with both of her thumbs. All four adults are roaring with laughter now, Dad's hand wildly slapping the table like he's struggling to buzz in on *Family Feud*.

"Yup . . . we're the worst!" Cam says over them, making a show of wiping his forehead. "Us teens don't like to advertise this, but until we hit the arbitrary age of eighteen, we're actually contracted minions of the Antichrist."

Everyone's grins vanish. Aunt Lori chokes on a sip of wine, glowering so hard her eyebrows almost touch. I keep my eyes on my plate, stuffing food into my mouth like I'm storing it for winter. Cam leans back—the only one who isn't uncomfortable.

"Let's calm down," Mrs. Haynes murmurs to him.

"This is calm," Cam says, folding his hands. For whatever reason, that's what does it.

"Enough of this crap. Go to your room." Mr. Haynes says it softly, but loud enough for everyone to hear.

Cam stares at his parents for a long time.

"Go to your room right now." His mom's tone matches his dad's.

I'm worried he'll fight even harder, but he stands without another word. Then he marches down the hall and closes his door as softly as possible.

Aunt Lori looks ready to kill someone.

Celtic Woman tells us to sleep in heavenly peace.

27

"It's five-oh-three," Cam points out, to no one in particular.

"How about that," Mrs. Lawson says, following his gaze to the wall clock. "We've gone over. Good catch, Mr. Haynes." She shuts her notebook, scooting her wheelchair back and folding her arms. "Nate, thank you—we're done for today. We'll pick this up tomorrow morning, same room. Go home and get some sleep."

She packs up her briefcase, sets it on her lap, and wheels out of the room without another word. Cam's attorney pats him on the shoulder twice, then follows suit. As everyone starts clearing out, my phone buzzes with a text from an unidentified number.

Attn: You've used almost 93% of your data for this month. Please visit our website immediately and avoid using the "back" button on your Internet browser. Thank you for choosing our service.

Dad and Aunt Lori stand on either side of me, each putting a hand on one of my shoulders. A casual bystander would think they're helping me to my feet—to be fair, I do have to take it easy—but their grips are just a little too strong for it to be for my sake.

We go.

I step out of the building and wince at the sunlight, rubbing my eyes with one hand and pressing on my stomach with the other. Walking is still a limited activity for me in this stage of healing. The soreness used to be a lot worse, back when I first got home from the hospital. The real bitch about an abdomen wound is that you use those muscles for literally everything, even just lying in place and breathing. My gut was in too much pain for me to walk or stand up for the first week, so I had to roll out of bed and drag myself to the bathroom—which is where the real fun would start. I also discovered that the waistband of my boxers pressed too much on the incision, so Aunt Lori had to pick me up a bathrobe that I'd wear when I could hobble out to the kitchen, unshowered and hunched over like an escaped resident from a nursing home.

Now, though, I'm able to mostly stand upright. I wiggle out of Dad's and Aunt Lori's grips.

"I'll see you guys at home. I'm going to run to the bathroom," I say. They weren't happy about it, but they agreed to let me drive myself to and from this thing. That was one of the conditions I'd set for agreeing to testify in a "cooperative manner."

"We'll wait for you," Aunt Lori says, just way too sweet.

"No, it's—I have to change the bandage," I say, putting my hand back over the area.

Her eyes widen enough that I see the tiniest bit of genuine worry. "More bleeding? It's not supposed to be—"

"It's only a tiny bit."

"Are you sure you're—"

"I promise I'm fine," I say, more rigidly. "Go ahead."

Dad convinces her that I can take care of myself, and they agree to leave. I watch as they march to their car, climb in, and pull out of the parking lot.

I count sixty seconds to make sure they're gone. Then I turn and amble around the side of the building. I'm sweating bullets, my head whipping back and forth. Anyone sees me and we're *fucked.* Then again, I figure we're fucked anyway.

I find Cam exactly where he's supposed to be: behind the trash bin next to the rear entrance of the building. He's leaned up against the wall, drumming his fingers on his knees. His eyes brighten when I approach.

"Hey, dude," he says, and his face splits into a smile. He tries to help steady me. I twist away.

"Seven minutes?" I murmur.

He nods. "Told my parents my stomach hurt. Snuck out the exit next to the bathroom."

This is the coded system Cam came up with months ago, shortly before the night of the incident: When he needed to meet up, he'd text me a service message from a burner phone. The amount of time we had was one hundred minus the percentage listed in the text. One hundred $-$ 93 percent $=$ seven minutes.

"Visit our website immediately" means meet up right now, this can't wait. "Back button" means "back entrance of the building."

"This better be important," I say.

"It's important," he replies. When he was released from jail, it was "on his own recognizance"—AKA zero bail—on the condition he have no private meet-ups with me. Naturally this meant he had Violet get him a pay-as-you-go burner phone the very next day. But even Cam wouldn't be reckless enough to actually use it—and risk jail time—without it being an emergency.

I wait.

"Listen," he says. "Tomorrow. You have to tell them about New Year's Eve."

"*Fuck* that."

"Nate, you have to."

This is so like him.

"Go home, Cam," I say. I try to sound gentle, but it doesn't work too well. I turn away from him and make it a few steps before he yells after me.

"Why are you here?"

I stop. Deep breath. Then I turn around to face him. He has his fists clenched at his sides, feet planted on the cement. The same stance he had right before I hurt him that night.

"I'm here because you texted me to meet you," I answer.

"Not that. I mean, why are you doing this deposition in the first place? They can't force you to answer the questions. You could just not say anything, and this all goes away. They'd have nothing."

"Aunt Lori wants—"

"I know what she wants," Cam snaps. "She wants you to paint me as a vagarious lunatic who spends my free time stabbing people. I'm asking why *you're* doing this. You."

My hand involuntarily trails back to my abdomen and stays there. "Come on. You know I don't get a choice with her."

"*I* don't get a choice!" he huffs. "I sit there in that room, and I have to listen to your version of the events—"

"What did I get wrong?" I ask, puzzled. "I didn't lie about anything—"

"The minute you sit down tomorrow and don't talk about New Year's Eve, this becomes a whole different story."

"Can I remind you of something?"

"Sure."

"One of the *first* things I said in there was how this is more my fault than yours. In case you didn't notice, that doesn't make me look great."

"Oh nooo," Cam coos. "Bless your little heart, Nate."

"Aunt Lori—"

"I mean, *God fucking forbid* you don't look great—"

"Aunt Lori ordered me to put it all on you, but I didn't! And oh yeah, another thing!"

"Can't wait for this—"

"STOP pissing all over the people who could throw you in prison! If you don't plead guilty, you don't get a deal, and, just, just—" I start to pant, my voice fracturing with real fear for him.

"Cam, maximum sentence is ten fucking *years*."

"Is it actually?" he asks, eyebrows knitting together. "Didn't get around to checking that."

"I'm trying to help you, asshole."

"Good!" he says, firing back up. "Tell them about New Year's Eve!"

"I just don't see how it's relevant. Look, I'm sorry, okay? I don't know if I've said that yet—"

"You haven't."

"—but I'm fucking *sorry*."

"I'm not sure you are. Sorry means you wouldn't do it again. Why are you here, Nate?"

"That's the third time you've asked me that."

"Then answer."

"I did answer!" I yell at him. He's really starting to piss me off. "I'm here because Aunt Lori, who's had control over every single aspect of my life—and you know exactly how bad it got toward the end—she *needs* this from me. She needs me to show up, to sit in that room, to tell them about everything. And by the way—no, shut up and listen to me! By the way, in exchange for doing that, she's giving me whatever I want. Anything I ask for. Why do you think we can talk right now? Because she let me drive myself here." I yank my car keys out of my pocket and throw them at him. I miss.

"Great!" Cam applauds me, his face twisted in anger. He picks up the keys and hurls them at my head, missing too. "So you told her you won't be moving to Ohio then, yeah?"

"I want to move," I say. "I need to get away from all this."
From you.

"You know, if we had more time, I'd tell you how much of a fucking asshole you are."

"The only reason I'm standing here is as a favor to you!"

"How will I ever repay you!"

"Jesus *Christ*, this isn't—"

"You want to do me a favor?" Cam is so frantic that he spits the word out—literally spits. Wipes his chin. "Tell every one of those assholes in that room what this is really about! Tell them about New Year's Eve! And everything after!" He steps forward, wringing his hands together. "Nate, you have to. Just—it's important, okay?"

"I don't even know how I'd—I'd word any of it. How I'd phrase the stuff we did—"

"Wh—It's a deposition, not the fucking *Canterbury Tales*! Just say what happened!"

"And the minute I do, both of our parents are going to know everything."

"So then both of our parents know everything. Why aren't you doing this, man? Why?"

"Because I have to go home!" I explode at him. "Whatever I say in there, I have to face them afterward. I have to go *home*."

"Well, it must be nice to have the option." When I don't reply, he keeps pressing. "This is your chance, man. For God's sake, just—please. Make this right."

Neither of us is budging, and we can both feel it.

"God," I say, "couldn't be farther away from any of this shit."

"Right now, He and us are the only ones who know what all of this is really about."

"I'm keeping it that way."

"What are you afraid of?"

"Oh, stop. Being afraid has nothing to do with it." I want to believe what I'm saying, but I really don't, and neither does Cam.

"No one——" he starts.

"Cam, stop it."

"No one——"

"We aren't discussing this. I'm not discussing New Year's."

"No one——"

"I'll tell them everything else, I swear," I say.

"*NO* ONE——"

"I want to help you, Cam, but this is the best I can do!"

"——GIVES A SHIT THAT YOU'RE BISEXUAL!"

I lunge forward—vision blurred, fist raised. Cam flinches and stumbles back. Then we both freeze—statues. Blood rushes through my ears, my wound burning and throbbing.

I lower my hand and take a step back, feeling dizzy. Cam just pouts at me, entirely smug.

"Get the fuck out of here," I spit at him.

"You know what? Fine. But we'll be back tomorrow."

I kick the ground as hard as I can.

"We," I say, "are done."

"Oh, we're not done."

"Yes, we are."

"No." Cam lifts his chin, already stepping out of sight. He looks grim—calculating. "Not just yet."

DAY 2

28

For a while, after I'm done beating him that night, he doesn't even move.

"Oh God," I whisper. "Oh God. Oh God."

A full minute since I hurt him. For the first time, I stop to take in the sight at my feet. *Cam.* Half conscious. Lying on the ground. My house to my back. My fists, trembling— painted in blood that shines under the faint streetlamp. His blood. *Cam.*

"Oh God," I repeat. I'm shaking all over. *We need to call an ambulance.* "Cam . . . Cam, I . . ."

I fall back against my mailbox, burying my face in my hands. I'm entering shock, I think. Cam, meanwhile, is coughing and clutching his stomach. His glasses are on the street, lenses shattered. I reach to help him, but he swats me away.

"Get the fuck off me," he chokes out.

I realize it's the same thing I said to him moments before,

when he was trying to take my hand. Moments before, when we both could have walked away from this.

"Cam, I'm so . . . holy shit. I . . ."

It takes him three tries, but he pushes himself into a sitting position on the pavement. He slides his empty glasses frames back onto his face.

"I don't know what to say," I tell him between rattling breaths. I feel more helpless than he looks. "How bad are you hurt?"

Cam spits onto the street. "Feels like bruising on my left eye, fracture in a thoracic rib—maybe two—and I think blunt-force trauma to both kidneys. *Fuck*—"

The rest is cut off as he pukes onto the street corner. He's making strangled whimpering noises, clutching his side in agony as he chokes out the vomit. Gasp in, gasp out. It's intermixed with miserable sobs.

There's no other way to say it: He sounds like he wants to die.

I did that.

I kneel beside him. He flinches, but I keep my hands low. Nonthreatening.

"Cam." I say it softly. "Hit me."

"What?"

"I want you to hit me back."

Cam looks up at me. I can barely meet his eyes. His left one is already swelling shut. His knees are tucked up against his chest, and he's rocking back and forth slightly.

"Seriously," I tell him. "Hit me back. Make us even. I, I . . .

can't . . . Cam, you have to hit me back."

I see him gather all of his strength, and he uses it to rise to his feet. I match his movements, our gazes locked. For the very first time, I see it in his eyes: genuine hate. For me.

I don't blame him, Mrs. Lawson, I don't. I swear to you I share it.

29

"**H**old on a second, Nate."

Today's setup matches yesterday's: same conference room. Same seating. Practically the same clothes. Cam is back, too, only he's not doodling on his notepad this time. I'm still in a bit of a daze—I couldn't sleep last night, and I didn't want to use my pain meds to do it, so I'm running on half a gallon of coffee.

I refocus on Mrs. Lawson, who's saying to me, "You're jumping ahead."

"You asked me what happened next."

"And you're jumping ahead. We left off in December. The alleged assault was July first. I'm asking you to show your math. Is it fair to say one or two things may have happened within those seven months to change the nature of your interactions?"

I can practically feel Cam leaping out of his chair. I glance between him and Aunt Lori, who has her grip on my shoulder again.

I take a deep breath.

"Only if my dad and aunt leave."

As expected, Aunt Lori stiffens. "Absolutely not."

"Nate, there wouldn't be a point," Mrs. Lawson says, surprisingly gentle. "Transcripts of this will be available to them anyway."

"I know. It would just be easier to talk about without them in the room." I clear my throat, my words strained. "My statements . . . can only be counted if I do it without my dad and aunt here."

It feels like Mrs. Lawson's eyes are reaching through my forehead, trying to grab hold of my brain and pull it apart for inspection. I fight the urge to squirm in my seat and turn my focus to Cam, whose chin bobs a fraction of an inch to give me the world's tiniest nod.

Apparently Mrs. Lawson decides she's satisfied, because she turns to my parents with an upturned palm and says, "Well, you heard him. Enjoy the day. Get some breakfast, catch a movie. . . . We'll have him back to you by five."

Aunt Lori sits forward with a little twitch, like someone pinched her. "Wait. You're not serious?"

"If Nate feels more comfortable doing this on his own—"

"No, no, hey—*excuse* me." Aunt Lori clamps down harder on my arm. "That's our call."

"The State is trying Mr. Haynes as an adult, and Nate's older than him. I think he can handle answering his own questions and picking his own bathroom breaks," Mrs. Lawson deadpans, sounding like a store manager refusing to accept an expired coupon. She flicks two fingers in the direction of the door. "We'll take good care of him."

Dad stands up. Aunt Lori doesn't.

"I'll report this," she warns.

Mrs. Lawson says, "I don't really care."

"I mean it. This is going straight to the ODC."

"I," Mrs. Lawson says, "don't care."

Dad gestures to Aunt Lori and says, "Hey, come on. Just let him do it. Nate"—he puts a hand on my head—"text if you need anything, okay? Check in with us."

I tell him I will and that I'll drive straight back to the house afterward. I keep my head down until I hear their chairs scrape. The door swings open, then slams shut.

Cam watches the whole scene like a hawk. Behind him, his mom glances from me to Mrs. Lawson, pointing to the door. "Should we . . . ?"

For probably the first time since Cam's arrest, I take a good look at his parents. I almost can't handle it. The pale, terrified faces they've been wearing for the past six weeks. I don't know if they want to hear this, but they deserve to.

"You guys can stay," I tell them, and so they do.

Mrs. Lawson nods for me to begin. I fold my hands.

Us and God.

"New Year's Eve."

30

Meghan Richter hosts another party.

Which isn't even a fair statement. *Another* implies that this party is anything like the Halloween event, which ends up feeling like a cute little third-grade playdate compared to the blowout of New Year's Eve.

Turns out Meghan is only the dainty little saint when Mom and Dad are around. (Halloween gathering = good example of this.) However, when Aria, Asher, Cam, and I pull up to her house on New Year's Eve, the place is already a cesspool of bad decisions. The windows flicker with colored lights, pulsating to the music blasting inside. Two guys in the front yard puke onto an object hanging out the window, which I realize is the still-decorated Richter family Christmas tree. A group of girls at the end of the driveway are smoking, looking bored.

"Oookay," Asher says as he parks the car along the street. "I don't want my little sister at this thing."

Aria rolls her eyes. "I'm older than you by sixteen minutes."

"Um," I say from the backseat. "Asher, you're not drinking, right? You're our ride home."

Asher makes a sound like *pffft*, which is not a reassuring affirmation.

"Worst case, I can drive us," I decide, since I'm planning to be sober anyway. I nudge Cam beside me. "Is that all right?"

He doesn't respond. His eyes are fixed on his shoes, and he's rubbing his hands together. His brain seems a million miles away. I snap my fingers in front of his face.

"Hey," I say. "Is that cool?"

"What's that now?" he says.

"Aw, he's distracted," Aria says as we get out of the car. She bumps her hip against his. "You nervous?"

Cam nods vigorously, flattening his sleeves. I realize how nicely he's dressed: striped button-down shirt with dark skinny jeans, his hair combed back like on Christmas. He pushes his glasses farther up his nose.

"Why are you nervous?" I ask.

Aria takes my hand, bouncing cheerfully, and says, "He liiikes Meghan."

We're starting toward the house now, and the music is already getting louder. The screen door flies open, and three people squish themselves out at once. One of them falls face-first onto the deck and doesn't get up.

"Meghan Richter? Seriously?" I say to Cam.

His face burns. "That information isn't approved for public release."

We all chuckle, including me, but I'm still wrapping my head around it. For starters, I don't know how I feel about him telling Aria that kind of secret but not me. What other private discussions do they have?

Before I can think any further, we squeeze into Meghan's house, and I'm caught up in the scene.

There have to be at least fifty people inside. The air is thick with smoke—the smell is a mix of weed and vape pens. I blink against a burning in my eyes. All the furniture in Meghan's living room has been shoved off to the side to make room for two massive speakers, a table full of snacks, and a set of strobe lights lining the wall. There are a dozen or so girls grinding on guys in the center of the room, with the rest of the people chatting, watching, or playing on their phones. In the other room, I spot a couple of people parked in front of a flatscreen with controllers in one hand and shot glasses in the other. Someone has a projector set up, broadcasting the New Year's Eve live stream from Times Square. The entire area is the temperature of a furnace and tastes like sweat.

"Wow," Cam summarizes, all matter-of-fact. His eyes are darting around.

"I'm gonna peel off," Asher says, waving to a group of his lacrosse buddies. He pats Aria on the shoulder. "Stay out of trouble."

Aria nods and draws a little closer to me. I know parties like this aren't normally her thing.

"Hey," I say to her. "If you want, we can go."

"Nah," she says. "We have to help Cam with Meghan, right?"

"Kissing on New Year's isn't even really a thing," Cam is muttering to a nearby lampshade. "I mean, yeah, people do it, but it never works out like you see in movies. Stop talking, Cam."

"Aw," Aria says, hooking her arm through his. "Let's look around."

Things don't get any tamer as we go deeper into the house. When we pass the family room, I spot couches and chairs packed with horizontal bodies. Picture frames up on the wall rattle with the beat from the music. We sidestep a giant stain on the hallway carpet, which I'm fervently praying is from a beverage.

The kegs are in the kitchen: three of them, all sitting in puddles of spilled foam and soggy potato chips. This room is the most packed—a few dozen people, at least. Most are gathered around the table, where there's an intense card game going on.

"It's called Kings," Cam says in my ear. He has to shout because of the music. "It's a drinking game."

"Neat," I say without enthusiasm. I glance to my left and see some guy using the stove to heat a can of soup. And by that I mean, he has an unopened tin can of tomato soup, label and all, sitting directly on top of the lit burner.

"Well that's not right." Aria frowns.

Cam straightens up suddenly, and I see all five feet of Meghan Richter gliding toward us. Even under the circumstances, I'm astounded by how little she's wearing. Her jean shorts are so short they're basically underwear, and her boobs are spilling out of her white tube top.

"Hey, guys!" she shouts, sounding impressively sober.

Aria gives Cam a none-too-subtle bump toward Meghan. He waves to her. "Hey there. What's up?"

I can't help but be impressed by how confident he's able to sound, given his nerves so far. He turns on his smile, and Meghan squeezes her shoulders together.

"How's it going?" she asks him.

"All right. Any reason we aren't using the basement?"

"So we *were*," she says, rolling her eyes. "But then the football players got too rowdy. All the lizards escaped."

I don't have the first fucking idea what she means by that.

"Those lizards do that," Cam says, eyebrows arched. "I'm going to take a shot in the dark and say your parents are out of town?"

"Visiting family in Minnesota. I convinced them I had the flu," she says, then gives a cute little cough.

"If you want to be convincing, you should get some antiviral medicine. A lot of people think they work if you take them in the first forty-eight hours, but a lot of physicians agree that they're just placebos."

Cam cringes at himself as soon as he's done talking. Meghan gives a nervous chuckle and says, "I'd better go check on the living room. But hey, have some beer. We got the good shit."

She moves past us without waiting for a response. I turn to

Aria, expecting a disapproving glower, but I'm shocked to see her already filling a cup from the keg.

"What the hell? You hate drinking," I say.

"Correct. It's not for me." She hands it to Cam. "Here. We need to loosen you up."

Meet the anomaly that is my girlfriend: hates drinking, but is totally cool with going to a wild party and pushing alcohol on her friends.

Cam stares at the beer in his hand like it's a sleeping tarantula. He takes a tiny sip, smacking his lips and shuddering.

"I'd hate to taste the bad shit," he says, giving it back to Aria. "I'll pass, thanks."

"Oh, come on," she says. "Drink it!"

"Aria, let's ask ourselves: What would Jesus do?"

"If He's as helpful as they say, He'd probably slap you and tell you to stop being such a pussy. Bottoms up, lover boy."

Cam glances from her to me.

"I will if Nate does too," he says.

"Me? I've never had alcohol before," I say.

"Me neither. I need a wingman."

Aria looks a little less comfortable at that, but bites her lip and says, "Fine. Just don't go overboard."

31

Two hours later, I'm convinced that "just don't go overboard" will be the epitaph written on my tombstone.

Beer number one leads to beers two, three, and then I lose count. Cam knows all the biochemistry behind how alcohol works, so he types out some quick calculations on his phone about BAC. I don't think they're quite right, though, because we both get a bit drunker than intended. I keep waving my hand in front of my face, absolutely astounded at how fast it's moving.

Aria heads home around my third drink (she leaves with her friend Stacy, who's okay to drive because she has to stay sober because her parents would *kill her*). Aria refuses to kiss me and doesn't seem particularly pleased with my behavior, but she hugs me tight and makes me promise to help Cam get a kiss with Meghan.

"Meghan? She might've hon gome," I say. I giggle; those aren't the right words!

"First of all, you mean 'gone home,'" Aria says. "Second of all, this is her house."

Right. Smooth one, Nate.

So Aria leaves, and it's me and Cam. I would've never been comfortable drinking like this on my own, but with him there, it feels more like one of our adventures. For once—for *once!*—since our first night stargazing, I'm not worried about what's going to happen tomorrow. At one point I suggest we slow down, and Cam responds with, "The liver is a naughty organ and deserves to be punished."

The peak of our drunkenness hits around 10:30 p.m. We both sit on the floor in the hallway, staring at our phones and snickering whenever we hear a funny noise from the other room. As my one smart decision of the night, I put my phone on airplane mode. The last thing I need is to drunk text my parents and be welcomed home with a beheading.

Cam insists that we drink water, which means we take about ten bathroom trips between us. We do start sobering up a little, though, and by 11:30 p.m. we're able to move around without stumbling.

"Cam!" I yell to him over the music. I feel a big, stupid grin on my face.

"Nate!" he says back, planting a hand on my shoulder.

"You know what you need to do though?"

"What do I need to do?"

"You need to get Meghan to make out with you. Aria made me promise."

Cam purses his lips. He sticks his head in the hall leading to the living room. Then he turns back to me.

"You really think she'll want to?" he asks.

"One way to find out. And hey, if she doesn't, the alcohol will, like . . ." I knock on my own forehead. "Erase your memory of failure."

Cam's eyes get superwide at that, and he looks at me like I'm a genius.

"You're *right!*" he cheers. "Okay. Okay, fuck it. Let's do this."

Despite the fact that our motor control is mostly back, I still see his hands shake as we make our way into the living room. He fiddles with his glasses again. Meghan is standing with one of her friends, chatting, cup in hand. I wait in the doorway as Cam clears his throat and approaches.

"Meghan! Hi," he says, waving.

"Oh . . . hey, Cam," Meghan says. She sounds sort of interested, but not head over heels. "How're things?"

"Things are things," Cam says, nodding vigorously. "Listen—"

He's cut off by some dude stumbling through the living room, held up by two of his buddies. The guy is in a T-shirt and boxer shorts, with a pair of jeans draped over his shoulder.

"Bye, Meghan!" he calls, followed by something about how he needs to get enough sleep for church tomorrow morning.

Meghan leans toward Cam, looking bewildered. "Who even was that guy?"

"That man is our class president," Cam informs her.

"Really?"

"How does this work?" he blurts out, leaping right to the point. "If I were trying to ask you out. This is the part where I use some cringeworthy pickup line or something, right?"

Easy there, Cam.

She raises an eyebrow. It's tough to tell if she's into it.

"Hmm," she says. She glances at the clock. "Eh, what the hell. It's twenty minutes till midnight and I need someone to kiss. Give me your worst pickup line."

Cam nods. I realize I'm holding my breath—I'm almost more nervous than he is.

"Okay, got one." He clears his throat, eyes locked on her. "Hey there, are you a mitral valve prolapse? Because you make my heart skip a beat."

Meghan's face twitches, and Cam grabs his chest. "Oof. That hurt, like, physically as it was coming out."

"I can tell," Meghan says, gesturing between the two of them. "Or maybe you just have a mitral valve prolapse?"

"You know, it sort of feels like it right now," he says. They share a smile, then a fit of idiotic laughter.

"I think you'll do," Meghan says. She taps his lips, says, "Twenty minutes," and flutters away.

Something in his face changes. He marches toward me, power walking like a man on a mission.

"Bathroom," he says. "Now."

"You have to pee again?"

"No. My stomach has stopped being nice to me."

"Shit. Uh, okay, let's get to a toilet. Long as I'm not holding your hair."

32

The downstairs bathroom is occupied by several people, so we head into the nicer one upstairs. Cam doesn't puke, but he dry heaves a few times and clings to the toilet like it's a life raft. I—after pausing to give myself finger guns in the mirror—kneel beside him and awkwardly grab his shoulders to keep him upright.

"Think I'm better," he says after a few minutes. "Can you shut the door?"

I do, which muffles but doesn't entirely drown out the beat of the music downstairs. Cam rinses his mouth out in the sink, flashing me a weak thumbs-up as he gargles and spits.

"All good?" I ask, not entirely convinced that he is.

"I just need a minute, is all," he says, wiping his face on his sleeve. He pulls the toilet lid down and collapses onto it, an ironic half smile stuck to his face.

"Anything I can do?" I offer. I lean against the wall to face him.

To be fair, I'm still a little tipsy, so I'm not exactly in the best position to assist him.

He doesn't answer.

"So why Meghan?" I continue. "I had no idea you liked her."

Cam shrugs. "I mean, she's cute, and I've been tutoring her in math the past few weeks. She's fun to talk to. Still in the early stages of liking her, but yeah. We'll see where it goes."

I nod, not sure what to do with this.

Cam runs his hands through his hair, chuckling to himself. Like he can't believe he's here. "This is . . . a little too much."

"Are you going to throw up? Because you should be facing the other way for that."

"Nah, man, more like . . . weird mood, I guess. I'm not used to being *inebriated*." He says the word all funny. "I'm just psyching myself out. For midnight."

"Try to relax." *Genius advice!*

"Yeah."

"Maybe more alcohol would calm you down?" I say, though I know it's a reach.

"Not a good idea," he says, echoing my thoughts. "I'd puke all over her for sure. *Exorcist*-level vomit."

We both crack up at that.

"What'd you do that time you were high?" I ask.

"Well see, I didn't feel sick then," he points out, wagging a finger at absolutely nothing. "I smoked a little with this girl I thought was cute, we felt each other up a bit, then I went home and jerked off while giggling to myself a bunch. So you could say it was a wholesome evening."

"You jerked off? Seriously?"

"She was a very cute girl." He swallows, then hiccups. "Plus doing it high, it was . . . different."

"Different how?"

"Not really something I can explain. I imagine it's similar to doing it drunk."

We share a knowing nod.

"You *could* test the difference," I say. "Then let me know what it's like afterward."

"I could," he says. "Or if you just did it, too, you'd find out for yourself."

"I could."

It dawns on me that neither of us is sure whether we're joking about this suggestion or not. We fall silent. Waiting. Both of us. Waiting on the time and the tension to coax our unspoken thoughts into something real—something safe.

Downstairs, the song changes.

"You know, I've always wondered what it's like while tipsy," I finally admit.

"You're still tipsy, then?"

I mull it over. "A little. Enough. You?"

"A little. Enough."

Another endless pause.

"We'd see each other naked though," I remind him. "I don't

know how serious you are right now, but if you are, and we both did it in here, we'd have to see each other naked."

"That's fine with me."

"Is it?"

"Yeah, it's just my dick. I don't give a fuck."

"You'd have to see mine though. Does that bother you?"

"No."

"You're sure?" I say.

Cam just shrugs, long and deliberate. "It's you."

We meet eyes for the briefest instant, then turn away. I freeze in place while he starts drumming both hands on his kneecaps. And I don't know how much time passes, but I know that once it does, we look to each other again and this time we don't look away.

"So," I say in a strangled voice. "Are we actually doing this or what?"

Cam crosses his arms, leaning back. "Sure."

Neither of us moves.

"So then," Cam says carefully. "Are you—"

I step forward and reach to put my hand over his mouth.

"Stand up," I direct him.

He's completely caught off guard. Instead of doing as I say, he waits until I let go of his mouth.

"Are you sure?" is what he says.

I realize I'm waiting for the question. My palms are slick with sweat.

Fuck it.

"Only this once," I say, reminding myself to breathe. "To see what it's like. While drunk, I mean. And to help distract you."

"Okay," he says.

"And we're not going to tell anyone about it, obviously. Not *anyone*. They'd get the wrong idea. Just our thing."

"Okay," he says.

"And it's not gay at all. Just two best friends helping each other out."

"Okay," he says.

"I mean it. Just this once, just because we trust each other, and we both *know it's not gay*."

"Okay," he says.

"So I guess . . . lock the door. And don't make it weird."

"Okay," he says.

33

Cam. "So like . . . where do I stand?"

Me. "I didn't think about it. Do we both stand?"

"I guess? Who goes first?"

"What do you mean? We go at the same time."

Silence.

Cam. "I mean, like . . . who takes stuff off first?"

Me. "Are we keeping our shirts on?"

"May as well do it right. Since it's just this once."

Silence.

Me. "Your shirt buttons are a pain in the ass."

Cam. "Well your T-shirt isn't exactly—geez, hold still."

"That tickled and I'm super cold."

"Pretty sure we'll warm up."

"Haw, haw."

Silence.

Me. "Why is your belt so difficult?"

Cam. "God, your zipper. Did you walk into the mall, pound your fist on the counter, and staunchly demand they sell you pants three sizes too small?"

"Stop whining. And don't make it weird."

Silence.

Cam. "You left your socks on."

Me. "You're making it weird."

"You're the one with socks on."

Silence.

Cam. "How does that feel?"

Me. "Stop saying things like that."

"Am I doing it right though?"

"Yeah. Hey, don't touch my leg."

"Why not?"

"That's gay."

Silence.

Cam. "We're going to have a talk later about that word."

Me. "No, we aren't."

Cam. "Okay."

Me. "Okay."

Silence.

34

I feel the headache before anything else. Opening my eyes only makes it worse.

I'm lying on clean wheat-colored carpet with no pillows and a fleece blanket thrown over me. I'm still in my clothes that I wore to the party, and my ears are ringing. My phone and wallet are stacked on the ground beside me.

A surge of panic hits me when I realize I'm not in my bedroom. I sit up hard and survey my surroundings. A desk is in the corner next to a bookshelf, which is full of framed photographs. My eye catches Cam's backpack on the ground, and my brain retrieves a few helpful snapshots from last night: Cam and I leaving the bathroom. Him getting yelled at by Meghan for missing the kiss. He and I getting driven back to his house by Asher. Me texting Dad where I was. Cam and I not saying a word for the rest of the night.

My mouth is rubbery and tastes like tinfoil.

The door creaks open, and Cam—freshly dressed, hair wet

from a shower—tiptoes in. He's in a loose red tank top with a smoothie in his hands.

"Morning, sunshine," he says in a voice that immediately irritates me. I groan, massaging my forehead.

"Wakey wakey, big mistakey!" he sings.

"I'm going to hurt you."

"Before you do, you need to drink this banana milkshake and at least one cup of water."

"I don't want a milkshake. It's—shit, what time is it?" I squint at my phone. "It's eleven."

"This will be the best milkshake of your life." Cam squats down beside me, finger-combing his hair. "Water first though. Come on. Doctor Cam says so."

He points to the window ledge near my head, where there's a glass of ice water all ready. I take it and sip, closing my eyes.

"We're super dehydrated. You more than me," Cam says.

"We drank all that water last night."

"Doesn't matter. When you're drunk, the brain slows down and makes less ADH."

"ADH?"

"Antidiuretic hormone," he explains. "Vasopressin. It's what keeps your bladder in check. Remember those ten trips to the bathroom?"

Shut up about the bathroom.

"So dehydration is why my brain feels like it's being pushed through a cheese grater?" I ask, blinking.

Cam perches himself on the edge of his bed, wiggling his toes at me. "That's actually because alcohol causes your blood vessels to dilate, including the ones in your brain. You can fix that with four hundred milligrams of ibuprofen, which I've crushed and mixed into this milkshake." He waves the cup in my direction. "That'll induce generation of stomach acid, so I also mixed five hundred milligrams of Tums to counteract that."

"Anything else in here I should know about?"

"Just an extra lump of sugar to get your glucose levels back up. If you feel weak and shaky right now, that'll help. The bananas will restore your vitamin B6 levels, which most definitely took a hit last night." He tilts his head, studying me. "Are you nauseous?"

I think on it. "Not really."

"Good. Not much I could do for that. When your liver processes your night of poor decisions, an enzyme called alcohol dehydrogenase metabolizes Meghan's cheap beer into a chemical called acetaldehyde. That's out of your system by the time you wake up, but tiny leftover amounts can give you symptoms similar to flush syndrome—cold sweats and vomiting. You'd have to deal with that on your own."

I take the milkshake from him and sip, grateful that at least one of us knows how to handle hangovers. Normally I'd have told him to shut up by now, but I'm just relieved he's focused on a biochemistry lesson instead of discussing the party.

"So that party though," he says.

Fuck.

"What about it?"

"Meghan seemed pretty pissed at me, huh?" he says, wincing.

"I guess. Are you going to text her?"

I can tell from Cam's expression that Meghan isn't the subject he really wants to discuss.

"Maybe," he says, sitting on his hands. "Depends. What would I tell her?"

"You'll think of something."

We sit in silence. I can tell it's killing him to dance around the topic, so I decide to put him out of his misery.

"Just so we're clear," I say. "There's nothing to discuss, right?"

"I'm sorry, what?"

"Nothing from last night, I mean."

"I'm sorry, *what?*"

"Well, what is there to even talk about?"

Cam blinks at me. "The part where we jerked each other off."

"Don't—" I cut myself off, sighing. "It was a one-time thing, no big deal. We were drunk. We didn't know what we were doing."

That last part tastes sour in my mouth, because he and I are both aware that we may not have been sober, but we absolutely knew what we were doing.

"So that's all?" Cam says. I can't read his face. "Nothing else?"

"I mean, what else is there?"

"Well, for starters," he says, "Aria."

A chill runs through me as I realize I haven't given her a

second thought since she left last night. She hadn't even been a factor when I'd . . .

Oh God.

"We can't keep this from her, Nate. I won't do that to her."

My panic regurgitates as a hot bubble of anger.

"You *did* do that to her," I snap back. "You brought me into this."

"It was your *idea!* It doesn't matter." Cam keeps his eyes on the wall. "It happened, and we need to—"

"To what? To—"

"Own up to it," he finishes.

"*Or,*" I say, drawing out the word, "we both agree that it meant nothing, *like we said.* Alcohol makes you forget what you're doing—"

"It doesn't make you forget how a dick works!"

"What I'm saying is, I wish I hadn't done it."

His face twitches, and I know I've just hurt him. For now, my thoughts are too jumbled for me to care.

"Hey," Cam says in a sugary voice, "do you think if I ask nice, you could bullshit me just a little harder?"

"Why are you being such a pain in the ass about this?"

"Because it didn't mean *nothing* to me."

"We agreed it was nothing," I point out.

"No, we agreed it was nonromantic. That it was friends experimenting, or whatever. That still means something to me."

I shrug. "Me too. I guess. But it's *not* . . . whatever you're implying. We're not lovers. You're like, my brother. It was a bro bonding thing."

"Remind me to stay far, far away from your family reunions."

"Will you fuck off already? You're missing the point," I snap. "It was *non*romantic, so we don't need to tell Aria."

"I don't feel good about this at all."

"Why?"

"Well, if nothing else, you're completely avoiding the fact that you and I are now best friends who enjoy getting naked together."

My stomach flips over as I realize those are the exact words I used to describe what "girlfriend" means to me.

"Do me a favor and don't ever fucking say that again," I tell him.

Cam bites his lip, latching his mouth shut. He's smart enough to know that for now, at least, the subject is closed.

"Whatever," he finally says, sliding off the bed. He heads for the door. "My parents will be back in an hour to drive you home. Meantime, a shower will help you feel better. I set out toothpaste, a spare toothbrush, soap, shampoo, and a set of your clothes you left when you slept over last week. And don't worry . . . the door locks."

I'm not sure what kind of jab that's supposed to be, but he's out of the room before he's even done talking.

35

I'm positive the day can't get worse. This beautiful delusion lasts all the way until I get home.

I mutter a greeting to my dad and lumber up the stairs, ready to pass out in my bed. Unfortunately, there's an aunt in the way.

Specifically, she's sitting near my pillow, arms resting on her knees. She's inspecting two painted canvases sitting on my bed: the first is a landscape of the view outside my window. The second is a multicolored, jagged spiral with flecks of black and white surrounding it. I'd set the paintings out to dry before I left yesterday.

"Hey, bud," Aunt Lori says, getting to her feet. "Before you do anything else, I want you to clean your room, all right? It looks like a tornado went through here."

"I'll have it done by tonight." I'm already yawning.

"Do it now, before you forget. What're these drawings?"

"Oh." I feel my face flush. "Nothing. I just . . . made those."

"Hm. Why?"

I shrug.

She shrugs right back, arms folded. "No conceivable reason? Just didn't have anything else to do, so you sat down and painted?"

"I guess so."

"Cut the attitude, Nate. I'm trying to learn more about your new hobby. Come on, tell me about these."

I can tell she won't let me go until I do, so I sit on the end of the bed with the paintings beside me.

"Well, this one is a simple landscape," I say. "No deep meaning."

"What about the spiral?"

"That's from something Cam told me. We had a conversation one time about how . . . well, this was weird. But we said how the more you get to know someone, it's like unpeeling the good and bad parts of them. That's the light and dark coming off there." I point halfheartedly. "It's stupid."

Even as I'm talking, I get the lurking suspicion that I've said something wrong. Aunt Lori pauses, but I can tell from her knitted eyebrows that she's deep in thought. It also doesn't help that Cam is the last subject in the world I want to discuss right now.

"Do you remember Violet?" she finally asks, stepping back to lean against my doorway.

My blood freezes. *Don't give her a reaction.*

"Like, *Violet*-Violet? Cantrell?" I murmur.

"Mm-hm. Do you remember what your dad and I told you when we said you couldn't talk to her anymore?" Without waiting for my answer, she continues, "We said that it wasn't good for you to have someone in your life who was such a bad influence, no matter how close you two were."

I blink and it's like I'm fifteen again, my dad and aunt sitting me down with grim expressions on their faces. Except this time it's just my aunt.

"We both love you," she continues. "And we want you to be surrounded only by positive role models. You know . . . good friends. Solid friends."

"I know that. I am."

But we both know where this is going.

"Cameron isn't a good influence, Nate. Don't pretend you don't know that. The way he talks to his parents is unacceptable. Whatever they want to do in their house is their business. But I'm your aunt, and Bill is your father. It's our job to protect you."

The serpent coils around my chest, poised for the kill. This is it. This has been the plan for months, and now it's happening.

"So you're protecting me from . . . Cam?" I say. "Seriously?"

Her eyes narrow.

"Don't just wave your hand and shrug this off, Nate. *Don't* do that. I've seen how he acts. It's like he thinks the world owes him everything." She counts on her fingers. "He has no discipline, he puts all these ideas in your head . . . I mean, *painting*? You?"

"Whoa," I say, getting to my feet with my hands raised. "He isn't the reason I did it."

I'm really not in the mood to defend him, but I can tell this is more serious than a simple admonishment.

"He has a lot of . . . positive qualities," I continue. "Stuff you don't know about him."

"Like what? Like *what?*"

"He's a good person, and he doesn't control my decisions."

"You're right." She gives one of her dry chuckles. "That's our job."

"That's a joke, right? I'm sixteen."

"There." The whip cracks. "You never used to talk back to us like this. We're losing you, Nate. And we're not going to let it happen."

"He's my best friend," I say.

"News flash, pal: Not anymore. You're allowed to speak to him at school as much as you'd like. But no texting, and no more hanging out at each other's houses. I mean it."

"What? Why?"

"Because I said so."

I want to be like, *Good one, Aunt Lori. They teach you that at law school?* But instead I say, "That's insane. You can't—"

"Yeah, as long as you live under our roof, we can."

"I have the right to have *friends!*"

She takes two huge steps toward me, cutting the room in half. "Let me be as clear as I've ever been. Okay? Once you're eighteen and paying bills, you can make whatever decisions you'd like. But for now, this is our house; our *stuff*—our rules. You own none of this, you hear me? You don't have rights; those are privileges, and we can take them away at any time. I—we—tell you how things will work, and you just have to make them work. Do you understand me?"

No answer.

"*Do you* understand?"

"This is not—this is not normal," I muster. "This isn't fair."

She gives a little fake sob that makes me want to punch a wall. "Are you treated well in the workhouses? Because you'll want to make sure you cover that in the *60 Minutes* special." She throws up her hands. "I don't know what to tell you, bud. Welcome to adulthood—we're happy to have you."

"Okay, well-well—" I stutter, racking my brain. "What about group settings? What if a bunch of us go to the mall or something? What am I supposed to do then?" I'm grasping at straws here. I feel like I'm a witness being taken apart in her courtroom.

She steps back without responding. No further questions.

"We won't check your phone," she says. "Nor your email, nor your Messenger account—yeah, I know about that one. Your father and I agreed that this is our way of showing we trust you. But if you lie to us, or act like a little brat, we have no problem taking the phone away. Don't make us be the bad guys."

I don't trust myself to speak. I don't know what I'd say if I did.

"I know you don't see it now, but when you have kids of your own, you'll realize that we're on the same team here." She softens. "Let's work together on this."

I stare at her until she leaves the room.

■ ■ ■

Dear Violet,

I'm sorry, but I can't see you this week. Next time you're back in town, I really need to talk to you. Don't reply to this. I'll be in touch.

Nate

36

The next six weeks are quiet.

There's only one upside to my aunt forbidding my friendship with Cam: Now I have a valid excuse to avoid him, which the voice in the back of my head has been urging me to do since New Year's.

I ignore all of his texts for the last few days of winter break. On our first day back, he practically tackles me when he sees me in the hall, bouncing up and down, full of questions and concerns and annoying Cameron sayings.

I tell him what happened.

I expect him to get all upset or nervous, but he just listens without interrupting, nods a few times, and says, "Well, sounds like your aunt just needs some time to cool off."

"Dude, you weren't there. I really don't think this is going to improve."

"We'll see. Long as we can talk at school, we'll be fine."

Except we aren't, because it's the last real conversation we have for weeks. We only have Biology and History together, so I make sure to be in and out of those classrooms as fast as possible. I ask Mrs. Koestler (I know . . . kill me) if I can study in her room during my lunch period. Turns out she's actually a nice lady when she's off the clock.

It's easy to mask all this behavior with the pretense of "my aunt is making me." That's what I tell Aria, and she buys it in half a second. But all of her comforting only makes me feel worse, because it feels like I've suddenly been dropped on a planet where no one speaks the same language as me. When I look at Cam—who's soon reduced to just doing the guy head-jerk thing when he passes me in the hall—all I can think of is the party. And it doesn't make me feel excited, or dangerous, or any of those fun sensations from when it happened. It makes me feel like someone is grabbing my stomach and twisting it. Or like Aunt Lori has her security camera following me around everywhere, waiting for me to screw up.

I did this.

No more lunch period. No more study hangouts or Saturday nights with Cam. No more going to church together.

One day I'm so worked up that I get home and punch a hole right through my bedroom wall. Well, not through it, but into the drywall. My hand hurts like hell, and I have to hang up a picture to cover the hole, and it still doesn't make me feel any less alone. It just leaves bruises that linger with a dull ache I can't stop noticing.

One night, I'm lying in bed and I consider what Cam said the morning after the party . . . how this makes us more than just friends. So—gay for each other, then. As much as the idea makes me squirm, I give it fair consideration. And I decide that no, that isn't possible, because my feelings for Aria are completely real. Not a cover-up; not some bullshit subscription to societal norms or whatever. When I met her, I wasn't even looking for a girlfriend. I was hit at a million miles an hour by all the best feelings, triggered by a fellow human, and they've been there every day since. They still are.

So not gay, then. Just guilty.

Dear God: I don't know what to do.

All this blurs together into one recurring question that's on my mind: What's running through Cam's head? We used to know each other inside and out, but that feels like ages ago. We could practically finish each other's sentences before Christmas. Now, with everything that's happened, he doesn't even feel like a friend. He feels like some abstract idea—a force for me to react to, rather than a real human being for me to chill with and share conversations.

I want to ask him what he's feeling about all this between us. Then I realize I wouldn't know how to answer if he asked me the same thing.

One day at the start of February, I see him sitting on a bench behind the school with his head in his hands. He isn't crying, but he's rocking back and forth. It's a motion I know all too well:

He's having a memory attack.

I wonder if he thinks about that night.

I wonder if he regrets it the way I do.

I wonder if he prays about it the way I do.

I wonder all of it and I don't help him.

37

No surprise here: Aria is big on Valentine's Day.

I personally couldn't give a shit about it, especially since I've spent the past six weeks lying to her. But she wants to have a nice dinner date all dressed up in red fancy clothes, so that's what we do.

After dinner, we decide to chill in the back of my car with the heat blasting and soft music playing. I have a blanket in the backseat for just such an occasion, so we huddle together under that.

"How have things been with your aunt?" Aria asks, immediately pinpointing the number-one subject I want to discuss on a date.

"Fine," I say in a lifeless voice. "Her law firm is doing a little better, I think."

"Oh. I meant with Cameron."

"I mean, we're still not allowed to talk." Why does everyone seem to think my aunt is just going to wake up one morning and change her mind? "Why do you ask?" I say.

"I just hate not having us all together at lunch."

At that moment, my phone buzzes with a text. I frown at the screen—it's from him.

"Speak of the devil," Aria says, tilting her head. "What's it say?"

I open the message with the screen angled away from her since I realize there's a good chance she shouldn't read what it says.

I know we're not supposed to text, so you don't have to reply, but I just wanted to say Happy Valentine's Day, ya nugget :P

And then, a few seconds later:

I really miss you.

"Aww," Aria says, managing to read it anyway. "That's sweet of him."

Sure, I guess. Except he knows how risky it is for us to communicate, and this isn't exactly an important message.

I punch in a quick reply.

Happy V-Day, fellow nugget. Miss you too :P

I'm not sure why I send it. I do miss him, I guess.

I delete the message thread in case Dad or Aunt Lori check my texts. Then I pocket the phone and turn back to Aria, my nose a few inches from hers. I gently poke her in the forehead, making her smirk.

"That probably meant a lot to him," she tells me.

"Good for him."

"Do you not care?" she asks, hesitant. She pulls her face away from mine.

"Of course I do," I say, because that's the short version. The long version is that I'm so sick of thinking about all this. And I want to turn to her and confess everything. But that idea only makes me feel more disgusting, because the only reason I'd want to tell her is so I could have someone to vent to about it all. And I could explain to her how complicated my feelings about Cam are. I could grab her by the shoulders and say, "Aren't people in your life supposed to make you happy?! So why would I care about having Cam around if all he does is make me cheat on my girlfriend, get bitched out by my aunt, and leave me apologizing to God every night for the fucked-up things I can't stop thinking about?"

I bury it all.

"I don't know," Aria says, wrenching me back to reality. "Sometimes it just seems like you don't want people around."

"Well, of course not. I despise all people," I tell her.

"Except me, obviously."

"No no, especially you."

"Wow, you're such an ass."

"Love you!"

We play with each other's hands some, which leads to kissing, which leads to making out. I forget everything else.

■ ■ ■

I think about the painting I showed Aunt Lori with the light and dark sides of a spectrum wound together. I'd love to say that I'm wondering which end I'm on, but the truth is I already know.

38

'm four minutes late for curfew. Aunt Lori is waiting for me in the kitchen in her bathrobe and reading glasses. I spot a stack of papers in her lap with the usual glass of wine on the table. I'm hoping the booze will induce a bit of mercy.

"Come here, Nate," she calls softly as I tiptoe toward the stairs. No dice.

"I know I'm late," I say, shuffling into the kitchen. "Traffic was bad. I'm sorry."

"Traffic was bad? At ten o'clock on a Sunday night?"

Rule number one in negotiating with a lawyer aunt: Never whip out facts that aren't true.

"I'm kidding," she says, pulling off a chuckle. "Hey, it happens. Did you have a good time with Aria?"

I nod.

"What were you doing around eight o'clock?"

"Huh?"

Aunt Lori sighs through her nose and tilts her head. Sizing me up. Her voice drops until it's almost a whisper. "Nathan. Is there something you need to tell me?"

I feel my blood freeze. What's scarier than being caught when you're guilty? Being caught when you have no idea what you did.

"Um, Aria and I were getting ready to leave the restaurant, I think," I say.

"Get your cell phone out."

"What . . . why?" I ask. It's worth noting that I'm entirely awful at lying to my parents. I can't even remember the last time I did. Unlike Cam, I have no practice at this.

"Your cell phone—go ahead, get it out." Aunt Lori gives an encouraging nod.

"Right now?"

"Yeah, why not?"

She waits as I dig my phone out of my pocket and wave it at her. I feel my palms start to sweat as she unlocks it, scrolls around for a few minutes, then clicks her tongue. When she's finished, she slips the phone into the front pocket of her robe.

"Wait," I say.

"I think the thing that gets to me," Aunt Lori says, holding up a finger to shush me, "is that I tried really hard to work with you, buddy. Your dad talked me into giving you your space, trusting you to follow our rules. We were clear about the rules, weren't we? We were *so* clear."

"Wh—there are no messages with Cam!"

"I *know*," she coos, frowning. "That's the worst part, right? I think so. The deviousness. Deleting messages after you send and receive them."

Aunt Lori stands, waving the papers that were sitting in her lap. She slaps them against my chest as she walks by.

I see our phone company's website banner on the front page and feel my stomach drop. It's a printed out list of every text my phone has sent and received this month, time-stamped, phone numbers included. There are two from Cam's number received at 7:56 p.m. and one sent to it at 7:57 p.m.

"I called your dad, and we've already discussed your punishment," Aunt Lori says from behind me, icy. "The whole area under the fridge needs cleaning. That's your chore—scrape all the gunk off. Also, we get your phone for the week."

I nod uneasily. Dad isn't home, so I expected worse. I start toward the stairs again.

"Where do you think you're going?" Aunt Lori calls after me.

I rub my eyes. "Bed? I have school tomorrow."

"You didn't seem to care about that when you stayed out late." Aunt Lori motions me back into the room, then hands me a box of plastic kitchen knives.

"These are your scraping tools. You'll go to bed when the job is done. This is how it works—real adults see their tasks through. Right?"

I'm still waiting for the joke.

She blinks at me, daring me to tell her off. "You want to say something?"

"You . . ." I choose my words carefully. "You said you wouldn't track my phone. You promised."

"You get caught sneaking behind our backs, and you want to talk about honesty? I don't think so." She pats me on the shoulder as she leaves the room. "I'd get to work if I were you. That'll take a few hours. Wake me up if you need anything else, all right?"

■　■　■

I crawl into bed just before three o'clock. I spend the rest of the night dreaming of taking one of the plastic knives and ramming it through Cam's chest.

39

Since I get just over three hours of sleep, I cancel gas station breakfast with Aria the next morning. I'm so tired when I leave for school, the very feasible prospect of falling asleep and dying at the wheel excites me.

Unfortunately, I not only make it to school alive but run into Cam as soon as I stop by my locker.

"Hey, man!" he says, flicking my shoulder. "Tell me all about Nate's Valentine's weekend." Which sets me off immediately.

"It sucked, actually. What did I fucking say about texting me?"

Cam's smile crumbles. He pushes his glasses up his nose.

"My aunt saw it," I continue. I'm jamming my books into my backpack as hard as I can, my ears roaring. I realize that for the first time, not only am I *not* pleased to see him, but I'm actually in a worse mood because of it.

"She saw?" Cam's eyes pop out of his head. "Oh my God, I'm so sorry. Listen, I can call her, tell her it's my fault. . . ."

"Yeah, *great* idea!" I slam my locker shut, and he squeaks. The sound elicits a satisfying surge through my chest.

"Okay, okay," Cam says. "Well, on the bright side—"

"There's no bright side, Cam!"

"Okay. But it's not fair that you get punished for something I did," he says.

"There's literally no one who disagrees with that. Including my aunt. Hey, get out of my way."

"Can we talk about this? If yelling at me is what you need to do, go ahead. But I don't want to leave things like this. And just . . . there's a lot I want to talk about too."

I just so, so don't feel like dealing with this.

"No, we aren't talking about it. You want to help? Leave me alone before you get me in more trouble. I'm not even joking."

I walk past him.

Great, I think. It's 8:00 a.m., and I'm already going to be in a shitty mood for the rest of the day.

"How long should I leave you alone?" Cam calls after me.

"I don't know. Give me the week at least."

"The week. You got it. Um, sorry again, dude. I'll talk to you later."

He sounds ready to cry, and I honestly couldn't care less.

40

Dear Nate,

Yeah, first weekend of March works. What do you need to talk about? Are you all right?

Love,

Violet

■ ■ ■

It's tricky coordinating a meet-up since Aunt Lori is doubling down with her patrols, but Violet and I pinpoint a coffee shop halfway between her house and mine.

The drive is about an hour, so I tell Dad and Aunt Lori that I'm spending the day with Aria. It's been two weeks since Valentine's Day, but apparently I've gotten better at lying, because I sell them on it.

I sweat the whole drive up. I haven't planned out how much

I'm going to tell her. And I have no idea how she can help. I just know that, even if she gives me a tough time, she won't judge me for anything.

She's waiting for me outside the coffee shop, dressed in a white skirt and lavender blouse. Smoke leaks from her mouth around the cigarette wedged between her teeth. As soon as she spots me, her eyes light up.

"This human!" she says, tackling me in a hug. "It's about time!"

Meet Violet Cantrell: about half a foot taller than me, so pale she's practically translucent, and a head full of red hair but not a single freckle. As soon as we break our hug, she scans me up and down.

"You're not any taller," she says, rubbing her chin like she's a detective examining a crime scene.

"You are. Are you wearing heels?"

"You wish. C'mon, I'm freezing my ass off out here."

"Put that out first." Cigarettes are her latest habit, and I hate it.

She blows smoke in my face, sending me into a fit of coughing. She stabs the cigarette into the ashtray on top of the trash can, and we head into the café. Once we've both got our drinks, I steer us toward a booth in the back where there isn't any chance of us being overheard.

"So," says Violet. "What's up with you? It sounded pretty urgent."

It takes a lot of shaky breaths and "ums," followed by "okay, just listen . . ." but I tell her everything. I detail the New Year's Eve party, giving enough vague euphemisms to let her know what happened. I recap Aunt Lori's punishments and unhinged behavior. With every sentence, I breathe easier. It's the first time I've told the story aloud, and before long I'm rambling at lightning speed, getting an odd rush from finally, *finally* letting someone into my head.

Violet listens.

When I'm finished, I realize I've been tearing my napkin into smaller and smaller pieces. Violet sweeps them to her side, folds her arms behind her head, and delivers her version of a supportive statement.

"Fuck, man."

"Yeah."

"So, which issue are you here about?"

I frown. "Huh?"

She speaks slowly, her icy eyes fixed on me. "Are you here for help with coming out, or tips on how to deal with Lori being a bitch?"

"I'm straight, and she's not a bitch."

"That might be the most wrong sentence you've ever said aloud."

God, not her too.

"I'm *straight*," I huff. There's that bitter taste again. "Don't do this. You're the only one I've told."

Something in my tone makes her raise her hands in surrender, which is rare. "All right, hey, if you say you're straight, no one else has the right to argue. And I guess people do . . . experiment, sometimes."

"Have you? With girls?"

"In your dreams." She rolls her eyes. "Okay—wait a minute. Are you *looking* for other people who have done this too? And you thought I might've since I've tried so much other stuff?"

I don't say anything. Truthfully, that's exactly what I thought.

"All right." Violet props both of her elbows on the table, ready for business. "Well, let me ask you this: What's your plan with Cameron? Long term."

That's a question I've been asking myself every day for months. I have no idea what my answer is.

"What do you think I should do?" I ask her.

"That's a no-brainer." She leans forward, serious. "Keep him around. Fix things."

"It's way more complicated than that."

"I can almost guarantee it isn't, but let's hear your take on it."

"What about my family?"

"What about them? They can fuck right off."

"Stop saying—"

"Look how simple that was!"

"*Stop* saying that like it's easy. I'm not just going to throw away my family. Cam's not *that* special."

Her face tightens until it reminds me of Aunt Lori's scowl.

"So what, then?" Violet says, swatting at an invisible fly.

"What . . . you're going to just piss away one of your closest friends, because of something you *think* you owe to a few adults trying to shove a rod up your ass? The fuck outta here, dude."

"Look—"

"No, you look. The thing you and Cam did wrong was not tell Aria—which you *need* to do. But don't beat yourself up for being confused about . . . stuff and things."

It's weird, but I like how hard Violet is pushing me. That's what she's always been best at: playing devil's advocate without coming off as a condescending asshole.

"I'm not confused," I say. "And Aria or not, what he and I did is still a sin."

"Isn't the church becoming more progressive on this?"

I shake my head. "Not how it works. The rules are written down. Argue all you want, but that's a fact."

"Says who?"

"Literally the Catholic dogma."

"So ignore that rule. The church already ignores a bunch of other ones."

"Okay," I say, rubbing my forehead. "Clearly you either don't understand why the church condemns gay sex, or you don't care."

"No, it's both. I don't understand and I don't care."

This conversation is shaping up how I was afraid it would: cathartic, but ultimately unhelpful.

Violet eyes me. "Tell me what I'm not getting, Nate."

"What you're not getting is that according to the church, sex only exists to reproduce." I karate chop the table from left to right with every other word. "Anything else, for any other reason—so, including what Cam and I did—that goes against the purpose. All that kind of stuff—gay stuff—it's, it's . . . filthy, and impure—"

"Well. If you're doing it right."

"You're not hearing me! This is important," I say.

"Yes," she says. "It is."

"Then can you just tell me what I should do? Like, specifically."

"Would you like me to give advice as an objective outsider or as a biased friend?"

"Both, I guess."

"Okay." She's looking at a point above my head, gears whirring. "As an objective outsider . . . I think, do whatever makes you comfortable. You want to call yourself straight, then do it. Being happy is the most important thing."

"Why do you say that?"

"Because trust me when I say no one gives a shit if you're miserable."

All right.

"And as a friend?" She fixes me with a sad stare. "I just think someone needs to tell you that it's okay to not have your shit together. Because everybody screws up, even adults. Lori never tells you that. She really should."

I snort. "Got any advice for taking her on?"

"Well that one's easy," Violet says. "Whatever you do, don't shoot and miss."

41

You have to tell Aria.

I can't.

Once you do, you'll make things right.

I won't.

You NEED to tell her.

I don't.

■ ■ ■

For the next two weeks, I avoid Cam completely and Aria as much as possible. Cam has gotten the hint that our friendship isn't going back to normal, yet every day in Biology he makes sure to wave hello and give me a polite smile. I know that all I'd have to do is ask to talk, and we could discuss everything. Try to turn it into words. I wonder if it would be like old times, like those deep conversations we used to have months ago. I don't have the energy to find out.

One day, just after the final bell dismisses everyone, I'm on the way to my car when I hear Cam and Aria arguing in the parking lot.

I'm not normally nosy, but of course I listen in.

". . . keep telling you," Aria is saying to him. She sounds exhausted. They're both shielded from view by Aria's SUV.

"I've told you a hundred times, you're such an angel for looking out for me. But I know what I'm doing," Cam says, very measured.

"You have no idea what this is like on my end," she says. "It's like . . . Nate's never been good with emotions. But he isn't just being indifferent anymore. He's being—"

"Aria, please."

"—he's being *mean* to you!"

"You make it sound like he stole my crayons."

"Last week. Remember last week? You said you two were supposed to meet up by the picnic benches after school because it was one of your memory days."

My heart sinks, because I know where this story is going.

"Except not only did he ditch you, but he ditched you to hang out with *me*," she continues. "And he lied to you about it. That's not cool."

Cam sighs. "He chose to spend the day with his girlfriend. No big deal."

"Yeah, no, that's *not cool*," she repeats.

"It was a mistake."

"You just said it was his choice—not a mistake. Those are opposites."

"Are you breathing okay?"

"You know, I've been better," she huffs.

I peek and see Cam put his hands on her shoulders. "Hey. Try to rel—"

"Am I dating an asshole?"

"Try to *relax*."

"The fact that you're not answering the question is the least relaxing thing about this conversation."

"I promise you're not dating an asshole. He's going through a lot with his aunt. Cut him slack."

Which makes me feel so great, of course.

"You trust him?" Aria asks. She sounds like she's trying to be gentle. Hearing her talk like this about me, of all people, feels like a knife right between the shoulder blades. I've been part of so many conversations where she's complained about how mean some people are. Only this time, she's not saying it to me, she's saying it about me. To my best friend. And, I've entirely earned it.

"He's *not* an asshole," Cam insists. "And yeah, I trust him."

Aria doesn't respond.

"What is it?" he asks, poking her in the shoulder.

"It just . . ." She sighs. "It seems like you think that when he treats you like this, the trick is to . . . make yourself not mind. And that's not how it's supposed to work."

I leave before I hear any more.

42

"Is it fair to say you and Mr. Haynes were no longer friends by this time?" Mrs. Lawson asks me.

Cam gives an empty chuckle, loosening his tie.

I clear my throat. "We didn't hate each other, if that's what you mean."

"That's not what I mean," Mrs. Lawson says. "I mean: Is it fair to say you were no longer friends by this time?"

"We were friends," I say, injecting some authority into my voice. "But we hadn't had a real conversation since the party. There were the texts on Valentine's Day, and after that we both kept our heads down."

"It sounds as though, by the opinion of others, you didn't treat Mr. Haynes very well."

"Okay, well, something he tended to forget—" I say, shooting Cam a look over the table, "—is what I put up with to stay friends with him. I got lectured every day, my phone tracked—all that stuff would've gone away if I'd just cut him loose."

"But you didn't."

"No."

"Why not?"

"I . . . I don't know."

"You aren't sure?"

"No. I . . . no. I don't know."

43

To celebrate the first day of spring break, Aria and Asher invite me and Cam to come biking with them at Stone Hill Park. They go there all the time, so they shoot way down the trail in a heartbeat.

Cam and I are evenly matched, so we bike side by side. We're both in gym shorts and tank tops that expose our biceps (or, in my case, my lack thereof). I stare at Cam's muscles a little, but in a way that's admiring—not romantic or anything; more like, "he looks how I want to look." But then my thoughts feel a little too close to the line, so I stop. I feel guilty enough that I had to lie to my dad and aunt about where I was going today.

■ ■ ■

The whole trail is shaded, so it's a pleasant trip. I don't say much until the four of us stop for a water break.

"Hanging in there?" Aria asks me, wiping the sweat off my brow with the back of her hand. "Damn, you're drenched. Don't overheat." There's something about having her and Asher here that makes all this feel a bit more like old times.

"This is why I recommended gym clothes," Asher says. I give him a thumbs-up.

"Seriously—who knew you'd ever wear a tank top?" Aria says, patting my bare shoulder. "Cam's really rubbed off on you."

Cam responds to this by ferociously choking on his water.

We make small talk for another few minutes as Asher looks over the list of trails. Cam catches sight of one he's done before, and his eyes light up with that familiar glow he used to get when I first met him.

We haven't been normal in months, but now he turns to me and uses that same voice as before.

"Hey, Nate," he says. "You down to try something new?"

I roll my eyes, but when he keeps staring at me, I play along. "For your level-ninety-six adventure?"

"Yeah, that thingy. This one is scary but I'm telling you, it's worth it."

"You haven't told me what it is," I point out. I glance over at Aria and notice her studying our interaction like she's collecting observations for a case study.

Cam puts his hand near my face, pointing. "See that giant hill?"

I smack his arm away. "Yeah?"

"That's Stone Hill. The park was named after it."

"Makes sense. What about it?"

"You need to ride your bike down it with me."

Asher whistles. "I don't know, man. You're basically pumping the breaks the whole time. Steep hill, flat road for a few hundred feet, then a creek at the end."

"That's the point," Cam insists. "It's an insane rush. Come on, Nate, you have to do it with me. *Dooo* it."

"No thanks," I say.

"It's something new!"

"Kill me."

"Right here?"

If he and I were alone, I would yell at him to shut up, but Aria is giving me a look that tells me I don't have much of a choice.

"I'll do it if it gets you to shut up," I grumble to him.

He immediately lights up. "*Yesss.*"

I follow him around the bend to get to the spot. Aria and Asher stay put at the picnic bench.

"You're going to love this," Cam says, hopping up and down as we walk. "Aren't you excited?"

"I'm wetting myself."

"Sounds like—"

"If you make a urine joke, I swear—"

"*URINE* TROUBLE!" Cam sings over me, his voice echoing through the trees. It's so ridiculous that I can't help but burst out laughing, which makes him laugh, and I realize with an old ache how long it's been since we've joked around like this.

I breathe in deeply through my nose, taking in the spring air. It's moments like this that help me understand what he was saying when he told me the woods are the place to escape from all your problems.

"Okay, so," Cam says, coming to a halt. "Take a look."

I do and nearly throw up. We're standing at the top of a dirt hill that cuts straight through the forest, dipping down sharply and leveling off into a creek. It's not too far, but the end of the path looks like a tiny dot.

"Is this safe?" I ask him, gripping my bike with sweaty palms.

"I did it all the time back in August. Why? You scared?"

"No," I say. His face scrunches up—I know he can tell I'm lying. I also know he'll pretend he believes me.

"That's the spirit," he says. "One more thing—"

"What type of coffin would I like? Thanks for asking. Mahogany is fine."

"Trust. Me. Okay?"

I'm very close to wussing out. But he looks more excited than I've seen him in a while, and we're already on our bikes, and—

"Go!" he calls.

For a minute it doesn't feel like I'm moving at all. And then suddenly my bike feels like it's dropping beneath me; time slows down, I'm gripping the handlebars—it's all I can do to stay on—but then I look at Cam long enough to see him leaning forward, so I do too. I don't feel like I'm falling anymore; I'm floating, floating and shooting ahead. The air is rushing through my ears, and I'm yelling with laughter. I can't see Cam, but I can hear him beside me. Then there's a spray of mist, which makes us both yelp, then laugh again, because HOLY SHIT WE'RE FLYING!

44

The four of us finish the trek a few minutes after sunset, so we need flashlights to find our way back to the cars. When Asher gets a text telling him and Aria to be home ASAP, they say their good-byes to us and drive off. Mr. Haynes will be here in about half an hour.

"You don't have to wait with me," Cam insists. We're kicking leaves along the ground, where the edge of the parking lot meets the first trail into the woods.

"I have a little time," I say. "My aunt isn't expecting me yet."

"You didn't tell her I was coming today, did you?"

"I said I was going biking with Aria. Technically true."

Cam tilts his head at me.

"What?" I ask.

"Nothing. You're just getting better at lying."

It starts drizzling, so we head over to the cluster of picnic benches under the pavilion. We choose one in the middle and sit on the tabletop side by side, about a foot apart. The pattering on the roof above our heads is oddly calming—the start of a storm is outside the canopy twenty feet in front of us, yet under here we're safe and dry.

We stare at the rain.

Then in a soft voice, Cam says, "Can I share a memory with you?"

"Is today one of those?"

"Yeah. Not too painful or anything, but . . . yeah."

"What is it?"

He gives me a grateful smile, then rubs his hands together before letting them rest on his lap.

"Remember the girl from back home? The one I had my first kiss with."

"Yup."

"A few years ago today was the second time I asked her out."

I frown. "Second time?"

"I asked her out twice. She'd rejected me a few months back." He shrugs. "It just got me thinking."

"About what?"

"How glad I am that I tried again later."

"Why did you?" I ask.

"I mean, she was worth it. You wait for people who are worth it."

And it's like, this might be the single best example of how naïve Cam can be. Yeah, I used to think waiting for your crush was cute too . . . when I was like ten. Then I actually grew up and learned that sometimes the nicest people can be the biggest assholes, the most loving God can be the most terrifying thing, and the most invincible mom can be killed for no good fucking reason.

Fuck Cam and his sheltered little cookie-cutter household.

"The real world doesn't work like you think it does," I spit at him. "And this doesn't either."

Our eyes meet. And we both know that when I say *this*, I'm talking about us.

"It could," he replies.

I look Cam up and down. I see him in his loose tank top and gym shorts, his glasses just slightly crooked, his blond hair messed up from the wind. It's the first time he and I have been alone together, in private, since New Year's Eve. And suddenly I feel like we're back in that bathroom again—where we can say what we want, do what we want, with no one around to misinterpret it. This indulgent urgency.

"Stop," Cam says to me.

I look down and realize my hand is on his inner thigh.

I lift my arm. We're still sitting side by side on the table, but he scoots away from me.

"No one's here," I say to him, glancing back and forth. The rain has picked up. "We could make it quick. I haven't done it in a while anyway."

It's as though being here, with him, has flipped a switch in my brain. I'll regret this later. But I need to do it now.

Cam says, "I want to. But not while you're dating Aria."

"What's that supposed to mean?"

"That when and if you two are broken up, I'll be elated to unpause this conversation."

"What's wrong with you? I thought we were cool," I say. "I thought this was our *thing*. Not romantic. No labels."

"We both knew that was bullshit, man," Cam says. He stands, starting to pace between the picnic tables. "So listen—real talk. I'm pretty sure I'm bi. And I think you might be too. If nothing else, I'd kind of prefer to not reinforce the stereotype."

"Wait, what?"

"The one that says all bisexual people are chronic cheaters."

"No, I mean . . . you're *bi?* Since when?"

"If you have to know specifics, I drew the conclusion on March seventh."

"Like, *bisexual?* So that's an actual thing?"

Cam squints at me like I've just suggested he give heroin a try.

"What?" I say. I'm not trying to be a dick to him, but no one ever explained this stuff to me. "You either like guys or girls. Now, if you're gay—"

"It's a legitimate sexual orientation."

"Since when?"

"The answer to your question is 'always,' you asshole."

I shake my head. "Dude, think about this. You messed around with a guy once. Everyone experiments a little. You still like girls, right?"

"Definitely."

"So, there you go. You're straight except for one little road bump."

"Well first of all, I'd enjoy doing it again; second of all, 'little road bump' isn't a very nice thing to call yourself, and third—"

"Cam, just stop—"

"*Third* of all, is now a good time to remind you your dick wasn't exactly soft?"

"No."

"Fine, well, even if you're only one percent into dudes, it can still count. 'Bisexual' is a pretty broad term."

"So who's to say if that's the right label for you?"

"On March seventh, I did."

I take a breath, then try again.

"It sounds like you just enjoy *acting* bi."

"*What else matters?*" he shouts, grabbing his own head in frustration. "Why do you think anyone has a label in the first place? It's to let other people know who you're okay being involved with!"

"So you'd be okay having sex with a guy, then?"

"Not having sex, no," he says. "I'm not into that. Maybe that'll change; maybe it won't."

"No offense, but I'm having a tough time believing you."

"No offense, but eat my entire ass. Why should I have to *prove* anything to you? Because I missed the part where you're suddenly the chancellor of LGBT validation."

"Dude—"

"HAIL!"

"Stop."

"*You* stop." His words catch in his throat. "You're supposed to be my best friend. Why can't you just be happy for me?"

I don't have time to decide if I'm angry, tired, or hurt. I just keep talking.

"I'm not happy that my best friend is turning his back on our church," I say.

"I have literally never felt as close with God as I do now," Cam says. At first I think he's being sarcastic, but he sounds entirely serious.

"You *can't* be a Christian like this," I tell him.

"Turns out I can; you're seeing me do it right now."

"Pretending to be one doesn't make you one."

"Hey, Father Copeland? Go fuck yourself."

"I'm just stating a fact!" I say. "How can you justify this?"

"I don't know what you're trying to ask, but if you're wondering why I'm not designing my sexual identity around a few sentences from a twelve hundred–page book that was last fact-checked two thousand years ago, I don't have an answer for you. Christianity is about love, and acceptance, and I'm as much a part of it as you are."

"You are *not* the same as me!" I'm shouting at the top of my lungs, like if I yell hard enough I can make this go away. And I want to throw anything I can at him to hurt him, to shut him down, to wipe that determined look from his face. "Listen. I may have jerked you off, but this is just a side distraction since Aria won't put out, you got that? This is *nothing* to me. So for fuck's sake, drop it."

Cam is frozen in place. His eyes are saucers. His hand flies to his mouth.

At first, I think it's a reaction to my words. And then I see what he's staring at. Or rather, who he's staring at.

Behind me, Aria bursts into tears and runs back to her car.

45

She had forgotten her cell phone under the pavilion.

She heard everything.

She cried for an hour.

She promised not to tell anyone.

She dumped me.

She didn't yell at me.

I wish she had.

■ ■ ■

I think that if there's any mercy left in the world, Dad and Aunt Lori will both be asleep when I get home.

She's waiting for me in the kitchen. Same bathrobe, same glass of wine.

"Hey, bud," she whispers when I tiptoe into the kitchen. "How was biking? Did you beat the rain?"

I don't even have enough energy to come up with a bullshit response. I open my mouth once. Twice. Nothing. My eyes well up, and next thing I know, I'm crying. I'm crying and Aunt Lori is immediately shuffling toward me, wrapping her arms around me in a strong cradle that smells of booze and bath salts.

"Shh," she says, patting my head as I sob into her shoulder. "Buddy, what happened? Hm?"

She lets me cry until I'm ready to sit, then eases herself into the chair beside mine. I whimper a few sentences about how Aria broke up with me, no I don't know why, no I don't want to talk about it.

She doesn't ask. She doesn't scold. She lets me cry and holds me.

■　■　■

Dear God: I deserve this. I'm sorry.

46

I call his house as soon as I wake up the next morning.

"Hey. Are you home alone?" I ask.

"Nate?" Cam sounds thoroughly shocked. "Is that you?"

"Yeah. I'm calling from my home phone. Are your parents around?"

"Nope."

"Mine either. I'm just chilling."

"Same," he says. "Yay, spring break. Listen, about yesterday—"

"I want to sneak over to your house. Is that cool?"

"When?"

"Like an hour. Noonish."

"Seriously?" He sounds surprised, but thrilled. "Um, sure. My parents won't be home till three."

"Perfect. And Cam?"

"Yeah?"

"Two things."

"Sure."

"One, when I get there, I want to talk about last night. Not for long, but . . . it would help me to talk about it."

"Of course," he says. "What's the other thing?"

"Shower. I'll do the same. And don't wear a belt. I don't want to deal with that this time."

I hang up before he replies.

47

Cam answers as soon as I ring the doorbell. He's in a bright green T-shirt with khaki shorts, his hair still damp from the shower.

"Two things," he says, echoing what I told him on the phone.

"Sure."

"One. I'm sorry about your breakup, and even though you were a colossal prick to me yesterday, it's my job as your best friend to forget about that and be there for you. So whatever you need to talk about, I'm here to listen."

"What's the other thing?"

In response, Cam fiddles with the front of his shorts and grumbles, "These are basically falling down without my belt."

"Good."

He smirks and taps me on the shoulder. I grin back, he lets me in, and for the next half hour I just talk. I ramble about what Aria really meant to me, and how, yeah, the physical stuff with her was great; but beyond that, I'm only just now realizing how much of my BS she'd tolerated. She was my partner in crime. Not in the same way as Cam, but equally important.

I pace around his living room the whole time while he stays planted on the couch like a therapist, listening.

"What do you think she's going to do about us?" I finally ask him, once I'm done venting. "You think she'll ever get past it?"

Cam stares at the floor, adjusting his glasses.

"I'm not sure," he answers. "There are some things you just can't take back."

"Do you think it wrecked your friendship with her?"

"I think it fed our friendship into a wood chipper."

His voice strains a bit. It occurs to me that I haven't considered how awful he must be feeling. Aria was his closest friend besides me, and he hurt her in the worst way possible.

"I'm sorry," I tell him. It comes out of my mouth in one crisp motion, without irony.

"It's okay," he says. "I'd say these are extenuating circumstances. So, you admit being bi is a thing?"

"I don't admit that that's what I am, but yeah. Whatever works for you."

He doesn't look satisfied with that. I wait.

"And what if," he says, getting to his feet and strutting toward me, "you're wrong about yourself?"

"Then isn't it your job as a friend to let me figure it out on my own?"

"I'm in this with you," he retorts. He leans against the wall to face me, arms folded. "You loved Aria. But you're also here to do this with me."

It isn't a question, and I don't deny it. I think more about the idea—being bisexual. I'll admit it: As I lay awake in bed last night, I Googled "Am I bisexual quiz" and found myself on some smart-ass web page with only one true or false question: "I consider myself to be bisexual."

Real fucking helpful, thanks.

"You think I'm half gay, half straight?" I ask Cam. "Half Christian . . . half going to hell . . . "

"Um, no." Cam strokes his chin. "Wait—how would half going to hell even work? Do you get to wear a halo but your legs are on fire? Or does Lucifer get you for Tuesdays, Thursdays, and every other weekend?"

"This *isn't* funny."

"It's a little funny. And being bi doesn't mean being half of anything," Cam says. "If that was the case, you could just—like, switch that part of your brain off."

"Maybe that's what I'm trying to do."

"Yeah? How's that worked out so far?"

"Well, every time I've left it switched on, I've either hurt Aria or gotten shit from my aunt. So that's some fantastic incentive."

"Call it what you want," Cam says, backing down. "But listen to me: This will *not* go away just because you like girls too."

I feel like punching something. Trying to beat Cam in an

argument is like trying to catch smoke between your fingers. It's even tougher when he has a point, which deep down I know he does. But it amazes me that someone who cares so much about my feelings can't tell how much it bothers me to talk about this.

"I don't even like kissing guys," I tell him.

"So? I might not either."

"You're labeling yourself as into dudes, but you don't enjoy kissing them?"

"The interest is there," he says. "But I don't know until I try. You don't either, by the way."

"I can guess."

Cam rubs his hands together, taking a step toward me. "Or we could find out. What do you think?"

"I think I'd rather shit into my hands and start clapping."

"Little too kinky for me. Can we work our way up?"

"Fuck you."

"That's more like it!"

"Stop it, okay? Just stop." We're both pacing now, circling each other. He takes two steps forward, trying to come closer, but I take two steps back.

"Can I point out something?" I say to him. It comes out sour.

"Sure."

"I'm being serious."

"Me too."

"This is about you," I say.

"Perfect."

"It's a criticism."

"Even better."

I pause, searching for the right words. I motion to him with both hands and say, "You do this thing . . . where you seem to think if you *wish* hard enough for things to be a certain way, they just . . . will be. Or that if you keep yelling at me to change my feelings, eventually I will." I bite my lip. "And I don't know who gave you that idea, but that's not how any of this works. Learn to take no for an answer."

He needs to hear this. Cam always acts like the reason I'm saying no is because I don't know what I'm missing out on. Like he has some privileged insight that I'm too stupid to see. But he's wrong. I know exactly what he's proposing, and I'm still not interested.

He doesn't reply. Just stares at me. Stares until it becomes uncomfortable.

"You're really not going to try it?" he asks softly.

"Kissing you? No. I'm sorry, but no."

He falls silent again. And I don't know if there's a way he can convince me of what he's saying, but I know it isn't like this.

Finally he says in a slow, shaky breath: "I'm doing the best . . . that I know how to do here."

"We all are!" I snap. "Have you thought about that? Me, you, my aunt . . . we're *all* trying to do what's best for each other. Quit bitching at me just because none of us are good at it!"

His face tightens. He clenches his fists, staring at the leg of a nearby couch.

"I'm going to start coming out at school," he finally says. "I already told my parents yesterday."

I hesitate. "And how'd that go?"

"They were . . . actually, they were pretty good. They said it doesn't change anything. School might not go as well. But for right now, before that, I want to formally come out to you. I'm not asking you to say anything. Just sit there and listen and don't be a douche."

Okay.

He looks right at me. "I'm Cameron Haynes, and I'm bisexual."

Even as he says it, his shoulders deflate, and he gets this calm look across his face.

"Long as you're sure," is my comment.

"I'm sure." He nods. "I could fall for the hottest girl in the universe and it wouldn't change the fact that I enjoy going down on a guy."

"Again. How do you *know?*"

"Guess I don't," he says. "To be fair, neither do you."

I get that same feeling as last night under the pavilion. New Year's. The phone call this morning. The tugging in my gut that tells me I'll regret this later, but *I want to do this now.*

"We . . . okay. That, we could find out," I say.

He arches an eyebrow at me. "So you're not willing to kiss me."

"Fuck no."

"But you're one hundred percent okay with blowing me."

"I mean—yeah. As long as it's only for like a minute. Maybe thirty seconds."

"Thirty *seconds?* Are you sucking a dick or solving the riddle for Final Jeopardy?"

"It just can't be too, like, gay."

"I'll make sure to say 'no homo' afterward. Are we doing this or what?"

I nod once.

"Fine. Whatever," Cam says. "But let me be the one to go on record and say how screwed up this has gotten."

As I motion for him to get over here, I realize he's right. And as we pry off each other's clothes, I wonder if I even care anymore.

48

I go over to Cam's house three more times before the week is over. Each time, we do the same things. And each time, I feel the same way: fired up beforehand, euphoric during, and like a piece of garbage afterward.

On Thursday my thoughts are too bad for me to go over there, and I don't like how it feels to be alone in the house, so instead I drive to church and go to confession.

For those who are unfamiliar with the concept, confession—also called reconciliation, one of the seven Catholic sacraments—is where you go to get conscripted into saying ten Hail Marys as punishment for touching yourself.

That was the joke among all the guys in eighth grade anyway. In all seriousness, it's meant to be a healing process where you reflect on the sins you've committed, confess them aloud to your priest, and contemplate how you can make yourself a better person to avoid repeating the same mistakes. The priest weighs in with some spiritual counseling, then assigns a penance, which is meant to be an act of contrition (and for the record, they do usually stop the "ten Hail Marys" thing after middle school). It's not fun to do, but it's meant to refine your conversations with God. Which I most definitely need help with.

As soon as I kneel in the confessional booth, the screen cover slides open. I cross myself and wring my hands together.

"Bless me Father, for I have sinned," I say through the screen, already struggling not to trip over my tongue. "It's been seven months since my last confession."

Father Parker replies, "May God the Father of all mercies bless you and aid you in the time of your unburdening."

Awkward pause.

"Father . . ." My voice gets jammed in my throat. I can't say it. There's no way I can blurt this out. *Damn it, he's waiting.* How do I even start this? Maybe throw some menial sins in there to grease the wheels?

I clench my hands even harder and try again. "I've been doing some really . . ." I swallow heavily. "Impure things."

"Mortal sins?" He says it gently, without judgment.

I squeeze my eyes shut against the image of the face Cam made yesterday. "Yes."

He knows I'm starting to lose it. "Take a few deep breaths," he says. He does them with me before continuing. "In the book of John, the Lord says if we confess our sins, He is faithful and just to forgive our sins, and cleanse us from all unrighteousness."

"That's why I'm here," I sputter.

"These impure acts—do you unequivocally renounce these atrocities?"

I breathe hard through my nose.

His teasing laugh. Defiant eye roll. Shared grins.

"I don't know if I can stop," I say. *Fuck*, I hate how I sound right now. Like a drug addict. Someone who can't help himself. "Can I just ask God to take these feelings away?"

"No."

"But I want them gone. *I want* them gone."

Father Parker takes a long pause for himself, so long that I start to wonder if he fell asleep.

"To ask God to take these away—that isn't the answer," he finally says. "It may feel this way, but it isn't. These feelings came from God, just as we did and everything does. To ask God to take them away would be in service to your own gratifications— not His."

I mean, yeah, that's why I asked. Can you tell God I'm trying to do what he wants without hating myself?

And it's almost like Father Parker senses my train of thought, because he continues, "Too many people today, they subscribe to the belief that to serve God is an easy task. But this isn't true. You are a servant, and your life belongs to Christ. Following Him requires personal sacrifice—sometimes every day. Every member of this church, no matter how they seem, has struggled with the same things as you. You aren't alone in this."

"So how do I fix it? How did they?"

"They taught themselves to *trust* the word of the Lord. To trust it completely, even if it seems to lead us down an impossible path. We need to be willing to give up not only our temptations for Him, but our *lives*, if we must."

I shake my head, loosening my hands. *"Why?"*

Whoa—that was a lot more attitude than I intended. Damn it—this isn't how confession is supposed to work. *Don't screw this up too. . . .*

"Because this is what Christ did for us," Father Parker responds, surprisingly unfazed. Maybe he's heard worse. "I would also remind you of something important: Committing immoral acts does *not* make one an immoral person. It isn't being a sinner that's unspeakable—we're all sinners, aren't we? You are, I am . . . we're all human. There is nothing wrong with you for being human, understand?"

"Yes."

"What's immoral is to willingly commit the sins without contrition. If an alcoholic, for example, feels the persistent temptation to drink—this isn't wrong. What would be wrong is to give in to the urges. To act in service of the self rather than in service of Christ."

Okay. Okay. So if I am bi—hypothetically, if I am, then being bi *isn't wrong*. It's giving in to the temptation. So I just can't act on any . . . urges. Or fantasize about them.

"This is difficult for us to remember at times," Father Parker says. "Which is why we all come here. We offer penance for the healing of the hurt caused by the sin. And through examination of conscience, we strengthen our soul against future temptation."

Damn it, this is going to be difficult.

"And therefore, to facilitate this examination, your penance is to carry out a reflection through a personal prayer of ten Hail Marys—"

Oh, for fuck's sake.

■ ■ ■

I spend the rest of spring break alone in my house not talking to anyone. On Saturday, I meet up with Violet, and she gives me an unprompted delivery: a disposable cell phone, preloaded with five hundred text messages. I tell her I won't ever use it, but she makes me take it anyway. I tuck it underneath my mattress without turning it on.

On Sunday, I go to Easter mass. During the homily, I'm plunged back into the feeling that's been building since confession—that I'm a hypocrite; an imposter of the purity my mom emulated so naturally. That this room is full of people who are holier than me, more deserving of forgiveness than I am.

I look to Cam, who sits in the church like it's his home. During the homilies, he'll nod, like he's really taking in these messages about living a moral life. Does he hear the same things I do? Does he have any doubts?

Church is a topic I've stopped discussing with him.

When I go home, I try to keep painting a piece I was working on for Easter—a sunrise with three crosses on a hill. I give up before I can finish it.

■ ■ ■

The next week I'm back at school, and I wonder how Cam and I are going to interact in the halls. The answer is readily apparent: We don't.

I still get my gas station breakfast every morning, but I do it alone now. I'm not expecting Aria to speak to me again, and sure enough for the first three days, she avoids me and Cam like the plague. No greetings, no little comments; she doesn't even look in my direction. On Thursday, though, I bump into her at a sign-up sheet that's been posted for Covenant Lake Bible Camp—i.e., the site of the Boathouse Incident last summer.

"Sorry," I say when I realize I'm blocking her path to the clipboard.

She clutches her schoolbooks to her chest. "Hi."

"Hi," I echo. My tone is appropriately solemn.

Aria waits until the last handful of kids empties out of the hallway. Once we're alone, tension drapes over the air like a thick fog.

Deciding to be direct, I say, "I'm guessing you're still mad."

She inspects me up and down, impassive. "Actually, I'm not.

I'm glad I found out. Because I'd had this feeling, for months, that there was something off with you. And it's good to know I wasn't being paranoid."

"If you could just let me explain—"

"No."

"No? As in, like—"

"As in no, you don't have my permission to explain it to me. I don't want you to try." She sounds cold in a way I've never heard before. "I really mean that. We aren't going to talk about this. The whole thing is disgusting, and so are you."

I grab the air in frustration. "I know. It's unnatural and wrong, and I'm trying to not—"

Aria lets out the loudest *pfffft* I've ever heard.

"Wait, wait," she says. "You think it disgusts me that you like guys?"

"*SHHH!*"

She's actually laughing at me. "Dude, it disgusts me because you *cheated on me*. And justifying it by saying I don't put out—thanks again for that, by the way. Because 'this walking baby factory can be fun to chat with, but when are we getting to the *good* stuff?'"

"I didn't mean to say—"

"You think you did this because of who you're attracted to, or whatever? No. You did it because you're a fucking asshole."

She scribbles her name along with Asher's on the clipboard, then brushes past me down the hall. I call after her, "Please don't tell anyone."

She stops dead in her tracks.

"Please," I say to the back of her head. "You promised you wouldn't. Did you mean it?"

She pirouettes in a semicircle until she's facing me. Her face contorts—pure revulsion.

"You know something, Nate?" she says. "Just because you're full of shit doesn't mean everyone else is."

49

As soon as I get home from school, I do two things: I confirm the house is empty, and I use the home phone to call Cam.

This isn't a risk I'd normally take, but Aria's comments in the hallway have been nesting in my brain all day. I need to vent. If there's one thing Cam is usually good at, it's listening to my problems.

Except for today, apparently.

"How would you like me to react?" he asks, as soon as I tell him what Aria said. He almost sounds more pissed than she was. "She has every right to be upset that we didn't tell her. *Like I said we should.*"

"I know."

"It's almost as if . . . exactly what I said would happen, is exactly what happened . . ."

"I know. I'm just surprised she didn't want to talk."

"I'm surprised she didn't saw off your head and throw it into traffic with Asher's lacrosse stick. You do know what cheating on someone is, right?"

"Oh my God—I *know*. But I'm scared she's never going to talk to us again."

He blows air into the receiver. "I have no idea what to tell you."

"Just . . ." I put my head in my hands, balancing the phone on my shoulder. "I guess I'm not sure why I called."

"No, it's fine," Cam says. "I can't—"

"This is just—hello?" I give the phone a shake. The line is dead. "Hello?"

I hop from the living room to the kitchen, where the base for the phone sits on the counter. I frown. The wire connecting the line is sitting on top of the counter, running around the fridge, to—

"You lying little *shit!*"

I scream and jump backward. Aunt Lori steps out of the corner, the freshly disconnected phone line in her hands. She's still in her work suit.

"I almost texted, that I'd be home early, you know. But I figured I didn't need to." Aunt Lori spits the words out, dripping with disgust. "Nathan Copeland, you've been lying to us. You know we check your cell, so you use a different phone, yeah? Thought you were being clever? How long have you been pulling this stunt?"

"I . . ." I'm fighting for words. "Where's—"

"Where's Dad? You want him? He'll be home after midnight.

The usual." Her voice drops to a hiss. "You're stuck with me for now."

█ █ █

My first chore is to scrape the kitchen floor clean again, with two differences from last time: I'm cleaning under the dishwasher instead of the fridge, and I have to use an old rag instead of plastic knives.

I try to see the bright side: I can take out some anger as I pick away at the dirt caked onto the tiling. But Aunt Lori stands over me the whole time, making comments like, "You can do better than that, can't you?" or "You missed a spot over there."

When she sits down to eat dinner, she watches me from the table, promising me I can eat once my chores are done. I don't know how many tasks are on her list, so I don't know when that will be. I finish the kitchen just before 7:00 p.m., so I'm sent to scrub the shower in the upstairs bathroom. I'm done with that in an hour, but she points out a spot about the size of my thumb that's permanently stained into the tiling.

"That isn't going to come out," I tell her. "You'd have to repaint it."

"Don't give me that," Aunt Lori says. "Scrub harder. And remember, this is a punishment. *Think* about why I'm making you do this. It's not for my own health."

In those hours, I decide I've never despised someone as

much as I despise Cameron Haynes. Nothing is nice about our friendship anymore. Nothing. Anyone who gave a shit about me would see all the damage they're causing and get the hell out of my life. Instead, he knows exactly how to keep roping me in, and I'm enough of an idiot to keep letting him.

I'm still scrubbing the tiling at 11:00 p.m. Aunt Lori doesn't send me to bed, despite the fact that it's a school night. She eventually decides that the stain really won't come out, so she next sends me to look for the remote to the Blu-ray player.

"We lost that five years ago," I tell her, keeping my voice as respectful as possible. "The player works fine without it anyway."

"Well, I didn't lose it, and your dad didn't lose it. And it didn't walk away on its own. So who does that leave?" When I don't answer, she adds, "Responsibility, Nate. That's the whole point of all this."

So I pick through the house square foot by square foot to find the fucking remote, which I never do. I'm so tired that I'm running on emergency power, and my stomach's growls turn into cramps.

By 1:00 a.m., I can barely stand. Aunt Lori allows me to eat so we don't break any child abuse laws. As I attack my plate, she pours me ice water and praises how hard I've been working.

"One more chore," she adds. "Then you can go to bed. Clean out the fishbowl upstairs. Okay?"

"Sammy's? I changed his water last week."

"Not the water, the bowl. I just emptied it out."

I chew my food, staring into space.

"So you flushed him, then," I say. A question without being a question.

"Responsibility, Nate. Okay?"

"Okay."

50

"**D**id your punishments continue after that night, Nate?"

"Yes."

"Was your cell phone confiscated?"

"Yes."

"Is it fair to say you had little-to-no contact with your peers during the next few weeks?"

"Yes."

"Did you continue eating lunch by yourself at school?"

"Yes."

"Did you continue attending church alone?"

"Yes."

"Is it fair to say you had little-to-no social life?"

"Yes."

"Is it fair to say Mr. Haynes was the cause of this?"

"Yes."

"Would you say this led you to feel more violent tendencies?"

"Yes."

"Earlier you denied that you hated Mr. Haynes. Is it fair to say that changed by this point?"

"Yes."

51

The second Sunday of April, I do something I haven't done in over a year: I visit my mom's grave.

I go at night, when it's dark and drizzling. I'll admit it's a little spooky visiting a cemetery under the moonlight, but it's right next to the church, so that makes me feel safe.

It's been a while, but I don't have any trouble finding her headstone. It's right near the back of the cemetery, almost up against the corner.

I sink down beside it and stare at the inscription under her name.

MARIA COPELAND.

HEBREWS 13:5.

NEVER WILL I LEAVE YOU;

NEVER WILL I FORSAKE YOU.

I ease down so I'm lying on my side, facing the marker, legs half bent.

What would you think of me?

I don't remember much about her. She was gentle. She kissed my scrapes and cut the crust off my sandwiches and let me sleep next to her when I had a nightmare.

"Mom." I say the word aloud, testing it. I hate how unfamiliar it sounds coming out of my mouth.

I tell her everything.

By the time I'm finished rambling, the drizzle has picked up to a real rain, but I'm close to crying so I don't mind.

What would you think of me?

I can't be like Cam. Queer. That's who he is and that's fine, but it's just not who I am. I'm not bubbly or girly like he is. That isn't *me*. I don't have a feminine voice or flamboyant walk. I'm Nathan Copeland, normal teenager.

"Think about this," I say under my breath.

I don't want to.

"I was in love with Aria for a while. And there was the Boathouse Incident. So I'm definitely not gay." I don't know who I'm talking to.

I'm not gay. I knew that already.

Would you still love me?

I squeeze my eyes shut.

"I really liked the stuff with Cam too. But I don't think I'd enjoy kissing him."

Mom, would you still love me?

"Maybe. I don't know. I don't think I want to have sex with him."

God.

I'm crying. The wind bites at the back of my neck.

"I don't think of him that way."

God.

It isn't until I ponder the name, by itself, that I realize how much it scares me. And it scares me that it scares me, because it never has before. I've always pictured God as a gentle old man, with strong arms and this warm, softhearted smile. Now, the name just makes me think about what's going to happen to me after I die.

Mom, will I see you again?

The idea of hell is incredibly terrifying, when you really stop to think about it. There's the fiery suffering part, which is scary enough. But what paralyzes me is the endlessness of it. Imagine that you die, wake up, and it's like, "Here I am, in hell." And then there's the torture, and maybe you can take it at first, but eventually it's so unbearable that you'd do anything to escape— even kill yourself. Splinter your soul and reshape it into whatever grotesque distortion this new world needs it to be. Except you can't do it, because you're already dead. *Here I am, in hell.* So you wait for the end of the world. But even when the planet dies, you'll still be here, a trapped soul for eternity; not just as long as you live, but for as long as existence itself, until entropy consumes us all. Forever and a day—the embodiment of infinity. No time, no being; only the choices you made. You.

Me.

I'm going to hell I'm going to hell I'm going to hell.

My clothes are soaked through. Chilling me. Mud pools around my head. I'm trembling so hard that I wouldn't be able to stand if I tried.

Dear God: Why did you make me like this?

I pull my arms closer to my chest. I repeat it again and again in my head until the words run together.

Why did you make me like this? Why did you make me like this?

I press my head against the headstone.

Dear God: I hate this.

I picture Cam's cute smile and the butterflies it gives me and like a reflex, it squeezes more tears out of me. I picture how I felt the day we rode our bikes down the hill with our faces to the wind. I picture us lying on his bed naked, holding each other, foreheads pressed together.

I hate him. I hate him. I hate him.

My hand clutches my mom's grave. It isn't enough. It's cold and wet and makes me feel tiny.

Dear God: I fucking hate him.

Without thinking, I throw back my head and scream. *Scream.* Until the air is scratching my lungs and all the breath is gone from my body. Nothing happens, so I do it again. And a third time. I don't know what I'm expecting.

It's right then that I realize: There's no worse feeling than to yell and yell and feel like no one can hear you.

Why did you make me like this, why did you make me this, why did you make me, WHY.

Actually, that's wrong. The worst feeling is that sneaking suspicion that people can hear you, loud and clear, and they still don't care enough to answer.

I breathe.

Dear God: I fucking hate you.

I breathe.

I breathe.

I breathe.

When that doesn't work, I just bawl my eyes out.

52

When I get home from the cemetery, Aunt Lori asks if I had a nice time sneaking around with Cameron.

She grounds me for the rest of the month and informs me that my computer has been dismantled.

She reminds me that real adults don't whine about their punishment.

When I tell her I wasn't out with Cam, she reminds me that real adults aren't liars either.

53

Two men show up one morning to collect the Wi-Fi router, cable box, and modem that we rent from our telecom company. Dad and Aunt Lori canceled all services except the phone line—Amish mode for me. They can still use data on their cell phones, which is more than I can say because they took that away from me too.

I keep myself from losing my mind by chatting with Violet over the burner phone she got me. I tell her how everything except my car has been confiscated, and that's only because I need it to get to school. I tell her how I come home every day to a list of chores, which I usually finish by nine if I'm lucky.

The last weekend of April, Dad and Aunt Lori let loose their cruelest punishment yet: They make me go to my junior prom.

Let's not mince words—I hate dances. They're loud, sweaty, and overcrowded. I find them especially unpleasant when I don't have a date, which is the case here. None of it matters to my dad and aunt. They both insist that prom is one of those vital experiences you never forget, and it's so important that I'm ungrounded for the night as long as I attend.

I show up an hour late, so I have to park in the auxiliary lot. That's about a five-minute walk to get to the school. Unfortunately I don't make it that far.

I'm walking across the lot when I catch noise of a commotion near the trash bins. Most of the area is obscured in the shadows of the streetlamps, so I step closer until I get a good look at the scene. My blood turns icy—I recognize one of the voices.

Three guys, all built like bears, are beating the piss out of a shape that I quickly recognize as Cameron. He's lying on the pavement, arms and legs pulled tight. It reminds me of how he looked that first night he shared a memory with me at the homecoming game, curled up on the trailer deck.

"Are you fucking crying?" one of the guys is saying. I can't hear what they say next, but I catch the word "fag" more than once.

In response, Cam turns his body over, aims his shoe, and drives it into one guy's kneecaps. The guy goes down, but his two friends keep up the barrage. One stomps on Cam's left hand, hard, eliciting a sharp scream.

I step toward them, realizing too late that they can clearly see my face. Everyone freezes.

In the half second I have, I size up the scene. I don't recognize the three attackers—they're definitely seniors, all decked out in suits and ties with boutonnieres pinned to the pockets. Cam, still curled up on the ground, is in a white dress shirt with purple suspenders and a matching bow tie. His lip is split, soaking most of his chin in blood.

The leader of the pack addresses me. "You know this guy?"

I shrug. "Not really."

"So you don't care if we finish up here?"

I shrug. "Not really."

They deal Cam a few more blows, but having a witness seems to have dampened the mood. They eventually slink off toward the gym. As they leave, one of them bumps into me. I don't react.

Cam lies quiet and still.

I kneel beside him. He grabs the side of the trash bin for support as he spits blood onto the pavement.

"Did they beat you up for being gay?" I ask. I don't mean to blurt it out like that, but I have to ask. Like seriously, what fucking year is it?

"First of all, I'm not gay," he mutters. His face is in the shadows, so I can't make out his expression, but he sounds deflated. "And second of all, I provoked them."

"Why?"

"They said I looked gay."

I sigh.

"The suspenders are a little much," I concede.

"Says the man in a black shirt, black suit, and black tie."

"Is it too serious?"

"Depends. Are you and your most trusted associates Rastelli and Garafolo about to make me an offer I simply can't refuse?"

I chuckle despite everything. Cam winces, then adds, "And it wasn't my suspenders."

He holds both hands in front of my face. It takes me a minute to realize what I'm looking at: All ten of Cam's nails are painted dark purple.

"Well . . ." I say, unable to contain myself. "I mean. Christ, Cam, why did you do that?" Maybe that's too harsh, but I can't believe he would be so naïve. Sure, our school is progressive and all, but *nail polish?* Of *course* someone is going to notice and give him shit for it.

"Because I wanted to," he says. "Okay?"

I don't immediately answer. I feel an intense mix of frustration and resentment toward Cam. Half feeling bad for him getting beaten; half wishing I'd been the one to do it.

He takes one of his hands and presses it up against my chest. At first I think he's going to shove me, but he just lets it linger there.

And we are both so, so tired.

"You need to quit acting like this," I finally say.

Cam tilts his head, studying my face. He presses his hand into my chest harder, like he's trying to reach through me. Then he lets go and shrinks away.

"Nate," he says, his eyes brimming with ghosts. "Where the fuck are you?"

54

I take Cam back to his house. Neither of us says a word the whole drive. Neither of us addresses the fact that I basically told those guys to keep attacking my best friend. He spends the whole ride not looking at me.

His mom, seated in the living room, notices us the minute we step through the front door.

"Oh my *God*." She leaps from the couch, her laptop thudding to the floor. "Sweetheart. You're bleeding . . . *Peter!*"

Mr. Haynes appears at the top of the stairs, takes one look at Cam, and makes a mad dash to grab the first aid kit. Meanwhile, I'm just in the background for all this, helping Cam over to a chair without saying a word.

"How did this happen? Who did this?" Mrs. Haynes demands as her husband appears behind her, unzipping a pouch of medical supplies. I scooch out of the way so I'm on the other end of the couch.

"I'm fine," Cam says. "It was some guys from school. I think they did it when they saw my nails." And he shows them.

"Oh, geez," I hear Mr. Haynes murmur. Mrs. Haynes, meanwhile, slowly gets to her feet and begins pacing the room, a hand pressed to her mouth.

That's the lingering snapshot for a minute: Cam's mom calming herself while his dad cleans him up and I sit there, a spectator.

Then Mrs. Haynes lowers her hand and turns back to Cam.

"Sweetie," she says quietly, "I'm sorry. But what were you thinking?"

No response.

"I mean . . ." she continues. "Leaving . . . leaving the house like that? At school, where everyone can see—"

"I was thinking," Cam murmurs in a dangerously soft voice, "that I wanted to wear nail polish."

She doesn't let it go. "But why? *Why?*"

"You know what, you want me to write an essay justifying it, go get me the fucking MLA Handbook," Cam snaps, louder this time. He swats at an alcohol wipe his dad is trying to press to his chin.

"*Oh,*" Mrs. Haynes says, freezing on the spot. "Oh, you are not going to do that, young man. You hear me? Not today. I will put up with your attitude on any other day . . . any other situation. But when my son comes home with the daylights knocked out of him . . . We're your *parents!*"

"Well, I'd be elated if you started acting like it."

Dead silence. Everyone is holding their breath. I'm waiting for Mrs. Haynes to fire back, and so is Cam. When she doesn't, he swallows and continues. "You said you're okay with me being bi, right? But now you're saying it's okay as long as I don't openly *express* it? As long as I don't bring it outside the house? Leave it in here where you can deal with it—"

"*Enough.*" If his mom cares about yelling in front of me, she isn't showing it. "It's our job to protect you. Do you understand that? It's our *job*, Cameron. As parents—"

"Protect me?"

"Yes, *protect* you! From—"

Cam leaps to his feet, fists at his sides. "What the fuck do you know about this? You have *no idea* how it is, Mom and Dad—honestly, do you get that? Both of you. If you knew what it's like—"

"Like what?" Mrs. Haynes interrupts, her eyes wide once more. "Who else has hurt you? Hit you?"

Cam spits out a dry laugh, pointing to his busted lip. "*Why* do you think it can't get worse than this?"

His mom pauses, and I can see her eyes welling up. I feel like I'm intruding on a private scene; seeing something I shouldn't.

"Cameron," Mrs. Haynes says. "We've . . . we've already lost one—"

"Mom, we've been over this," Cam says, impatient. "I *know* you lost a kid—"

"YOU DON'T KNOW—*you do not know!*" Mrs. Haynes erupts. Everyone jumps. "You can't know what it's like! None of you." She points to Cam, then me, then her own husband. "Until you lug a kid around inside you for nine months . . ."

I see the tiniest nostalgic grimace pass over her lips. Mr. Haynes steps close enough for her to clutch his arm.

"Cameron," she continues, facing him directly. "You think your father and I care who you love? Seriously? I know there are parents who take issue. . . . I can't wrap my head around it, and I would never . . . but I will do this. This, I'll do."

Cam clears his throat. "What's 'this'?"

"Telling you how it is in the real world. Telling you that you aren't allowed to wear nail polish outside this house. And you shouldn't hold hands with another boy in certain public places, because not everywhere is safe. You *need* to see—" Her voice catches. "It's the hardest thing, but it's our job to make you see that you need to be careful with some of this. If you walk around without . . . Baby, we're protecting you. And you know what, you always wanted us to treat you as an adult. Well . . ." She shrugs, halfheartedly. "Here we are. You *can't* be yourself in certain times and places. And if you think . . ." She trails off, sniffling twice. "Your dad and I would give *anything* to make this better for you. Anything."

That makes Cam crack a smile.

"But this is how it is," Mrs. Haynes says. She lets go of her husband so she can kneel in front of Cam, stroking his hair.

"Hiding means they'll keep doing it," Cam says, keeping his eyes on his knees. His lips are set in a thin line. I pick up on what he isn't saying: *That's why I wore nail polish.*

"I know," Mrs. Haynes says, putting her hands on his cheeks. "But trying to tackle that at this age . . . it isn't worth the risk. That's the one sacrifice your dad and I can't make. Some parents, better parents, could do it. If we could, we would—but we can't. I'm sorry, sweetheart, but that's just going to have to work for now."

Cam's eyes finally meet his mom's. And together, they stand up.

55

My birthday is almost entirely uneventful. Then Violet Cantrell gives me the strangest gift I've ever received.

By complete happenstance, she was born on May nineteenth, same as me, except one year later. Because of this, we make it a point every year to see each other on our "day of twinning," as she calls it.

This year, we meet up at the usual coffee shop after school, which is a risk I'm willing to take for today. She's chopped her red hair short for the summer, but otherwise it's same old Violet.

"Happy you-exploded-out-of-a-vagina day!" she greets me, hugging me tight. She smells like a mix of perfume and cigarette smoke. "Except that's right, you were a C-section. So you were just removed."

"Har-har."

"Happy Removal Day, tumor baby."

"You about done?"

We get our coffee and grab a table near the back, as usual. She tells me about a cute boy she met at a party who might be the new Mr. Violet Cantrell, and I fill her in with news about Aunt Lori, which is that there is no news. She's been traveling for various legal conferences nearly nonstop for the past few weeks, putting her out of the house even more than Dad. If I'm lucky, I'll get to spend my birthday in an empty home tonight.

"I don't think Garner-Stowell is doing very well," I add.

"What about Cameron?" Violet asks.

I shrug. "Haven't talked much, I guess. I don't know." I decide not to tell her about prom, and that he and I have barely said two words to each other in the weeks since. We've texted here and there using the burner phone, but no real conversations.

"Do you think things will get better with him?" she asks me.

"Why do you ask?"

"I don't know." Violet pauses. "I just feel like you can't keep doing the same thing hoping for a different result, you know?"

I chew on that as she reaches into her purse and digs out an envelope with my name on it.

"What's this?" I ask as she hands it to me.

"It's for you."

"Yeah, I got that. Is it a birthday present? Because I only got you a gift card."

"Kind of—no, don't open it here," she says, grabbing my arm. "Read it when you get home."

"O . . . kay?" I say, sufficiently confused. "What is it?"

For the first time in a while, she turns serious.

"It's—I don't know how to explain it. It's assistance. Help," she says.

"Help with what?"

"Your family."

"I'm so confused."

She tries again, slower. "It'll make sense when you read it."

"That doesn't make me less confused. Should I be worried?"

"No. If anything, I'm worried about you."

"Don't be," I say. "And don't worry about Aunt Lori either. She's trying as hard as she can."

"I know she is," Violet says, her arctic gaze far away. "That's why I'm worried."

56

Mrs. Lawson leans forward.

"What was in the letter?" she asks.

I'm clutching the table so hard I can barely feel my fingertips. I loosen my grip but don't answer her because *no, I'm not going there. I'm not doing that. I'm not spilling a story that's not mine to tell.*

"I decline to answer."

She, for once, wasn't expecting that. "Mr. Copeland, we need a response from you."

"He has the right to decline the question, Nora," Cam's lawyer reminds her sternly. "Asked and answered."

She scowls at the clock.

"We're almost done for today," she remarks.

"Time flies when you're having fun," says Cam.

Mrs. Lawson pulls out her phone, dials a number, and presses it to her ear. When someone answers on the other end, she says, "I need you to start drafting a subpoena for the Haynes depo.

It'll be for all correspondence between Copeland and Violet Cantrell. I'll fill in the blanks when I'm done here. Thanks." She pockets her phone and turns back to us like there was no interruption. "What happened next?"

Shit. Subpoena. You most definitely can't ignore those—as I learned when I was personally served one for this deposition in the first place. Are they going to send a search party to my house? Confiscate my phone? I could hide or destroy Violet's letter, but I'm pretty sure that's obstruction of justice or something.

"Nate?" Mrs. Lawson prompts.

I expect Cam to jump in, but he's silent. I shrug, letting my hands thud against the table.

"There's one last thing before summer. There was a party on the last day of school," I say. "I was allowed to go because it was technically a class event."

57

Meghan Richter's first party was the tame little Halloween chatterfest. New Year's Eve was the raging blowout. Word is that her end-of-school-year beach party will be somewhere in the middle.

The word, as it turns out, is accurate. There are parents crawling around everywhere, so alcohol and drugs are off limits, but there's still music blasting through a set of massive speakers under the pavilion. The adults are in charge of cranking out burgers and hot dogs. A game of volleyball is in play farther down the beach. The rest of the kids are either lying around or splashing in the lake.

The sun is just starting to set when I get there. I spot Cam sitting on the other side of the crowd by himself, head in his hands. He's in a bright orange tank top with yellow board shorts—the epitome of good summer vibes—but he looks miserable. More upset than when I saw him in AP Bio today, but then again I didn't actually talk to him, so I'm not sure what the deal is.

"Nate!" Meghan calls, distracting me. She bounces up to me and gives me a quick hug. "You are *just* in time. We need one more player for volleyball."

I try to back out, but it quickly becomes clear that this isn't a request. So I play, staying near the corner and not doing much. As much as I try to focus, my eyes keep darting back to Cam.

The months of limited contact? Those have been tough. But it's even worse seeing him sit by himself, damn near tears, and I'm fifty feet away knowing that anything I say will just result in an argument. Which will make him feel even worse. No matter how close he and I have been, physically or otherwise, we've never been able to fix each other's pain. A voice in my head tells me that's because it can't be fixed. A much darker voice tells me that's because our worst pain comes from each other.

The volleyball smacks me in the ear.

I curse, then take myself out of the game.

"Nice moves. Fucking amazing. Catlike reflexes, dude."

I turn around to face the source of the voice: Aria, dressed in a white lace tank top and jean shorts. She has a burger in one hand and a drink in the other. The sunset is hitting her face at just the right angle so every freckle stands out, and oh my God does she look gorgeous.

"Hi," I say to her.

"You play volleyball now?"

"They just needed an extra player. It was boys versus girls."

"Sounds perfect for you."

Okay, I walked right into that one.

"I didn't know you were coming," I say.

"How would you have had any way of knowing that?"

"Fair point. Sorry. Being weird." It's bizarre talking to her—I feel like someone has dropped me back in tenth grade. My last conversation with her was when she yelled at me in the hallway the week after spring break. That was months ago, and with everything that's happened since, this may as well be a whole new girl in front of me. Twelve weeks—that's all it took to turn my girlfriend and my best friend, the two people who used to be my whole world, into complete strangers.

"It's been a weird school year," Aria notes. She's fixated on the sand at our feet. I can tell there's something she wants to say but isn't sure how to bring it up.

"You've got that right," I say. "A lot changed."

The background ambience feels so out of place—people cheering, dance music blasting behind us, and here we are having a serious conversation.

I just say it.

"I'm sorry, Aria. Like, I could tell you that you misheard things at the park, or that it wasn't as bad as you think, but it just was. Is. Literally *no one* deserved that shit less than you. No one." I make a point to keep eye contact with her during the last bit, because if this is our final conversation and I can only leave her

275

with one sentiment, I need it to be that. And it's a lame apology, for sure, but it's about the best I can do.

She chews on her lower lip, lobbing her head from side to side.

"That's nice of you to say," she says. "I mean, don't get me wrong. We needed to break up. But thank you for saying that."

"I don't know if this helps," I add, "but for what it's worth, I wasn't, like . . . I wasn't faking our relationship. I mean, I fucking *loved* you. I get it if you don't believe me—"

"I do," she says.

"I'm glad. Because I did. And I really was, like . . . attracted to you too. Physically. I wasn't faking that either."

"Dude, I know. Boathouse Incident, remember?"

My face boils. I shake my head, pinching the bridge of my nose. "That's going to follow me forever, isn't it?"

She shrugs, her lips hinting at a thin smile. "Your secret's safe with me."

I can't tell if she means the Cam situation or the Boathouse Incident, but I'm so floored by how much I appreciate her in that moment that I don't really care.

"You fucking rock," I say. "I hope you know that."

"You know what? I do."

I glance over to Cam, who's still sitting on the other end of the beach. He's drawing in the sand with his toes, looking like he wants to bury himself alive.

"You should go talk to him," Aria says.

"Do you know why he's so upset?"

"Well, it may have something to do with the fact that his grandparents just found out about his sexuality and pretty much disowned him."

Oh.

"I . . . take it that probably hit him hard," I say.

"Probably," she agrees. "It doesn't help that I've been a bitch to him about the whole thing."

"Yeah, wait . . . When did he tell you all this?"

"About half an hour ago. I sat with him and we fixed things." Her smile loosens. "You have to understand, Nate . . . With the way I found out about everything—"

"Yeah. I get it."

"I was pissed and in shock and didn't exactly think the queer stuff was something to be happy about, you know? I felt like everyone had been lying to me. My anxiety went through the roof."

"You don't have to explain," I tell her. If anything, it's making me feel worse.

"Okay. Then just go talk to him," she says.

I look her up and down. I remember what Cam said to her back in the parking lot that one day: *You're such an angel.* Then I remember the much worse things that were said after she found out. I think about how she changed. How Cam changed. Where they ended up.

"I should see where my friends went," Aria says, stepping back toward the sunset. "But it was good to see you, Nate."

I can't help but cringe. It sounds like she's saying farewell to a former acquaintance she ran into at the grocery store.

"What is it?" she asks.

"Nothing, just . . . 'it was good to see you.' It sounds like we're distant classmates or something. Instead of friends."

"Well, we're not distant classmates and we're not friends either," Aria says, finally turning away to face the crowd. "But it'll always be good to see you."

58

Turns out it's easy enough for me to sneak away from the party. The beach is a big place.

Aria tells Cam to meet me. Three minutes later, he's shuffling toward me along the shoreline, kicking his feet through the water with his head down.

"Aria said you wanted to talk?" he asks, lips pursed.

"Not about anything in particular. You just looked upset."

"I don't need your help," he says.

"Your family just pissed all over your sexuality, dude. That's tough."

"So am I."

"Why don't you want my help?"

Cam kicks at more sand.

"I don't want to argue for the millionth time," he tells me.

"Why don't you want my help?"

"The answer is going to piss you off."

"Try me."

"Fine." He balls his hands into fists. "It's because I don't *want* to talk about this with someone who barely acknowledges that being bi is a thing. Is that so tough for you to understand?"

I take a calming breath. "I agreed that it was a thing, remember? I'm trying my best here."

"That's not good enough anymore. You grant me that my sexuality exists—congrats. Do you have any idea how much *work* you still have to do? Do you understand how many other people I could talk to about this?"

"Work to do?"

"You think that what we did is something straight people do! You think that everyone does it—"

"Okay, okay. So I'm bicurious," I say. Even the one sentence elicits an odd twitch in my stomach. "There, happy? Is that what you're trying to get me to say?"

"You don't get it," Cam says. He's looking at me sadly, like he knows bad news that I don't. "Whatever your sexuality is, it's not your *uncertainty* that I have a problem with. It's this . . . refusal to accept anything else."

"My opinions shouldn't affect me trying to make you feel better," I say. God, he doesn't have to rail on me just for offering help. "I don't agree with your choices, but I accept you. You're still the same person to me."

"Oh, bullshit. You think I'm a freak. You can listen to me; you can't understand what I'm saying. You tolerate my sexuality; you don't accept it. There's a difference. You don't see yourself as the *same* as me."

"I'm sorry, okay? I really hate how I've been acting—"

"Where can I trade that in for you never doing it again?"

"I'm trying to get my shit together."

Well, here we are again. Arguing.

"You couldn't admit what you are even if you knew it," Cam says. "No—even if you *wanted* this, same as me, you couldn't say it. You wouldn't be able to look at me or any other guy and say, 'I love you.'"

I stare at him. Has he lost his mind?

"Well, you're right," I say. "I'm not going to say that."

"See? I'm not having this same conversation again."

"Okay, I'm confused. Are you pissed about me not admitting I'm bi, or not saying I love you?"

"You're operating under the wildly false assumption that I'm incapable of being pissed about two things at the same time."

"Jesus Christ, *where* is your 'off' switch—"

"Where's YOURS?" he demands. "Why do you have to have this . . . this tough-guy act up *all* the time? Just *once*, drop face. Admit that you care about me."

"No. I'm sorry."

"Please." He's pleading with me. He grabs the air like he can throw it in my face. "I won't tell anyone, I swear. There's no one else here; it'll just be our thing."

"No. I'm sorry."

"You have to! JUST SAY IT!"

"It doesn't even mean anything!"

"Oh, fucking hell." Cam resumes pacing along the sand, clenching and unclenching his fists. "So, just to make sure I have this right. You're willing to hook up with me, but not say three little words that you claim mean nothing to you but I claim mean *everything* to me? Please. I can't tell you how tired I am of fighting with you. Just once, tonight, say it. I'll drop the subject, I'll be happy, the night will be fixed."

He studies me as I stand there thinking. I want to sink into a world where I'm considering doing as he asks. But I'm not.

"I'm not going to say it."

Cam nods, rubbing his chin. Then he turns away from me, picks up a fistful of sand, and slams it into the water as hard as he can.

"MOTHER*FUCKER!*" His voice cracks.

"Let me ask you this," I say, holding up a hand to calm him. "No, hey—why does it matter if I say it or not?"

"You cannot expect me to believe that's a real question."

"It is," I say, sincere. "*Think* about it! What do you think is going to change if I admit it? Do you expect suddenly everything will be better? Huh? You think suddenly we'll be in *love*?"

"We already are! THAT'S why it's so important!"

"We're in love, really? *Really*. Why? Because you say so?"

"No." Cam sharpens his voice like it's a weapon of war. "We are because of how things were *before* New Year's. Before all the guilt. And I see how scared you've been by it since. You think I'm not scared too? I'm *terrified!* I'm just as confused by all of this—"

"Not confused—"

"And *every* time you deny it, you're hurting yourself more than me. We've done everything else together, haven't we? Why shouldn't we handle the most important thing that's been thrown at us?"

"Because it wasn't *thrown at us.*" I say the last part through gritted teeth. "We chose it. And then we chose it again, and again, and I have no idea why it's so tough for you to understand how I feel! Why don't you see what I see?" Now it's my turn to plead with him. "Why can't you see that I'm fucking *sick* because of what we've been doing?"

"I know that's how you've been feeling," Cam says. "And that's why I'm not giving up on you."

"I'm telling you to!" I scream. I'm out of breath even though I haven't moved. "Why can't you do that?"

"Why?" Cam catches the word and throws it right back at me. "Because this, you and I, it used to fucking *work!"*

"Says *you,*" I point out. My raw, unfiltered rage is at an all-time peak. Is this seriously his grand plan for us? "You want to know something? Everything wasn't perfect before New Year's. The reason I hung out with you is because you'd bug me until I agreed! God, why don't you get this? This imaginary relationship that you want to return to *never ex-is-ted. Stop* seeing things that aren't there. I've been telling you to let this go for months now, but you're so scared of being alone that you'd rather put up with *this shit*, trying to pretend you have a boyfriend—"

I never finish the sentence. Because instead of crying like I expect him to, he draws back his fist and nails me in the jaw.

It's the first time I've been punched in the face, and it's a shock. I yell and stumble back, my hands flying to my face. My vision is rocking back and forth. *Oh my God, Cam hit me. He really hit me.*

By the time I can see again, I'm standing alone.

59

I go home.

My house is quiet and dark. It's only 7:00 p.m., and I remember my dad will be getting home from a long shift around midnight. I touch my face, checking for swelling. There's some, but it shouldn't be noticeable for a few hours.

As always, Aunt Lori is waiting at the table. She's not in a robe this time, and there's no wine. Just her in her work clothes, arms folded, facing the front door. She has a red folder in front of her on the table.

"You're home early," she remarks when I stumble into the hall. "Everything all right?"

"Just really tired," I mutter, rubbing my forehead. "I'm going to bed."

"Come here real quick first."

I don't want to, and it's probably the closest I've come to telling her off. But of course I don't. I amble into the kitchen and face her.

"Could you hand me your cell phone, please?" she asks, still seated. "It's on the counter behind you."

I feel a chill run through my chest. She stares at me, unblinking, as I take my phone from where she's placed it on the countertop. I hold it out.

"Here . . . " she says. She nods her head to the table surface, indicating I should slide it. "Here."

I push it toward her. "Wh—"

"*HERE!*"

The scream is ripped from Aunt Lori's throat as she lunges forward, grabs a cast-iron frying pan from behind her, and slams it down on my cell phone. I scream, too, yanking my hand back barely enough to avoid it being crushed. She throws the pan off to the side as she stands, towering over me.

"You. Are. Done."

"Aunt Lori?" My voice is tiny and terrified.

"You have no idea how much time I've spent trying to figure out what's happened with you," she says in a low growl. "Because we both know something's happened. Don't we?"

"Aunt Lori—" I try to repeat.

"I felt bad, you know. When I kept track of your texts after I said I wouldn't," she continues, talking right over me. She begins to pace back and forth like a caged animal. "But then on Valentine's Day, you and Cameron swapped messages behind our backs."

"That was literally just—"

"So I take your phone away, you get it back one week later, and our obedient Nathan is here again. Right?" she coos. "I thought you were. So we got back to normal. And during that first week of March, there was an afternoon where you went over to Aria's house. Do you remember that?"

"I—"

"Actually, that's not fair," she cuts me off. "You wouldn't remember that because you weren't at her house."

She reaches for her folder, pulls out a paper, and hands it to me. I feel my stomach drop. It's a printout of a page from our cell phone company, with a time-stamped map showing a small dot over the coffee shop where I met Violet.

I open my mouth, but she keeps going.

"I thought maybe you and Aria went on a road trip. Drove an hour north for some reason. So I called Mrs. Harrington, and not only were you never at their house, but Aria had a dance retreat. You didn't see her at *all* that day. And then I got to thinking . . . What's he doing up north? Who's up north?" Aunt Lori stops moving long enough to face me directly. She lets out a slow, dangerous breath. "You saw Violet, didn't you?"

"We just—"

"If I were you, I wouldn't finish that sentence." Aunt Lori resumes pacing. "So after that little stunt, I knew our good Nathan wasn't back at all. Someone was in his place. Scheming Nathan."

"Please let me say something," I plead.

"You've done enough of that. Scheming Nathan telling me anything I need to hear. Scheming Nathan visiting Stone Hill

Park with his girlfriend. That *is* who you went with, right?" She fixes me with wide eyes, almost pouting, daring me to contradict her. "But you forgot to mention something."

She reaches into the folder again. Hands me another piece of paper. My stomach drops a second time. It's a printout of Aria's social media page, which has a selfie of me, Aria, Asher, and Cam at the park that day.

"Aw . . . Did you forget to mention Cam being there?" she says in a voice that's sickly sweet. "Cam and scheming Nathan—two peas in a pod. Laughing behind our backs—*hahahaha!* Because lying is A-okay as long as it's for a really, really good reason."

"I didn't lie—"

"Which time?" Aunt Lori snaps. "The park? Is that the answer we're going with?"

I don't respond.

"Good answer," she rules.

"You found Aria online?" I ask. I don't know why I get the courage to say it, but Aunt Lori doesn't get angrier. Instead, she fixes me with an ironic smirk. Playful.

"I'm glad you're fascinated by social media," she says, reaching a third time into the folder. "Because you're going to love what I got from Cam's."

I know what it is before I even look at it: Cam's profile picture, which is of him beaming and wearing a rainbow tank top. The caption reads, HAPPY PRIDE MONTH, LOVES!!!

"See, then . . ." Aunt Lori nods knowingly to the paper, like it's a medical report of a fatal prognosis. "Then I knew what we were dealing with."

"That's not what he is," I say, with much less authority than I intend. "He's not gay, I swear."

Instead of responding, Aunt Lori walks over to the far kitchen cupboard and points to our Wi-Fi security camera underneath. I stare at it, dumbfounded, as she swipes around on her phone and clicks. And that's when I remember that, for the week of spring break, I was home during the hours the camera was on.

My blood chills as I hear my own voice from her hand.

"Hey. Are you home alone?" A pause for a few seconds, then: *"Yeah. I'm calling from my home phone. Are your parents around?"* Another pause. *"Mine either. I'm just chilling . . . I want to sneak over to your house. Is that cool?"*

Aunt Lori tilts her head, trying to meet my gaze.

"Is that cool?" she croons. "I don't think it's very cool."

"That was one time," I mumble to the counter, completely numb. This feels like a bad dream. "You seriously *checked*—"

"*One* time? You were only over there one time?" She nods. "I had to believe that, didn't I? Let's not focus on the teachers I emailed who told me they saw you two talking in the hallways, socializing *after* I forbade it—"

"What the *hell*—"

"No, instead, let's talk about prom. How you spent it over at Cameron's house. That was a big night, wasn't it? Scheming Nathan almost pulled it off. He gave us a good story when he got home. About having fun at the *dance*, talking with your *friends* . . ." She's doing a lispy impression of me. "But then you made the mistake of taking a picture on this."

I freeze. Aunt Lori reaches into her pocket and pulls out my second cell phone. The prepaid one Violet gave me. My background is a selfie Cam and I took after we'd gotten him cleaned up from his injuries that night. I'm still in my prom gear, pressed up against him as we both give a thumbs-up.

"It's a shame you deleted all your messages on this thing," she says, waving it in my face. "I bet there were some gems. I found it about an hour ago. Know what I was doing? I was looking for your suitcase to see if you need a new one for the Covenant Lake trip in a few weeks."

"That isn't what you think it is," I say, grasping at straws.

"Well, thank God. Here I was so sure that it was a cell phone Violet gave you to communicate with your boyfriend in secret."

"He is *not* my boyfriend!"

Aunt Lori throws the phone at the wall with all her might.

SMACK! I jump. One of the hanging picture frames crashes to the floor.

"Listen—" I start.

"Yeah, that'll happen—"

"Listen to me!" I shout over her.

"No, *you* listen to *me. You listen to me!"* she roars. She takes huge steps toward me; I stumble backward, tripping over my own feet and slamming back into the wall. *THUD*—I'm cornered.

She continues, "That's your problem right there. Always 'me, me, me.' Never mind that I've had to deal with this on top of work. Never mind that Garner-Stowell went under a few days ago."

"I'm sorry," I squeak.

"Shut up." Aunt Lori grips the kitchen table. "Your father and I have been preparing for this, and we agreed on the plan if it does. No discussion here. There's a position for me as a junior litigator at a private firm in Ohio. We're moving there by the end of this summer. All of us."

"*What?*" I splutter. "That is *not* fair! Aunt Lori, you can't—"

"ONE MORE WORD! *I FUCKING DARE YOU!*"

My mouth snaps shut. I bite my lip to stop it from quivering.

She stands over me for a minute, then retreats all the way back to the doorway.

"You're still going on that trip to camp. God knows you need it," she says. "I'll make sure you and Cam won't be assigned to the same bunk. And in the three weeks until then, you'll help us get this house ready for sale. You'll replace the upstairs faucet. Fix up the basement and the bathroom. And above all, you'll think long and hard about what type of man you want to be."

We stare at each other. Two boxers who have just finished a fight.

"But for right now, you need to go to your room," she says.

■ ■ ■

I make sure not to cry until I'm up the stairs. My door has been removed, so I do it under the pillows as I pretend to fall asleep.

60

Dear God: I want to die.

61

"That's enough."

Mrs. Lawson's voice cuts into my head. I sit forward and catch my breath—too much talking. Cam has his eyes closed. His parents aren't looking at anything.

"Five o'clock," Mrs. Lawson says, scribbling one last note. "We'll pick this up tomorrow. Nate, do you expect we'll be able to finish up by the end of the day?"

I nod absently.

"All right. See you folks at nine."

I feel her brush my arm as she wheels past me—almost patting it, not quite. I watch her leave.

I check my phone, which has two unread texts.

The first, from Aunt Lori: We ARE sitting in there with you tomorrow. End of STORY.

I decide I'll deal with that tomorrow.

The second, from an unlisted number: Attn: you've used almost

98% of your data for this month. Please visit our website immediately and avoid using the "back" button on your Internet browser. Thank you for choosing our service.

■ ■ ■

My injury is more sore than yesterday. I'm holding it as I find Cam behind the building, same spot as yesterday.

"Your parents are going to get suspicious if you get sick two days in a row," I say.

"You don't think that's believable?" he asks, jerking his head in the direction of the deposition room. Then his face softens. "I'm really proud of you, dude."

"For what? Telling them about all our shit?"

"Yeah." He's being sincere.

"As long as you're not here to tell me to spill the rest."

"Spill the rest."

"God damn it."

"Please," Cam says, the same way he's pleaded with me so many times. He reaches a hand toward me.

I ignore it. "They're sitting in there with me tomorrow."

"So?"

"So?" I repeat the same thing I said to him yesterday. "So I have to go home, Cam. Are you hearing me? This isn't just about pissing them off or whatever. I could be kicked out of the house. Tell me you understand that."

"You want to stay there? The way they treat you? You could—you could move in with my parents and me, maybe. Or just my parents if I get—if I'm not living there. I don't know, we'll figure it out. But you have to tell them the rest, Nate. Please."

I throw up my hands in frustration. "I want to. But I can't. I can't."

"What if I get Violet to tell them about the letter she wrote you? Or bring a copy of it in?"

I scoff. "Yeah, right. You don't even know how to find her."

"She gave me the phone, remember? Plus I know her email," he shoots back.

"What? How?"

"Remember that time we were in my bedroom on October twenty-third, and I saw you emailing her? We listened to the Kooks and talked about urine trouble."

That memory, I swear to God.

"I can message her to come in tomorrow," he continues. "With her letter. That's admissible."

"No Violet. No letter. Leave it alone."

"Promise you'll think about it."

"I'm sick of making promises I can't keep." I step back. "Sorry. Like I said yesterday, you and I are finally done."

Once again, Cam shakes his head.

"Oh, we're not done," he says. "Not yet."

DAY 3

62

"**H**it me back. Hit me back. For fuck's sake, Cam."

He's still trying to recover his breath. I can tell he's struggling to keep himself standing upright. I spread my arms wide.

"Come on," I say, reassuring myself as much as him. "You can hit me as much as you want until we're even. We're both dead anyway. Please, Cam, *please.*"

I keep saying that word. *Please.* I wonder how many times I've said it to him tonight.

I'm just starting to let my guard down when he does it: He picks his backpack off the ground, hoists it by the straps, and swings it as hard as he can at my chest.

"Ow!" I grunt, knocked back. It's nothing compared to the hell I just unleashed on him—at most, it feels like a hard bump with a shopping cart. Still, it sends me to the ground; I pull the backpack down with me, and Cam down with it.

Amid all the tussling, the contents of his pack spill out onto the sidewalk: clothes. A sleeping bag. Something ceramic—a plate decorated with a tie-dye pattern. It shatters on the sidewalk, cracking into four or five thick pieces.

"The hell is that?" I grunt, trying to shove him off me.

"It's a—craft plate—I painted for you—on the first day—you dick!" Cam hits me between words, but he's so weak that it feels like one of his trademark playful punches. Nothing that does real damage.

I push him back, and he falls to the pavement. *Thud.* He grunts; his hand reaches out, and at first I think he's trying to grab my shoulder, but instead I see him pick up the sharpest, thickest shard of the ceramic plate.

As soon as I see what he's doing, I grab one too.

We both climb to our feet, wobbly, weapons in hand.

"Fuck with me," Cam spits.

I stomp my foot forward. There's barely anything between us.

63

The door to the deposition room springs open.

The serpent clamps down on my wrist. Dad wheels around in his seat.

"Excuse me!" Mrs. Lawson barks at the doorway. "You're interrupting a legal matter, miss. You can't be in here."

I've never heard Mrs. Lawson yell until now, and it scares the hell out of me. She has a set of pipes that rival Aunt Lori's.

Violet Cantrell steps into the conference room, kicking the door shut behind her. "I'm not interrupting. They asked me to come."

I glance between her and Cam, who's wearing his widest triumphant smile. His attorney begins to explain how Cam asked Violet to sit in on the deposition with them.

God damn it, Cam.

My eyes trail to a folder in Violet's hand. She keeps it at her side, just enough to make it clear to everyone in the room that she brought it.

Meanwhile, Aunt Lori's jaw is on the floor.

"*Violet?*" she splutters.

Violet wrinkles her nose, sliding into a chair. "Hey Mom. I hear you're still a miserable cunt?"

64

The lawyers are immediately at each other's throats.

"Oh what the hell do you call this?" Mrs. Lawson fires off. "Dan, you don't get to introduce someone into Mr. Copeland's deposition without having the courtesy to give proper notice—"

"Easy, Nora," says Cam's attorney. "It was my client's decision—"

"Your client is sixteen—"

"And we didn't even expect her to show," Cam's lawyer continues. "Hell, she's a relevant witness—"

"The *state* decides who's a relevant witness. We don't just go around deposing everyone," Mrs. Lawson snaps. "She can't be in here."

"You know there's no law restricting—"

"I don't care about that; you're tampering with my depo!" she fires back. In a way, it reminds me of Aunt Lori—something is deviating from the plan, so it's being corrected.

"Quick question: Did you, a lawyer, just say you don't care about the law?" Cam interjects, half raising a hand. Everyone ignores him.

"I'll get the judge to back me on this," Mrs. Lawson says.

"I agree," Aunt Lori jumps in.

"God's sakes, a protective order?" Cam's lawyer shouts, grabbing his hair like he's about to rip it out. "His own cousin? Are you out of your mind?"

"You're tampering with my depo," Mrs. Lawson repeats, icy.

They go on like that for another five minutes. Meanwhile, Cam, Violet, and I all look to one another. Despite everything, in the cacophony of adult banter, the three of us exchange weak smiles. Like we're in a middle-school classroom where the teacher just left the room.

Eventually, Cam's lawyer points out, "Nate has to be the one to request the PO." He snaps his fingers in my direction. "Is that what you want, Nate?"

"P-O?" I stammer.

"Protective order," Mrs. Lawson says. "A restraining order to keep Violet out of the deposition. Do you want that?"

"Yes," Aunt Lori answers for me.

"No," I say.

"Yes," she repeats.

"*No.*"

We meet each other's eyes for the first time since the deposition started. I expect to see her cold control there, but I don't.

Instead, it looks like someone has reached into her chest and wrapped their hands around her spine.

"Can . . . can I start again?" I ask, turning back to Mrs. Lawson.

"If we're all settled, then fine. Go back to where you left off yesterday," she instructs, apparently admitting defeat on the Violet debate. "What happened after the argument with your aunt?"

I stare across the table at Violet and Cam. I've never seen the two of them in the same room before. Their eyes are saying the same thing:

Go.

"I left for Covenant Lake summer camp the last week of June. Cam was still pissed at me about our fight at the beach, but I told him about Ohio on the bus ride up."

"Meaning, your family's intentions to relocate at the end of the summer," Mrs. Lawson clarifies.

"That's right."

"How did he respond to that news?"

Across the table, Cam massages his forehead.

"He, well . . ." I search for the right words. "He suggested we run away."

"From the camp?"

"Yeah. I told him he'd lost his mind."

"And yet . . ." Mrs. Lawson double-checks a note. "That's precisely what you did."

"Okay, yeah, but not at first."

65

The bus is supposed to pick me and the other campers up from the school parking lot on Monday, 8:00 a.m. sharp. Dad tells me—under no uncertain terms—that he wants to take me out to dinner the night before the trip. When I ask him why, he dodges the question and is all, "I just want to spend a little time with my son."

I can't tell what this is. Maybe some sort of shakedown? A chance for a tough-love lecture like, "Stop giving your aunt a bunch of crap?" Or maybe it'll be some sort of apology gesture on his end for being gone five days a week. Or for the move. So much shit has hit the fan in the last month—he's got a lot of options to pick from.

The car ride is mostly quiet. I don't have my phone, so I spend a lot of time staring out the window. How much does my dad know? I've barely said two words to Aunt Lori since the night she confronted me, and she left to visit our Ohio home a few days ago, so I'm not sure what info they've swapped. He doesn't ask me anything in the car except where I want to eat. I tell him I don't care, so he takes us to a sports bar.

"Get whatever you want," he says, thumbing his goatee as he scans the menu. I end up ordering chicken wings, and he gets a loaded burger.

"And two glasses of your best stuff on tap," he adds.

Well, there's surprise number one: my dad, drinking. It's not that he doesn't do it, I've just only seen it a handful of times growing up. When the beers are delivered, he slides one over to my end of the table and raises the other.

"Cheers. Hey, cheers," he repeats, waving his glass toward mine, which I haven't touched.

"Seriously?" I raise an eyebrow. "You know I'm seventeen, right?"

"Nonsense," Dad says, his bald head whipping back and forth. "Turned twenty-one just last month, didn't you?"

He's trying to put on a serious face, but the edges of his mouth are twitching.

"*Didn't you,*" he repeats through gritted teeth, all exaggerated, like I'm blowing our cover.

Surprise number two: my dad, being a goofball. There used to be a lot of that, but it's been a while since I've seen that side of him.

"I *did,*" I play along, matching his sort-of smile. For a ridiculous second, I wonder if this is a test, like I'll be immediately grounded when I touch the glass. Then I pick it up. *Clink*, sip. It's much richer than the stuff at Meghan's party, but I still can't shake the taste of fermented urine.

"My first beer," I say.

"Sure it is," Dad says. Hard to tell if he's kidding. "Just don't let Lori know about this."

The mention of her name robs the mood almost at once. This is a good example of how my dad works as a parent: He's chill about me bending the rules, but he never has a problem letting Aunt Lori punish me if I'm caught. He never challenges her because for most of my rule-breaking, all he has to go off of are her versions of the events.

"How's she doing with the Ohio stuff?" I ask. My voice is back to its flat, fake inflection.

"She texted this afternoon that she met with the senior partners at the new firm. Said they seemed nice."

We swap nods.

"So, hey, listen," he says, after a long sip from his glass. "I wanted to talk to you about the move."

I don't answer. They signed a lease on the new rental last week, and half of my stuff is already in boxes.

"I get it." Dad's arms are crossed tightly. "I'm not going to feed you a bunch of BS about how great this is. It's not."

He's trying to get through to me. But all I can think about is how "a bunch of BS" is precisely what we've been dealing with for months. It's been our first and only language. I stare hard at my beer glass. My dad doesn't want BS? He and Aunt Lori don't know the first thing about what's been going on with me. I wouldn't even know where to start—if I could even tell them, which I can't. There's this act I have to put on for them both.

And if that's how it is, fine. But don't pretend that it's not.

"It's not," I repeat, aloud this time.

"What's been going on with you?"

He says it too fast, clearly working up the nerve to blurt it out. Our waitress zips by to drop off glasses of water. We wait until she leaves.

Dad tries again. "Hey, Nate—can you look at me for a second?" Once I do, he continues, "I know I haven't been around much these past few months. There's a lot of stuff at work that's been going on . . . which I won't get into, but that's why. When we move, I'm done. I'll still work, but . . . different place. Regular hours. That's part of why we're moving. So I can be around more."

I'll admit, I hadn't considered that.

"It's just . . . messed up that we're leaving," I say. "It's my *senior year*. All my friends are here. I'm going to graduate with a bunch of people I don't even know—I mean, are you kidding me? And what, I'm going to have a new room for . . . a year? Then I leave again. And I go off to some private college that you guys make me go to, majoring in whatever you decide for me—"

"Whoa, whoa," Dad says. "You can major in whatever you want, bud."

"Well, I've got no idea what I want, Dad. None. Except to not move. So that worked out great."

He spends some time digesting that, nodding to himself.

"What about the painting thing?" he finally asks.

"What about it?"

"Well, is that what you want to do?"

I scoff, ready for the punch line, but he's just waiting to hear my answer.

"It doesn't matter if it is," I mutter. "No one makes any money with art."

"Unfortunately not," he agrees. "But you know, I've actually been rethinking all that. How I feel about you doing that."

I smack my lips from another sip of beer. "What brought that on?"

"Something I saw online the other day. It was actually a concert—you heard of the group AC/DC?"

"Oh my God." I snort so hard it hurts. "Yes, Dad, I've heard of AC/DC."

"Hey, I couldn't assume," he says, all defensive. "I'm an old shit, remember?"

"*Yes*, I know them. They did 'Back in Black.'"

"Oh, man, they did a lot more than that. First live show I went to was AC/DC. And that was back in 1978, with Bon— that's their original singer."

"So if you were a teenager in 1978 . . . that would make you . . ."

"*Old.* And these guys are even older. Now, understand, the video I saw the other day was from 2009. *Live at River Plate.* Thirty-one years after I saw them. I figure, they've gotta be slowing down. But let me tell you—they get up on that stage, and it's like they're more fired up than ever. The camera shows each of 'em up close, and they just have these huge smiles on their faces, playing their asses off . . . and they do this for *two hours.*"

My dad is grinning from ear to ear, talking so loudly that he's almost yelling. I realize I'm matching his expression, completely caught up in his excitement.

"Two hours?" I echo him, almost as loud.

"At *least.* And right toward the end, when they do 'Highway to Hell' . . . oh man. This huge stadium—has to be thousands of people—all jumping at once. It's just this sea of hands, everyone screaming, fire on the big screens . . . and Johnson, the singer, he's this sixtysomething old fucker jumping right along, the rest of the band running around the stage . . . and you look at these guys and you can just tell. They're still going almost forty years later, because they're doing what they love. I saw that and I thought, *This stuff here. This is what it's about.* You have to find something you *love.* Don't get me wrong, I'm not saying run off to art school and forget about making money. But don't treat it all like it's nothing either. Just get the hell out there and *try* it while you still can. Just think about it."

From there, Dad shuts his mouth and gets back to his drink. But I'm still processing that whole speech. He's never been the type to give speeches, especially not ones like that. I look at him sitting across from me and realize this was a growing moment for him too . . . a genuine instance of being caught up in something that changed his perspective. Sometimes I forget that adults even have those.

"It'd be really hard," I finally say. "With stuff like art or writing, there are no guarantees. Even if you're good at them. What if I suck at painting?"

"Then you won't get anywhere." Dad shrugs. "Least you'll know something you don't know now, right? The point is, I just don't want to see you stick with a path that's 'safe' if it keeps you from getting anywhere interesting. Don't be afraid to rip off the Band-Aid. You like a hobby? Try it. You like someone? Tell 'em. You care about something? *Go* for it."

"What about Aunt Lori?" I ask. "She wouldn't be cool with me being an artist, would she?"

"I'm not sure," he concedes. "You have to understand that she's trying, buddy. It's not like she's against artists. It's just . . . it's different when it's your own kid. Or nephew."

Translation: She's tolerant toward every person except the one who matters. Sounds about right.

"There's just something about being a parent and realizing your kid's life isn't going to turn out the way you expected it to," Dad continues. "It happens to everyone. But that's how the move will help. It's all about fresh starts. New changes."

Something in there is the right thing to say.

"Well," I tell him slowly. Carefully. "I guess . . . there is something new. Or, someone new. Who I like. But I can't just tell them. It's gotten really complicated. And what if it all gets screwed up?"

Dad gives the same nonchalant shrug as always, but it feels different now.

"Hey man, what if it doesn't?" he says.

66

The first few days of Covenant Lake camp are hot and boring.
A lot of people probably hear "Bible camp" and picture a
bunch of God-fearing ladies telling us how we'll burn in hell for
touching ourselves. The truth is, this one is a lot like any other
summer camp. The bus drives us the two hours north, drops us at
the camp check-in, and we're collected by a group of counselors
barely older than us. We're also given our tenting assignments
for the week. Each site is a little clearing in the woods that has
a handful of tents, set up army style with wooden floors, leather
flaps, and two cots. Me, Cam, Asher, and a boy named Leo are
assigned to Cherokee, a site near the very top of the hill. As Aunt
Lori promised, Cam and I are separated, so I'm paired with Asher.

Considering he and I haven't talked since before Aria broke up
with me, it's a little awkward at first. Around lunchtime on the first
day he just says, "Oh, hey—my sister told me you guys are chill
again after the beach thing. Good to hear, man." And that's that.

Cam is paired with Leo, a shortish Hispanic guy with jet-black hair. I recognize him from the football team—he's one of those people I've seen around school but never really interacted with.

The four of us are scheduled for different activity sets during the first few days, so we barely see one another until the end of day three. By the time dinner wraps up that evening, it's dark outside, and we're told we have a free hour before bed.

"All right, my dudes," Asher says to me, Cam, and Leo, after we're all showered and sitting around our site. "You know what we have to do? We've gotta make the sickest fire these fuckers have ever seen."

It's not a bad idea. Our site is at the very top of the hill, and between the tents are two picnic benches sitting on either side of a fire pit. It's isolated and roomy enough.

"Let's do it," Cam says. He's in his traditional tank top and gym shorts, an orange bandana tied around his forehead. "I know how to start one as long as you bitches aren't afraid to get kindling from the woods."

"We're the bitches, really?" Asher mutters, smacking him on the head as he walks by.

I join them in gathering firewood.

Sure enough, Cam is able to use his flint and steel kit to light a small fire, which before long fills up the whole pit. He and Leo sit across from Asher and me on the other side of the flame.

"You guys want to see something?" Leo asks, rubbing his hands together.

"You'll have to be more specific," Cam says.

Leo pulls out an unopened can of soda and starts dangling it over the fire.

"*Don't* do that shit!" Cam shouts, sliding away from him.

"Son, be careful," Asher says, sounding uneasy.

"Fucking relax, it's fine. I saw a guy do this in a video," Leo says. He fakes dropping the can in, which makes us all yell. I scoot away a little bit.

"Seriously, dude," Cam says, clearly trying hard to sound calm. "Pressure from the carbon dioxide—"

Leo throws the can in. Immediately there's a *pop*, the can flies upward, and embers are kicked up on all sides. All of us fall back, yelping at first, then laughing with relief when the can lands on the other side of the site.

"You," Leo says, making a point to jab a finger at me, then Asher, then Cam, "are all pussies. But, dude, it actually exploded!"

"Imagine!" Cam says. "Fucking moron."

"Fuck off, fag," Leo says, flipping him off as we all pull ourselves back onto the seats around the fire.

"You work hard on that one?" Cam asks, sounding supremely unfazed. He pushes his glasses up his nose. "I mean, that's like the third-least creative insult in the English language, but props for putting yourself out there."

"He's got you there," Asher points out, grinning and giving a small conciliatory nod to Cam. Leo rolls his eyes.

"And I'm sorry, what's *your* girlfriend's name again?" Cam spits at him.

"Eat a dick, Haynes."

"What is that—Swedish?"

"Guys," I say. I'm trying to throw Cam some support, even though it seems like he can handle himself. I turn to Asher, trying to change the subject. "What about you, man? You and Erica still a thing?" Girl he met in History a few months back.

"Dating, no. Hooking up, yes. I haven't seen her in like two weeks though."

"And now you'll be here for the rest of this week." Leo pats him on the shoulder. "My sympathies, sir."

"*Yeah,*" Asher says, grabbing his head with a frustrated smirk. "Haven't jacked off for like five days either. It's been a long fucking week."

"Should I be worried about sharing a tent with you?" I quip. Everyone laughs. It feels good to be able to contribute, but I still feel a little uncomfortable by the whole thing.

"Nah, man, no worries," Asher says. "Why, how long has it been for you?"

I decide to be truthful. "Well I haven't had a lock on my door for three weeks so . . . about three weeks."

"Jeeesus!" Leo yells, way louder than he probably should at a Bible camp.

"You wouldn't even believe how strict his parents are," Cam says to the group. Then he adds, "You should get that taken care of, Nate," with this coy little smile that's borderline torture.

"You'd like to see that, wouldn't you, Haynes?" Leo says, grinning.

"You know me. Always the slut," Cam says, tossing a twig into the fire. "Not like Copeland the prude here. You're not even going to let anyone get in your pants until your wedding night, yeah?" He raises his eyebrows at me without a hint of irony.

"You got me," I say, giving the same look right back.

"Goddamn, I wish there were more girls around here," Leo says, either not noticing the subliminal exchange or not understanding it. "Take them over to Moonshine Cabin—boom."

We all give him puzzled looks.

"You guys don't know about it? Oh shit. Listen to this." Leo rests his elbows on his knees. "You see that river on the edge of camp, near the dining hall? On the other side of the river is this old cabin that's been there since, like, the '60s. Some old lady lived there for a while, but anyone who visited her disappeared. Forever! Rumor has it she just shoved people into her oven. Even *kids*."

"Is there any chance that your source on this story is a children's book titled *Hansel and Gretel*?" Cam asks. "Because if you're about to tell us her house was made of gumdrops, I have some terrible news."

"Fuck *off*, pansy—this was legit. She didn't have any friends or anything. Want to know how I know? Because no one realized this bitch was dead until someone *happened* to look in the cabin and found her skeleton. It was like a year later. They cleared it out but never tore down the building. Shit's just been rotting since the '90s. And rumor says it's haunted, so the campers are too afraid to go near it. I bet you anything that's where the counselors go to bang."

Leo mimes pelvic thrusting, making us laugh. Then he does it toward Cam, who immediately shoves him back.

"Come on, Haynes. How much for a night?"

"However much it costs to buy a hazmat suit," Cam deadpans. He still sounds completely calm, bored even. Like all this is rolling right off his shoulders. It just now dawns on me that he's been out to everyone at school for three months, and he's probably well practiced at dealing with this.

"Least when *I* get laid I won't be bent over biting a pillow," Leo mutters. He uses a stick to flick a cluster of embers at Cam, who squeaks sharply.

"You *know*," Cam retorts hotly, brushing off his knee, "I had my doubts, but I can tell you and I are going to get along swimmingly for the rest of this week."

I glance over to Asher, who looks just as uncomfortable as I feel. We're in the same boat: wanting to support Cam, not wanting to piss off Leo, completely unsure of when or how to jump in. And with every second, I can feel Cam barreling toward one of his trademark, royally pissed-off outbursts.

"Just stay on your own side," Leo says.

"Yo," I jump in, seeing that Cam is getting pummeled. "Don't be such a prick, dude."

"Yeah," Asher agrees.

I study Cam, who's staring hard at the fire. The funny thing is, he and I have joked about this kind of stuff before. But Leo isn't laughing with him, he's laughing at him. And everyone can tell the difference.

"I'm going to call it a night," Asher says, standing up and dusting off his knees. "We forgot to get water to put this thing out. Leo, come help."

The two of them slink off down the hill. The water station is a ten-minute walk each way, so I know it'll be a bit.

Once the two have disappeared, I turn to Cam to ask if he's okay. But before I can, he repeats the same thing he said to me at my bedroom window, ten months and ten lifetimes ago.

"Nate," he says, his gaze reaching across the fire. *"Adapt, migrate, or die."*

67

"**W**e packed. We didn't think. We just ran."

"You ran away from camp because of the insults?" Mrs. Lawson says, very controlled.

I nod. Violet is still seated across from me, right next to Cam.

"Is it fair to say Mr. Haynes was upset by the use of the word 'faggot'?" Mrs. Lawson asks me. Everyone in the room gasps a little, but she doesn't flinch. The question throws me completely off.

"What?" I ask.

She repeats herself.

"Yeah, he was upset. You don't believe that?"

"It doesn't matter what I believe. I'm asking because of"— Mrs. Lawson cuts herself off, then rummages through her folder and pulls out a paper—"this."

I take it and read it over. It's my written account of the incident that I submitted to the court two weeks after Cam's arrest. By then he'd been arraigned, released, and they were starting his preliminary hearing to determine whether or not to go to trial. Which meant they needed a statement from me formally accusing him—but I had only just been released from the hospital and could barely sit up on my own, let alone show up in court. The solution: I submitted my story in writing—or rather, Aunt Lori submitted one for me.

Mrs. Lawson takes the paper back and flips to the fourth page. "In this signed affidavit, you allege that right before Mr. Haynes attacked you, he grabbed your neck and repeatedly called you—and I'm quoting here—'a fucking faggot; you're a fucking faggot.'"

She lets that linger for a minute before saying to me, "So I'm naturally curious about what happened on your trip to cause that kind of transformation."

68

L *eft, right, blink, breathe. Left, right, blink, breathe.*

I can't remember the last time I've been immersed in such a simple routine. But for hours and hours into the night, that's what Cam and I do. We walk. Blink. Breathe.

I raise a good point somewhat early on: "So, uh, where are we going?"

Cam points out that the one good thing about Leo being assigned to our site was that he told us the story of the abandoned cabin.

"You want to go to the worn-down building that everyone avoids?" I ask him.

"Why not?" he says. He's reading from his phone. "Google says it's just a tourist attraction, but a tour hasn't even been offered since 2012. And if it's on the other side of the river, we'll be separated from the camp. No one will come across us by accident."

"It also means we'll have to cross the river."

Cam nods, already on it. "I've got the map pulled up here. There's a hanging bridge about three miles away that we can take. Another three and a half miles from there is the cabin."

The hike is as long and draining as it sounds. We both have about ten pounds of belongings on our backs, and neither of us are world-class athletes. It's also pitch-dark, and Cam refuses to let us use our phones for light in case someone sees us. So we have to feel our way through the woods bit by bit, scraping through thorns, branches, and roots. A few times, I have to grab his wrist to keep track of him.

In a way it's peaceful, being out here with nothing but the sounds of night critters and the wind in the trees. It's better than dealing with Leo and camp bullshit anyway.

At one point, Cam breaks the silence.

"Sky looks nice," he says. I tilt my head back—sure enough, the sky is free of clouds and full of stars.

"It's like that first night with the trampoline," I remark.

"True, yeah. I'm just realizing, I don't think I've been stargazing since then. I used to do it all the time when I was younger."

"Because of your family's camping trips, right? That's what you told me."

Cam seems impressed that I still remember that.

"That's part of it," he says. "But I also didn't know you super well when I said that, so I didn't really tell you the rest."

"The rest?"

"It's not even a huge thing," he says. "But I did it a lot after Chloe died. She really liked the outdoors."

I nod—makes sense.

"I don't talk about it much, but she died from something called osteosarcoma. What you have to understand is that's *nasty* stuff to treat, especially because of—well, I don't want to get into it. But it was really bad. About six weeks after she was diagnosed, her right leg had to be amputated.

"I stayed with her after. At night when she was awake, she'd stare out the window of the recovery room and just go on and on about wanting to go camping again. I talked about it with her every night to help her get to sleep."

He's close to crying. He holds out his hand, and I let him take mine.

It's not exactly a monumental gesture, because it's pitch dark and we're completely alone. No one to see us or even know it happened. As I feel our fingers lock, I wait for him to comment on it, but he doesn't. He just breathes a little deeper and resumes the story.

"She died a week later from a blood infection—complications from the surgery, they're pretty sure. She was in a *lot* of pain, Nate. She cried a lot. She screamed a lot. But something about the window, just . . ."

He never does finish the thought. He trails off, and we hold hands, and I don't speak. I keep listening, even when he's out of words.

■ ■ ■

At one point we have to cross a small creek, so we let go of each other's hands. When we get to the other side, I'm the one who reaches for him this time.

69

"**O**h, nice!" Cam points straight ahead. "Shit, there it is— look."

The entire hike has taken just under five hours. I'm about ready to keel over and sink into a coma when I squint and . . . sure enough, there's the cabin. Even in the dark, I can tell why people avoid it. It may have been a home once, but now it's essentially ruins. Ivy crawls up every surface, and the roof is nothing more than a few stray boards. A fallen tree is buried in the back wall, its branches reaching over the structure. The windows have boards hammered over the grimy, cracked panes of glass. I spot a pile of bricks, presumably once a chimney, spilled beside the empty doorway.

We approach.

"This doesn't look safe," I say, leaning to peer in the empty doorway.

"We made it this far," Cam argues. He clicks on his flashlight, wielding the beam like a weapon as he steps inside.

I follow him into the pitch-dark room, and I'll admit it: I'm scared. More scared than I can remember being in the past few months, which is saying something. I reach down to find Cam's hand again, which folds around mine snugly.

"Shit. Look at this place," he breathes.

It's small—essentially one room the size of a kitchen. It looks like there may have been another room toward the back, but the roof has collapsed over the area, blocking it off. The remains of an old stove and basin sink are shoved against the front wall. Moonlight shines through the tree branches above, spilling onto the dirt floor. The only good news: The space we do have available is big enough to spread out our belongings.

"Welcome to Moonshine Cabin," Cam says in a creepy-old-man voice, shining his flashlight over his face and wiggling his fingers at me. I swat at him as he pulls two tarps out of his pack, hanging one over the doorway and spreading the second on the ground. Then he plops down onto it and says, "We should take inventory."

It starts to hit me that we didn't think this trip through very well. First of all, as soon as Leo and Asher wake up, they're going to notice we left. Second of all, we don't have any sources of food, drinking water, or means of sustaining ourselves.

I tell all this to Cam, who's nodding and smiling like he was hoping I'd bring that up.

"Don't you worry your pretty little head," he says. "Asher is going to cover for us. I already worked it out with him."

"What are you talking about?"

"I texted him as soon as we left. Explained things . . . well, sort of. He understood. I think he feels bad about what happened. He agreed to cover for us if anyone asks where we are, which they shouldn't, since from now on we're just rotating stations. I offered him twenty bucks to make sure Leo doesn't snitch."

I nod, impressed, though I don't know why I should expect anything less from him.

"As for supplies, we're all set," he says. He dumps out his pack onto the tarp.

"Holy shit, dude," I say, squatting down. Cam has apparently been carrying a pack crammed full of instant soup mix, camping bread, pouch cereal, trail mix, and corn chips.

"Should be enough to keep us going for a day or two, at least. For drinking water, we have this," he says, brandishing a dark glass bottle that looks like cough medicine. "This is a chemical called tetraglycine hydroperiodide, and it'll treat the water from the stream. We have enough for five gallons."

Fucking Cam.

"*Where* did you get all this?" I ask.

"From the camp store."

"Why though?"

He lowers his eyes, devoting extra attention toward unrolling his sleeping bag. "I knew we might need to get out of there."

I've known him long enough to pick up on the unsettling context: He made the decision up front that if he wanted to leave, that's what would happen, and I would just follow him out here no questions asked.

He bags the food and hangs it up outside. From there, we're so tired that we crawl straight into our sleeping bags. I see Cam take off his glasses, then cross himself and fold his hands—saying a quick prayer before bed. I don't follow suit.

"Can I tell you something weird?" Cam asks me when he's finished.

"Sure."

"Before the New Year's Eve party . . . Well, obviously I'd never done anything with another guy before. But I always kind of wondered, you know?"

"About yourself? If you'd like it?"

"No, not even. Just like, how many of my classmates did that with each other. I guess I assumed a lot of guy friends did that together, but no one ever talked about it."

I smirk, eyes closed. "Same here, actually."

"How're you holding up with everything now?" Cam asks.

"Scared," I summarize, feeling myself slowly drift into a numb sleep.

"I know what that's like," he says. "If it helps, remember I'm in the middle of this with you."

"Sometimes it doesn't feel like anyone is."

"Well, I know what that's like too."

70

I'm woken by the sound of birds chirping overhead. I blink and sit up, rubbing my eyes hard. It takes me a few seconds to remember where I am. Sunlight pokes through the gaps in the roof, spilling over us in strange patterns that warm my skin.

"Morning," says Cam. I whip around to find him leaned over a table he's fashioned from the ruins of a much larger table. He raises his camping bowl, full of—

"Is that cereal?" I ask.

"Yessir," he says, handing me the bowl along with his spork. "Instant granola blend, technically. Saved you some. I only have one bowl with me, so."

It tastes disgusting, but it's sustenance, so I don't complain.

"How long have you been awake? What time is it?" I ask.

"It's twelve thirty," he says matter-of-factly, crouching down beside me as I sit in my sleeping bag and eat. "I woke up about two hours ago. I found a way down to the river, which is where

I got the water. Assuming it doesn't contain *cryptosporidium*, I can one hundred percent promise it's safe to drink. I also checked out the outside of the cabin. We have some repairs to do today."

I finish the cereal, set it down beside me, and shake my head.

"What?" Cam asks, flicking me in the shoulder.

"This is insane," I say, holding my hands in front of me and staring at them. "We have to go back."

"What? Why?"

"Because we're in the middle of nowhere! I'm not Bear Grylls!"

I expect us to launch into another argument, but Cam just shrugs.

"If you really want to, we can," he says.

"Seriously?"

"I wanted to wait another day or two until the end of camp, but yeah. It's your call."

I narrow my eyes, feeling like I've stepped into one of Aunt Lori's traps. All the arguing from before, and now Cam couldn't be more agreeable. What's his play?

"Here," he says, gesturing to the exit. "At least help me patch up the cabin while you think on it."

Even when it's just me and him in the world, I'll never understand him.

■ ■ ■

The cabin needs two things it doesn't have now: a door and a roof.

The obvious choice for a roof would be trees lain across the top, but that's not something we can make happen by ourselves. We search the woods and fortunately find a few dead limbs that are small enough to drag. We haul them to the cabin and prop them up against the outside wall, so the branches are overlapping to form a sort of canopy over the structure. It's full of holes, but it's something.

"All we can do," Cam points out. "Let's focus on getting the door."

That one, luckily, is more realistic. Cam has a Swiss Army knife with a saw attachment, so we take turns: one of us cuts up midsize branches while the other works on binding them together with camper's twine.

The work is slow going, draining, and not very fun.

"This better be the best door ever," I mutter, sawing away at a branch a little thicker than my arm.

"It will be," Cam says, squatting down a few feet away. He's still wearing his orange bandana. "We work well together."

I snort. "For once."

"For once in a *while*," he corrects me. "We worked great, way back when."

I know that's easy for him to remember. But to me it feels like another century.

"Maybe," I say. "I know I liked it better back then."

After a minute of silence, Cam says, "I'm not sure if I did or not."

"You don't wish we could go back to September?" I ask, intrigued. I grunt, sawing through the branch. The two pieces fall at my feet, and Cam picks them up.

"I have this theory," he tells me. "I think that how you feel toward someone doesn't really change. More like, your feelings eventually get to where they were always going to end up."

"You really think that?"

"Yeah. But I'm also not delusional, Nate," he says. "You and I aren't much of anything anymore."

It's the same thing I've spent months trying to tell him. So why does it sting when he's the one saying it?

"We used to be though," he adds, in exactly the type of wistful tone I've come to expect from him.

He cuts a new branch, hands it to me, and picks up another. I watch him work. He carries on without noticing.

"Admit something to me," I finally say.

"Oh boy."

"It's super simple: Admit that you know it never would've happened with us. Becoming a couple."

Cam fixes me with a wry smile. "You get pretty introspective when you spend some time with the trees, my friend."

I wait, and his smile relaxes. He shrugs. "Yeah, sure. But that doesn't mean I'm not still hung up on the idea of it. Us."

"Why can't you let it go?"

"That's tough to do when the idea feels so close to being a reality."

And then silence falls between us, filled only by the birds and wind through the leaves.

"I've been a major asshole to you," I finally say. "I'm sorry about that. I guess it doesn't matter now, since we won't see each other after I move. But for what it's worth, I didn't mean to put you through any of this."

"I know," Cam says, gentler.

"Really?"

"Well, I don't think anyone wakes up one day and says to themselves, '*You know what? Today, I want to fuck up the life of someone I care about.*'"

"You're definitely persistent," I grant him. "You know that?"

"I do."

"I take it that's your only move?"

"Oh, you unenlightened man," he says with his most devilish grin. "You don't have the first idea about my moves."

I feel my face burning, so I break the gaze. I crouch down and arrange the chopped branches into the right pattern before binding them all together.

"Interesting question though," he tells the sky.

"Interesting answer," I say to the ground.

71

At one point during lunch, I lean toward Cam to grab a piece of beef jerky and wrinkle my nose.

"What is it?" he asks, half smiling.

I move my nose a little closer. "Did you know you smell very, very bad?"

We both do. After eating, we head down to the river to rinse off. I don't have a bathing suit, so I just go in my boxers. Judging by the look of the water, it's debatable whether or not the bath helps or hurts our hygienic state.

At one point, I mess with Cam by running my fingers over his foot in the water, which makes him yelp and nearly kick me in the head.

"Oh shit . . . I didn't hit you, did I?" he asks, wide-eyed.

"Not since the beach party," I quip, giving a teasing smile to show I'm not seriously hung up on it.

Cam whistles. "That's dark. That's some dark humor there."

"Eh, I deserved the punch."

"Things did get pretty creamy," Cam says. At first I have no idea what he means, then I catch his smirk and remember the Mrs. Koestler autocorrect joke from forever ago.

I cup my hands around my mouth and yell, "WE ARE CREAMY PEOPLE!" out into the water. My voice echoes a few times, then fades.

I do a double take.

"What're you looking at?" I ask. Because Cam is staring at me like he's just met me for the first time.

I give him a little splash, but he doesn't snap out of it. Instead, his eyes shine with this fervent relief that I can't quite describe. I just know I haven't seen it until now.

■ ■ ■

We get back from swimming a little after five o'clock, so we decide to utilize Cam's fire-building skills and my wood-gathering skills. It takes a few tries to get it going because we don't have any lighter fluid, but by the start of early evening, we've got something. Enough to start cooking soup, at least.

"Do you have fresh clothes?" Cam asks me. We're still in our wet boxers from swimming earlier.

"In my pack, yeah. Why?"

Cam dips into the cabin and emerges with my clothes stacked on top of his. Without missing a beat he sets them on the ground, strips off his boxers, and lays them out near the fire. He notices me staring as he pulls his new clothes on.

"Oh, sorry," he says, eyebrows perched. "In case you haven't seen it before, this is what my dick looks like."

And that gets us both laughing even as I say, "Stop making it weird."

"You're planning to change too, right?"

"I will if you promise not to make it weird."

"Promise."

I strip off my underwear.

"IT'S YOUR BUTT!"

"God damn it."

I resist the urge to rush or cover up as I re-dress. I'm halfway done when I just mutter, "Fuck it," and take a little half step toward Cam, feeling just like I did in that bathroom on New Year's. "Okay, come on, dude. Let's just do this."

But unlike New Year's, Cam backs away a little, tightening the drawstring on his gym shorts. "Hold up. I wasn't trying to— sorry. My bad. I don't want to do that right now."

"I mean—okay," I say, giving my best *like-I-give-a-shit* shrug as I finish dressing. Smoke trails my way, burning my eyes. I step aside and wave it in Cam's direction. Then, not quite wanting the subject to die, I add, "It hasn't happened in forever anyway."

"March twenty-second," he says.

"Yeah." I bite my lip. "I've thought about it a few times since then." I don't know why I'm telling him. Maybe because he's the only one I can tell.

Cam nods but doesn't give a response.

"And when I say 'thought about it,' I mean like, picturing it," I clarify.

"Yeah, jerking off. I know what you meant," he says. Uncharacteristically terse.

The flames fill the silence with violent crackling. Cam seats himself on a log but doesn't add anything and doesn't look at me.

I sit beside him. "Did you ever do that? Picture it."

"I used to," he answers. "I stopped after a couple weeks."

"Why?"

"It made me feel too shitty afterward."

I feel that familiar internal squirming again. "Me too."

"Not in the same way," Cam points out. "Your feelings were all guilt. Mine were just—I don't know. Feeling *shitty*."

"I had a bit of both," I say. I wish there was a better way to phrase it, but the truth is that it all just felt . . . bad. Pain, self-blame . . . it all runs together eventually.

"Here's what I'm wondering," Cam says.

"Yeah?"

He pauses. "Is the guilt because *you* think it's wrong, or because you're afraid of going to hell? Because the religious stuff is up for interpretation."

"Hell is *not* up for interpretation."

"It can be. One example: The Orthodox Catholic Church

teaches that God doesn't send us to hell as punishment; He just lets us choose to go there or not. If we choose to reject Him, and His love and all that, then we send ourselves there. Completely up to us."

"It's supposed to be scary," I argue. "You're supposed to be scared of God. That's how you know what's right or wrong."

Cam doesn't respond to that.

"You don't think that's true?" I challenge.

His eyes drift toward me and stay there. "I just don't think it's possible to love someone and be afraid of them at the same time."

I think of Aunt Lori. How I've gutted my own life by submitting to her rules, the ones she has only because she loves me. I think about what the point is of following those rules if they're going to turn my life into hell on earth. I wonder why it's *wrong* to assume she might be wrong.

I remember my love of painting—how it started on one ordinary day when I was about five, and I just decided to try it for the first time. And when my mom saw, she cheered and told me it looked great even though it was garbage, and that made me feel good, so I just kept doing it. She saved every painting I made in this little cedar chest until the day she died. If she hadn't cheered for me that first time, would I still want to paint now? If I'd tried other things, like singing or baseball, and she'd praised those . . . would they be my passions now instead? And why does it matter since she didn't praise something different, and I am where I am now, whether or not it's where I was supposed to end up?

I think of last night when Cam—openly, proudly queer Cam—prayed to God before going to sleep, when I haven't been able to do that in weeks. I think about how much I wanted my life to be over a few days ago, and I realize that I never hated myself for who I am. I never hated myself for being bi. I hated how my family made me feel about it.

And it hits me—maybe all at once, maybe a gradual build—that if you think you have to earn enough points on someone's rubric for them to accept you, then either you're wrong to assume they won't love you for who you are, or they never loved you in the first place.

The pot of water starts to boil. I feel Cam slide a little closer to me so our knees touch. I take a deep breath. The closeness, his confident words, the calm evening air . . . it all just feels *right*. Like this is where I was designed to be.

Cam and I each grab a plastic spoon from his pack, and we pour the soup into our one bowl. We manage to balance it on our knees, still pressed against each other.

"Turns out camping is astronomically more fun without Leo joining us," Cam remarks, dueling my spoon with his. "Who knew?"

"He was an asshole."

"Yeah, well. You called him out," Cam points out. "That meant a lot, by the way."

We both slurp our soup.

"You're so different when you're out here," Cam adds. And

the tension between us is back, because I know we're both thinking of all the little moments from today. I've become so used to arguing with him these past months. The sensation of sharing an honest experience with him feels lost, but familiar. Like it's from a dream that I'm starting to remember.

"I *want* this to work," I finally admit. My voice is so quiet. Suddenly I'm very aware of the flames next to us, the heat on our knees. I turn to face him. Our eyes find each other and stay there.

"This," Cam simply says.

And I kiss him.

My hand, already behind his head, pulls his face against mine in one quick motion, and he makes a little surprised squeak but doesn't pull away. The taste is supremely unsexy—river salt and chicken noodle soup—but it's on both our lips and it only makes us draw closer. It doesn't physically feel any different than kissing Aria, except the stubble on his chin scratches my face.

We pull apart, then back together, then apart, then together again. At some point we break the cycle, and he's studying my face, both hands on my shoulders. His smile quietly tries to wrap around me—prodding with timid exuberance—and for once, finally, I let it.

72

It's not until nighttime that I realize how fast the day has gone. I haven't spent any of it thinking about Aunt Lori, Dad, or what's waiting for me once the trip is over. My bedroom feels like it's on another planet; something from another life.

The sounds of birds turn into the sounds of crickets, and Cam and I shut ourselves in the cabin. He consolidates our light sources and sets them around us so we can see each other. It turns out I have a handheld radio in my pack, so we put that on SCAN. We sit cross-legged on our sleeping bags, facing each other. Cam teaches me how to play a game called Egyptian Ratscrew with his deck of cards. Except every time our eyes meet, we both giggle stupidly for no reason.

"No one ever plays card games anymore," I comment. The radio hums in the background. It's mostly static, but occasionally bits of an oldies song will play through the white noise.

"It's a very outdoorsy thing to do," Cam replies. "Although we kind of killed the vibe by bringing the radio into this."

"It'd be better if there were music."

"Man, you and I haven't listened to music together in ages. You remember when we used to do that?" he says. He sets down his cards, letting himself fall back onto his sleeping bag. I do the same, so we're both staring up at the holes in our treetop ceiling with our game set aside. We can't see much of the sky, but I count seven stars.

Wordlessly, the two of us slide off our dirty clothes from the day. We don't touch each other; we don't get each other off. We just get naked and that's what it is.

"You and I always talked about going to a concert, you know," Cam says. "I don't know if you remember. It was back when we first met."

I put my arms behind my head, breathing deeply.

"I would've loved to go to a concert with you," I say.

We both pick up on my phrasing: *would've*. In another life, maybe it would've happened. In a life where this is our first time watching the stars instead of our last, and the world is kinder to people like him and easier for people like me. But that's a fantasy world, and it isn't the one waiting for us outside these woods.

"What a good fucking day," Cam says.

I slide my right hand behind his bare shoulders, letting my other rest on his stomach. He lays his fingers over mine, intertwining them.

As we refocus on the sky, I ask, "How many galaxies did you say there are again?"

"At least one hundred billion," he answers. "And those are just the ones we can see."

"So there could be other worlds with life on them?"

"Probably."

"They'd think they're alone. Just like we do."

"Probably."

"I've never even been out of the country."

"Me neither," Cam says.

"I'd love to go someday though."

"Where?" he asks. Softer, now.

"I don't even know where to start. There's so much out there."

"You'll see some of it when you move," he points out. I can't tell if he's joking or not, since we're talking about Ohio.

I swallow hard. Out here the hours have felt like days, and it's been ages since I thought about the move. The move—a thing that only has meaning in that other reality; the one I put on pause when I took Cam's hand instead of him taking mine, and when I ran with him instead of looking for reasons why I shouldn't.

Cam kisses me on the cheek, then on the spot between my neck and my shoulder, which makes me shiver. My arm has gone numb under his weight, and I don't care one bit.

This is me right now. Not forever, not for much longer, but for now. NOW. A now that feels so vividly like our first night star-gazing. *That night—a memory strong enough to fold me in its arms, lifting me through time to lay me back beside the boy I love—except it couldn't be more different this time, and all I can do is think about how things changed and wonder what will be next.*

Someday, weeks or months or years in my new life, I'll lie under the stars and close my eyes, and I'll want this back. But I'll never have it, because Cam's fingers won't be laced through mine, the arms that hold him won't be mine; nothing of his will be mine except for these woods and this cabin and this moment and the memories of this moment later.

Someday I'll exist in a now that feels so vividly like this night. *This night—a memory strong enough to fold me in its arms, lifting me through time to lay me back beside the boy I love—except it couldn't be more different this time, and all I can do is think about how things changed and wonder what will be next.*

I ask him, "How many memories do you have in your head?"

"Too many. It's literally thousands of . . . like, tiny little bits and pieces. It'd take forever to explain them all to one person." Then he says to me, very gently, "But I wish I could tell you everything."

I pull him as close as possible, squeezing until I feel like I'm breaking his ribs. He squeezes back, and that's how we stay.

"I have a serious question for you," I tell him.

"I'll give you a serious answer."

I pause. "Did you always know, with us? Those times we flirted before New Year's . . . I mean, I honestly didn't know that's what it was. Did you?"

He contemplates that for a while. I don't rush him.

"Honestly? No. I just didn't think about it. There wasn't really this moment where I thought, *This is the one!* I didn't really think about what I wanted it to be called. I just wanted it to keep going."

"Almost sounds like you settled for me," I tease.

"I mean, no one wants to admit they've settled, but everyone does," he says. "Everyone weighs the pros and cons of the person they may or may not love, and then they just . . . decide. Back when we first met, you saw me with all my weird quirks, and you know what, Nate? Whether you decided to or not, you loved me for them."

I don't know what to think of all that.

"So if it's all arbitrary," I say slowly, "Why didn't you give up after shit hit the fan?"

"Why didn't you?" he asks.

I'm not expecting that one. And the truth is, I still don't know. I've spent every minute of these past months trying to figure out what makes me fall for someone, and why I feel the things I feel, and if there's a way to put that into words, I won't find it. I am who I am. I've never acted on less than that, and I never want to.

"I honestly don't know," I say, my head still leaned against his. "If you hadn't pushed so hard, I probably would've."

"I held on because none of the stuff that came between us was our fault," he says. "I'm not going to lose my favorite person just because your aunt orders it to happen. That's not a good enough reason."

"How can you be sure we're not just bad for each other?"

"Because of today. When it's just us, Nate . . ."

He trails off without finishing the sentence. I nod against him, like, *I know what you're trying to say.*

"And this is what a relationship would be like," he continues. "Existing together. Just like this."

"This isn't the real world, Cam."

"Someday it will be though. Someday we'll be older and we can be anything we want."

"We're not adults yet."

"Fair enough." He shrugs against me. "So let's just try a date, then. A tiny little date."

"Hm." I choose my words carefully. "So. If we were to do something as small as get ice cream and chill on the beach or whatever . . . that would count as a date?"

"If you wanted to call it that? Hell yeah. What else matters?"

"Hm," I repeat. "Because I do like ice cream. And I mean, sitting here is nice. So I could get on board, I think. Except we wouldn't be naked next time."

"Unless you wanted that part too," he says. The breath of his laugh tickles my skin.

"Not at first," I say, sliding my hand over his chest. "But. You know."

"I do, in fact, know."

We're both whispering, and I don't know why. It's like we're speaking in our own language. Like our words finally mean the same thing to each other.

"I know the perfect spot we could go to at Rhiney Point," Cam says. "It's a little far though. You'll have to drive. Not to mention sneak out."

"I can do that."

"And you'll have to wear flip-flops. I know you hate those."

"I'll make an exception. Don't you dare get used to it though."

We both shut up after that. We don't kiss. We don't have sex. We simply close our eyes and exist, and the rest is splendor and starlight.

■ ■ ■

The flashlight in my face jolts me awake.

The counselor's jaw drops.

"What the *fuck*, guys?"

73

"Asher tried to cover for us, but the camp staffers took attendance. I guess he or Leo caved, figured out where we went, and told them where to look for us. They said it was the smoke from the fire that actually gave us away."

"You're lucky the police weren't called," Mrs. Lawson comments, setting down her pen. "Then the parents would've had to collect you in person."

"They didn't have to do that, but the camp left messages at both of our houses. Cam's parents were camping on the other side of the country, my dad had already moved into our Ohio house, and my aunt was staying there for the week to set up her office at the new job."

"So none of the parents got word of what had happened," Mrs. Lawson says.

"Not at first. We knew that as soon as we got home though...." I trail off, then restart. "There was only one day left at camp, so they had us wait it out in the staff lounge and go home with everyone else that night."

"Did any of your friends or classmates hear about this?" Mrs. Lawson asks.

Across the table, Cam has his head in his hands.

"The whole camp did," I answer, swallowing. "Everyone talked about it. About us. They couldn't get enough of it."

Mrs. Lawson pauses, slowly picking her pen back up. For the first time, she seems worn out by all of this.

"We both sat alone on the bus back. When we got to the school, Cam needed a ride home because his parents were out of town, and he didn't have his license."

"So you drove him home," Mrs. Lawson says. "You didn't have to do that."

"I know. I'm not sure why I did. We didn't even talk during the drive. I hated him so much for the mess we'd gotten into— I couldn't stop shaking."

"Hated him."

"Yes. Hated him."

"You dropped him off at his house, then?"

"No," I say. "We didn't get that far. I . . ." I pause. My stab wound burns like a hot poker, setting my stomach on fire.

"Nathan," Mrs. Lawson says.

"During the drive, I remembered that my aunt was due back at the house from her trip in a few hours. So we went to my place first, before Cam's. So I could get inside and delete the voicemail from camp before she heard it."

"Mr. Haynes was with you at that time," she says, writing carefully.

"Yes."

"And you two got out of your car?"

"Yes."

"And that's when the fight happened. In your front yard."

"Yes."

"When did Mr. Haynes stab you, Nathan?"

My hands are trembling in front of me. My entire right arm has gone numb under Aunt Lori's grip. Dad finally notices and motions for her to loosen up. Her fingers spring open, releasing me, which only leaves me shaking harder.

"Why don't we take a break," Mrs. Lawson says, her voice surprisingly soothing. "You've answered a lot of questions today, and we can finish—"

"No," I say, cutting her off. It's by complete reflex, and I don't know why I say it.

"I'm sorry?" she asks.

I have to go home.

"Nathan," she says. "Is there something else we haven't covered?"

I can't tell the truth because I have to go home. But I can't go home without saying this. No. I can't. I won't. *NO.* No more of this. None. *NO.*

My eyes meet Cam's. His are full of tears.

"For fuck's sake, say something," he chokes out.

It's the very first thing he said to me at the start of the deposition. I knew what he meant by it then. And I know what he means now.

74

We don't say anything during the drive back, but as soon as we get out of the car in my front yard—that's when we start arguing. And it feels like everything that's been building up since we got caught, since summer camp, since the beach, since prom, since New Year's, since before—I'm feeling it all at once. Thinking that because of how much pain I'm in, it doesn't matter that I'm causing more of it for him.

I feel unrestrained humiliation and smothering hopelessness and so many things I haven't felt before, and I do things I haven't done before; I call him a fag even though I don't mean it, I beat him half to death even though I don't even understand why I want to. But I *want* to. So that's what happens.

He's bleeding and throwing up like I described earlier. And the plate breaks on the sidewalk. A bunch of big pieces. We're facing each other, and then I tell him:

"Do it, Cam."

I tell him to hurt me even though She'll be here soon. I don't understand why I want him to do it. But I want him to. So I tell him to because I need it to happen, and I know that's not a good reason but I can't explain it more than that. I'm squeezing the shard of ceramic in my hand so tight it's cutting my palm, and I loosen my grip but I don't let go even though blood slides through my fingers and drips onto the sidewalk.

And Cam. Cam is struggling to keep upright, but he doesn't let go of his shard either, and *this is it*. This will happen. This will happen because I need it to, and Cameron Haynes is my best friend who has always helped me, and I want to tell him to help me now. I want to beg him to do it. So that's what happens. I beg him to do it, to hurt me to help me.

But he steps away from me. Looks at me. And I've never seen him look more disgusted at anything before. And between his gasps for breath he tells me, "You aren't someone I want to help, touch, or know, you incogitable fucking psychopath."

As soon as he gets out the last word, he drops the shard onto the sidewalk—it disintegrates completely—and his shoulders deflate like he's just said the last thing he needs to. Like he's going to collapse any second. So that's what happens. He falls flat onto the sidewalk. Unmoving. Unconscious.

So I scream, "CAM!" and I don't care if I wake up the neighbors, because he needs help—he's breathing, at least, thank God. He's breathing. But I don't think he's waking up and SHIT, She's going to be home any second. She's going to see all this.

Oh my God oh my God oh my God. I put my free hand over my face, and I want to cry but I don't, because Cam needs HELP. I need to get him HELP. So that's what happens. I run straight through my front door and I think, *First aid first aid.* I check the downstairs bathroom except FUCK, we've already packed everything up. So I run upstairs because there has to be something—come on, COME ON; there's nothing, no supplies anywhere, and I can't even use my cell phone to call 911 because it was taken away, so I go to use the house phone. Only it isn't there. The house phone isn't there because it was already packed up last week. Tucked away in a box where no message from camp would have ever reached it.

No message from camp. No answering machine to erase. No danger that was ever real. No reason to have stopped here with Cam.

CAM. I need to go outside to check on him! So that's what happens.

But something is wrong. Something is *wrong*, but I don't know it yet as I run through my living room, and I look out the window to my front yard.

There are things I should have noticed—and I even SEE them! I *SEE* THEM! I see things like Aunt Lori's keys in the living room and the purse on the countertop and the light in the kitchen that's just clicked on. But I don't think about what they mean because I'm staring out the window, to my front yard, to CAM, who's picked himself up and—he's leaving!

Don't leave! *Cam, DON'T LEAVE!* But he wants to. So that's what happens. He drags himself across my front yard and now he's standing up, steadying himself, limping down the street away from my house and toward his own. He limps away and he's gone, and I'm yelling that he's gone, and I'm so focused on it that I don't hear Her; I don't know someone else is here until She grabs my neck, and I don't know She's drunk until She slams my head into the living room wall.

■ ■ ■

My voice is so shaky that I'm barely understandable. Messy tears spill all over the papers in front of me. The only one in the room crying harder than me is Cam.

Mrs. Lawson puts her hand on my shoulder.

"When did your aunt stab you, Nathan?"

I sob harder.

■ ■ ■

Run. It's Her.

She feels unrestrained humiliation and smothering hopelessness and so many things She hasn't felt before, and She does things She hasn't done before; She calls me a fag even though She doesn't mean it, She beats me half to death even though She doesn't understand why She wants to. But She *wants* to. So that's what happens.

I try to yell for help, but Her forearm is crushing my windpipe; *I can't breathe; I can't fucking breathe.*

"A—fucking faggot!" She says it twice, and each word is accompanied by a bare-knuckle punch, and I gasp for air, and I—

"*I can't,*" I choke out, only instead of my voice it's a brittle rasp. *"Aunt Lori . . . I can't—"*

The edges of everything darken, and all I can focus on is the purple of Her bathrobe. She's leaned over me now, blocking everything else.

"I knew it." Her fingers tighten around my neck as She says it again, slurring. "I *knew* it."

IT'S ALL UPSIDE DOWN NOW and my arms knock against the floor as I choke. I try to shove Her off me, and I realize too late that that's going to make Her lose balance, and that's what happens; She *falls,* falls straight into me, and all at once my stomach is splitting open and—

"*FUCKKK!*"

I scream harder and louder than I ever have before. *It tears open my throat, but I can't even FEEL IT* because there's something hot and wet coating the front of my shirt, and I can feel that it's my own blood, and I see the piece of ceramic that had been in my hand, now almost completely lodged in my abdomen.

Now my whole front is on fire, and She sees what She did, and Her hands fly to Her mouth as She yells, "OH MY GOD! Nate—*Nathan! Nathan! NATHAN! NATHAN! NATHAN!*"

My own name is the last thing I hear before I pass out.

75

Screaming.

76

I'm standing and crying.

Cameron's parents are sitting and crying.

Violet is lunging at my aunt.

Cameron is stopping her.

Mrs. Lawson is calling someone.

My aunt is sitting and crying.

My father is screaming and crying.

With the weight of the world beneath my feet, I close my eyes and feel myself fall.

■ ■ ■

He catches me.

77

DEPOSITION EXHIBIT 4

Dear Nate,

I'm sorry to spring such a dark birthday gift on you, but I hope you understand the thought behind it once you read this. There are some important things I need to tell you.

You probably remember that I stopped living with you and your dad when I was fourteen. By that time, Lori had made your house into her own. It's where she wanted to be, so it's where she went. What you didn't see though, was the stuff she did during my last few years there.

Lori caught me sneaking out to my first house party in eighth grade. And when she did, she hit me across the face with the book she was reading. A few months later, she started using other things—her hands, cooking utensils, and that long electrical cord behind the couch in your living room.

That kind of stuff kept going for the next year. You mentioned how scary she is when she drinks—dude, been there. She was careful about hiding it from you and your dad, and instead of saying something, I just made more stupid decisions. I felt shitty and alone. The only thing Lori didn't have complete control of was her own temper.

She sent me to live with my dad after I started hurting myself, a little after I turned fourteen. But I know what you're going through, Nate, because she did it to me too. And I'm so, so worried for you.

I'm writing this down for you, telling you, because I'm tired of keeping all this to myself. So I want to make a deal: I'll say something if you do. Bring this letter to the right people (your dad, the cops . . . whoever), if you choose to take that step. We'll figure out the rest from there.

Nate, you poor idiot. Please take that step.

Love,

Violet

78

The charges against Cameron are dropped.

Aunt Lori is arrested.

I don't know what the exact rules are in terms of whether my deposition counts as evidence, but now people know.

They know that Aunt Lori called 911, then carried me back into my yard so the paramedics would find me there.

They know that when I woke up, she told me Cam had been arrested for her crime.

They know that she told me he would be released if we all stayed quiet—"don't lie, just stay quiet."

They know that when he wasn't released, she warned me how heartbroken my dad would be if he found out the truth.

They know it now.

■ ■ ■

It's a week after my deposition, and the wood of the church pew is digging into my forearms. I scoot back a few inches on the kneeler. The overhead lights are dimmed and the building is vacant, which is why I chose to come here in the early evening. No people.

For a long time—I don't know how long—I kneel with my hands folded, but I don't speak. I don't even really think. I let myself relax, eyes closed, feeling the atmosphere all around me. I imagine all the quiet hymns that blanketed my childhood, the ones I sang alongside my entire community in this room. Songs of peace and purity.

I lift my head to look to the altar, and I smile even as my eyes well up with tears. This place has been my home my whole life, and tonight is the last time I'll set foot in it before the move. The church I find in Ohio will hold the same mass service, I'm sure, with the same layout and same teachings. Because they mean more than I thought they did. But I'm not scared to learn anymore—I'm excited.

Tonight I stop running from this. Tonight I ask the question.

I take deep breaths in through my nose, steadying myself.

Dear God—

I'm still here. Are you?

I wait and listen for an answer and then I get one, I swear on my life I get one—two words that turn my tears into soft crying and my smile into exuberant laughter, right there in the middle of the church.

The path I'm on is leading me somewhere. To someone. I don't know who I'll find, but I know I won't be alone. And I don't know where I'm going, but I know I'll get there soon.

■　■　■

My dad finds me in my bedroom after I get home. There's barely anything left in our house because the movers have taken most of our stuff, and I only have enough clothes to last for the few days we have left here. But Dad finds a chair to pull up.

"Hey," I say to him. I'm lying on my bed tossing a rubber football in the air.

"How's the battle wound?" he asks. I've managed to wind down from pain meds to Tylenol since the deposition, and now the soreness is barely noticeable. No more bleeding either—all scar tissue.

"Doesn't hurt too bad," I answer, spinning the football on my palm. Dad motions for me to throw it to him. He catches it, then studies it for a while.

"I've been trying hard, you know," he tells the football, "to think of the right thing to say about all this."

"I don't think there's a right thing to say. It's a pretty unique situation."

"Yeah." Dad grimaces to himself. "Your mom was a rockstar with these. Unique situations. She was a unique woman."

I nod.

"I'm sorry," he says, lifting his head to look at me. His eyes are full of pain. "God, Nate, that's all I know to say. I'm sorry. If I'd been home more, I would've known what she was doing to you. What she did to you. And I'm going to be around more from now on——"

"Hey," I say, raising both hands like, *Whoa, bucko.* "This wasn't your fault."

"Someday, bud, if you're a parent, you'll understand it doesn't work like that. When it comes to my kid—my son—everything is on me. It's my job to protect you. I didn't do my job."

He says a lot more like that, and I keep telling him it's okay, that it doesn't matter now. It's strange to hear my goofy dad talking like this. I can't decide if I like it.

"I promise to do better," he concludes. "Okay? I'm going to work on it. And I want you to see a professional."

"A professional dad?"

He smirks before turning serious again. "A therapist, bud. I know you came out to us and everything, but I think you should see someone who can help you . . . finish sorting everything out."

"I'm just glad you're cool with it," I say.

Dad looks floored by that.

"For Christ's sake, why wouldn't I be? You're my son."

"Your son is bisexual," I tell him.

It sounds strange. But I say it.

I say it. I say it.

"I won't pretend I understand all of it," Dad tells me. "And it's not what I pictured for you. At all. But I love you just as much, and I hope that's good enough for now."

I tell him it is.

"And I hope you understand why I still want us to move," he adds.

"I do." And I really do. I realize that I have some things to work out. And there's no way I can do it in this house, in this school, with everything that's happened. Our town is small— people are going to talk. And every time they do, it'll remind me of all this.

Fresh start.

"We'll probably be a bit back and forth between here and Ohio, depending on what happens with Lori's case," Dad continues. "You may have to give another statement if it does go to trial. We'll do everything we can to avoid that. Nora—Mrs. Lawson—is taking the case."

"That's confirmed?"

"There was a bunch of red tape, but it's confirmed. She and her wife came by in person yesterday to let me know."

I nod.

"Something that crossed my mind," Dad says, starting to stand but easing back down. "Cameron knew it was Lori."

"Yeah. I mean, he didn't see it, and he never asked me, but he totally knew."

"He could have told the police. Made things easier for himself."

"The state offered him a plea deal, but he had to plead guilty.

Cam would've never done that. He told them everything he knew. He told them, 'I didn't do it.'"

"Why didn't he say who did?"

I bite the inside of my cheek. That question has crossed my mind a hundred times, and I know the answer. It's because he realized that telling the police would tear my house apart, and he didn't want to do that without my permission. It had to be me.

"He wanted it to be my decision," I say. "Trust me, he pushed me pretty hard."

Dad mops sweat off his brow, shaking his head.

"That boy really loves you."

I nod.

"That's one of the big Dad goals, you know. For their kid to be loved that much by someone else."

"He asked me on a date," I say with a smile. "I don't know when or if he still wants to. But I think we're going on a date before the move."

"Well? Go figure it out with him."

We hug for a long time. And then I go to do as he says.

79

Mrs. Haynes answers the door on the second knock. Without saying a word, both she and Mr. Haynes hug me.

"We're going to do better with him," Mrs. Haynes says, using the same words as my father. I don't know why she's telling me this or why she feels she needs to, but I nod.

They don't thank me for everything but they don't ask for an apology either. And I agree that about sums up where we are.

I jerk my head toward their backyard, as if to say, *Is he out there?* His parents tell me he is.

Cam is sitting in the big tree that overlooks their street, balanced just above a thick branch that obviously doubles as a step. He's taking in the view of the horizon, his feet dangling from the edge of his perch.

"Hey," he says when he sees me. He doesn't seem overly surprised that I'm here. The neutral tone sounds strange out of his mouth.

"Can I join?" I ask.

"I'm just sitting, but sure."

I climb and plant myself next to him with my legs also hanging off the edge, both of us facing the open view. The sky is streaked with fiery orange—the start of a sunset.

"Summer's just about over," I say, letting out a long breath.

"Yeah. You do anything fun?"

We both chuckle, trying to make a joke of it, but the territory still feels raw. Dad's right: This will take time for us to work through. Maybe if our first date goes well enough for a second date, or a third, or an official relationship. But not quite yet.

"What's going to happen with your aunt?" Cam asks.

"She might take a plea deal. We don't know yet. What's going to happen with your . . . Well, I guess, everything?"

Cam blows a strand of hair aside, which looks adorable. Then he counts on his fingers. "With parents: obviously we're all on a learning curve, but things are good. I don't have to wear a jacket to football games anymore."

We laugh, remembering the old joke.

"With friends . . . Well, Aria's made peace, and I think I'll be able to clear things up with Asher. So I'm set there. With school, I'm just going to go back and ignore anyone who gives me shit. It's pretty hard to worry about that stuff after all this."

He's got that right.

Cam bites his lip, which I notice is quivering a little.

"Can I share a memory with you?" he asks. It's the same

earnest tone he used when he first met me: *Would you like to be friends, Nate?*

"Of course."

He looks out to the horizon.

"August twenty-sixth. It's my first day of eleventh grade. I walk into Mrs. Koestler's class and I'm nervous—like, super fucking nervous. I don't know anyone. And I see one other guy who doesn't know anyone either. So I start a conversation, and I put on some bullshit confidence. Which turns out to be the best decision because we're joking around in a few minutes." He nudges me in the side. "Say 'what' again, mothafucka."

I smile, blinking fast.

"And this was way too optimistic of me, but by third period I was already thinking of movies and music I could introduce you to and memories that I would maybe be able to share if we got close enough. I pictured all that." Cam exhales, still not looking at me. "And then . . . then it actually happened. And it kept going, until I couldn't predict where it was going anymore. And at some point it stopped working, but until then, oh my God was it fucking beautiful."

I brush my knee up against his. "So what is it now?"

His lip is definitely trembling.

"Screwed up?" he offers to his lap. "I can't figure out when it stopped working, exactly. I know we *almost* got there—but your aunt was right about one thing: We're bad for each other. And I know that maybe she was the reason for that in the first place, but it doesn't matter how we would've worked otherwise because now we're here, and what I'm trying to tell you is that we both need to move on."

"What?" I blink, confused. "What's happening? I was going to ask about our date. The one we talked about. Rhiney Point?"

Cam gives the tiniest shake of his head. "I'm sorry, man. But that's not a good idea right now."

"Okay . . ." I squeeze the branch above my head, keeping myself calm. "Do you just need time, I guess? Because I get that. Really. Take as long as you need. I can wait."

He doesn't answer right away.

"I have no idea how to put what I'm feeling into words," he says. "But I'm going to try, okay?"

I wait.

"I went to an LGBT youth group a few days ago. I painted my nails, and right after I sat down, one of the guys said something to me. Know what it was? He said, 'Nice nails, dude. What's your name?'" Cam smiles at the memory, looking somewhere past me. "Like it was normal. And Nate, this whole thing . . ." He catches himself trailing off. "My whole coming out, and everything after, is all tied to what happened with us. It's tied to you. I think we can agree this was pretty much the opposite of normal, right? And for now . . ." He gives a one-armed shrug. "Normal is what I need. It just is. I need to be around friends who don't give me shit for wearing nail polish. I need a girlfriend or boyfriend who dates me without me having to convince them. And I'm proud of your progress, but you're just not . . . you're not *there*. Not yet."

"You——" I clear my throat to level my voice. "You won't wait for me to get there?"

"Nate . . ." He takes my hand and presses it to his chest. I feel his heart beating rapid-fire, matching mine. "It's not cute when people try to 'fix' each other. It's cringey and dysfunctional. We both need to already have our shit worked out before we bring anyone else into it."

I'm panicking now, absolutely panicking, because he's really serious about this, and I've never had to be the one to convince him to give this a chance, but I need to do it now.

"We've always helped each other work our shit out," I tell him, pulling my hand back and holding it up like I'm trying to calm a wild animal. "Since the day we met, we——"

"Say what you want, Nate, but all we've been doing since the day we met is suffocating each other," he says. His eyes are shining and looking at things I can't see. "I adore the idea of us; I really do. What we had for that day in the woods—oh my *God*. But the reality of us, out here, is toxic. I hate that word. But it's true."

"So . . ."

"So, I love you and always will. But I have to let you go now."

My vision is starting to blur. I want to say something, but my throat is too tight. I swallow a huge lump but still can't get my voice to work, so I just look at him. His eyes. The cryptic world that lives behind them. And I know he knows what I'm thinking of from the way he stares back.

"Someday." Cam pokes me and says the word so delicately, like it's the most fragile thing he has. "Maybe someday when we're adults, we can reconnect and catch up—talk. Maybe it'll be enough for us to get close again, and maybe we'll get close enough to bring up this conversation again. Maybe we'll do everything we did before. But we can't do any of it right now. Does that make sense?"

Now we're both tearing up. I can't think. This is the most important conversation I've ever had, and I can't even fucking think about what I need to say.

"Can . . ." I wipe at my face with my T-shirt. "Okay. Listen to me. Can we at least try the date? One last day together. If it doesn't work, you can totally say no to date two, and I swear I'll stop asking."

"I'm sorry," Cam says. "But no."

"Okay." I'm getting desperate. "How about . . . we give it six months and try it then. How about that? I can be in town for winter break. New Year's Eve reunion."

"I'm sorry," Cam says. "But no."

"Jesus Christ, can we at least swap addresses? Can I write you a letter? Can we stay *friends*?"

Cam squeezes his eyes shut. He takes off his glasses to wipe them.

"I'll always be your friend, Nate," he says. "But you and I are done now."

I don't know what to do.

"Is this just nothing, then?" I ask him.

"You won't ever be nothing," he says.

Despite myself, I scoff weakly. "That doesn't seem like a compliment."

"Okay, yeah, I realize how that sounded," he says. We both laugh—genuine for a second, then superficial. Empty. He turns to me and puts a hand under my chin, lifting it slightly. "I just meant that you're always going to be, like, the person who made me realize who I am. Which makes you one of the most important people I've known. I'm not sure if that makes you feel any better. But you'll always be that."

He turns away from me, and there we sit, side by side.

"Can I kiss you one more time?" I ask, leaning toward him.

"No."

"Just once. I promise."

"No," he says, gently pushing me back. "I'm sorry."

The sun touches the tree line. We look without watching it.

"I'm glad it happened," he says. He's talking to the air now. "Much as I hated some of it. To get here, I'd do everything again."

"So would I." I try to take his hand, but he doesn't let me.

"It was the best thing I've ever felt," he continues. "I think it was love. I'm still not sure. But thank you for it. Thank you for being my . . ." He grimaces, searching for the right word. "You."

I tenderly touch his shoulder and pull him into one last, long hug. And I start to really lose it, which makes him really lose it, and we stay against each other like that until we've both dried our soaked eyes and pulled ourselves together. Soon I know it's almost time to let go, and I feel him take deep, deliberate breaths against me. I squeeze my chest against his, rocking us back and forth as he murmurs, "It's okay. It's okay."

And the more I think about his words, the more I do understand. Because we did help each other, and we did have our days and nights together, but we can never be anything normal after all this. Maybe sometime later, I'll have time to be pissed at the world for being how it is. Because the idea that this is the last time I'll talk to him, or touch him, or be with him, hurts more than I can comprehend. So for now I don't think about any of it. For now I just hold him and God do I hold him tight.

"Know that I'll remember this," I say into his shoulder.

Eventually we break apart and he's the one who lets me go. Then he lifts his hand to his mouth, kisses his fingers, and presses them to my cheek. They linger there as we look into each other's eyes one last time.

And for a second, just a second, I swear I see us become the whole universe.

"You're going to be so many things someday," Cam tells me.

80

The last night in my old house, hovering on the edge of my old memories, I paint the stars.

I want to have a proper visual reference, so I climb out of my bedroom window just like I did almost a year ago. It's obviously a bit different than last time. There's no trampoline and no Cameron. But the nighttime ambience is still there, and it hasn't changed a bit.

I lie down and let myself sink into the sky. I wonder how many other people are doing the same thing right now. How often they've done it before and how many times they'll do it again. I wonder if one night Cameron and I will be watching the same constellations, hundreds of miles apart. Never to speak again, but still admiring the same thing. Understanding the same idea. Being the people we are now because we knew and loved each other back then.

I close my eyes, letting myself remember. And as I bathe myself in memory, I see the ghosts of him and me on that first night we spent out here. Us. Climbing out the window. Lying on the trampoline and basking in the nebulousness of a world we knew nothing about. Not the people we became, but the people we used to be.

Sic itur ad astra.

I watch the two make each other smile and laugh and fall in love without realizing it. Us. Two guys sharing who they are, connecting without the weight of the world to stop them. Two boys who will find themselves but lose each other. Two people joined by love: painted into the stars, protected by memory.

God, they're going to live forever.

ACKNOWLEDGMENTS

I t feels impossible to properly express my thanks to everyone who made this book what it is, but I'm going to try my best.

First and foremost: to my superstar agent, Allison Remcheck, whose fierce passion for this story rivals my own. Thank you for being one of the first people to believe in it, and in me. I could not feel any luckier to have my writing in your forever capable hands.

To my wonderful editor, Lauren Knowles, for fighting to get this book published, and for helping me with every step to get it there. I also owe enormously warm thanks to Will Kiester, Rebecca Behrans, Sara Pollard, and everyone else at Page Street for building this book into what it is. You all are incredible.

The next people that belong on this list are my teachers, mentors, and professors. Thank you to Dr. Taryn Bayles and Dr. Mariajose Castellanos, for your relentless support of my writing goals during my college years. Pauline Owen, for inspiring my love of chemistry. And of course, my unforgettable English teachers, Denise Daly Mandis and Colleen Gill. You slogged through every God-awful piece of writing I handed in and, where almost anyone would have laughed or rolled their eyes, you unironically reiterated that I—and every other student in the room—could be extraordinary. Know that I still think of you and always will. You changed my life.

To all of my GIS classmates at Leonardtown High, including and especially the ones who told me I would be a published author someday: I wouldn't have made it through high school without our weird little family, and there's no one I'd rather have built a plane in mid-air with than you.

To all of my fellow scouts in Troop 427, particularly Brendon Maldonado, my first blog reader and one of my strongest supporters, and Tim Kieber, who wins "most enthusiastic reaction" to each of my publishing milestones—and most especially, Mr. Mac: You taught me and countless others how to act honorably, accept ourselves, and live with decency. I intend to spend the rest of my life helping people because of you.

To the many friends who make every day worth living . . . Emily Rittenour: for being my first friend in high school, and for all the wonderful years that followed. Phillip Scassero: for reading my earliest stories and promptly building a sword replica inspired by them. Callie Flowers: for being one of the sweetest friends I've known, and making each morning of twelfth grade a bright one. Andy Zhao: for being a great roommate and one of my best friends. Allison Basiley: for your inspirational creativity and supporting everyone exactly as they are. Kevin Whitley: for being one of my closest friends, supporters, and sharer of countless inside jokes (not to mention Prequel Memes). And Paige Nelson: for taking my stagnant dream of being an author and breathing it into being. My words first became something real under your care, and I'll never forget it.

To Marlee Thorogood: for being one of my best college friends, and the first person to join my side for the querying journey. To Jon Riewerts: for being the first person to know who I am, and for your unconditional acceptance when I needed it the most. To Michael Rowley: for being the first person to read this book, and for helping me shape it during its early days in summer 2016. This story wouldn't have gotten off the ground without you. To Claire Ruble: for our Panera lunch conversations; and Mary, Scott, and Margaret Ruble, for always welcoming me into your home. To Michael Waters: for being my first friend in the publishing community. And to all the friends I made during my time at UMBC: Jackson Kotch, Alexander Al-Jazrawi, Morgan Busch, Alex Dolan, and Olivia Benton.

And of course, to Brodie Spade: for being the answer to every day I spent wondering what kind of person I'd want to share my life with. I love you for that and I always will.

Finally and most importantly, to Mom and Dad: for never judging me, especially when I deserved it; and for always listening, especially when I needed it. Nothing ever has, nor ever will, make me prouder than I am to be your son.

ABOUT THE AUTHOR

Zack Smedley was born and raised in southern Maryland, in an endearing county almost no one has heard of. He earned a degree in chemical engineering from UMBC in 2017 and currently works within the field. As a member of the LGBT community, his goal is to give a voice to marginalized young adults through gritty, morally complex narratives. He spends his free time building furniture, baking, tinkering with electronics, and managing his obsession with the works of Aaron Sorkin. *Deposing Nathan* is his first novel. You can find him online at www.zacksmedleyauthor.com.